Plus One

Sarah Phelan

Plus One
By Sarah Phelan

Published by
BlanketFort Publishing
117 Lake View Avenue
Lynn, MA 01904 U.S.A.

All rights reserved. No part of this book may be reproduced or transmitted in any form or by any means, electronic or mechanical, including photocopying, recording, or by any information storage or retrieval system, without written permission from the author, except for the inclusion or brief quotation in review.

Copyright © 2013 by Sarah Phelan

Library of Congress Cataloguing-in-Publication Data
Library of Congress Control Number: 1-960946611
Phelan, Sarah 1973-
Plus one
ISBN 13 978 0 9779927 2 0

Printed at King Printing, Lowell, MA
Set in Times New Roman, Palace Script MT, Century Gothic, Copperplate Gothic Bold

Cover Art by Peter Phelan

Publisher's Note: This is a work of fiction. Names, characters, places, and incidents either are the product of the author's imagination or are used fictitiously, and any resemblance to actual persons, living or dead, business establishments, events or locales are entirely coincidental.

ISBN 13 978-0—9779927-2-0

For Peter Phelan

CHAPTER 1
And They Lived

Inevitably, the young bride-to-be would ask to hear *her* story.

Either they had been briefly blinded by the sparkle and shine of Julia's unmistakably extravagant - yet, very tasteful - diamond anniversary band that anchored her left honey-skinned, manicured hand, or they had glanced up behind her sprawling mahogany desk just beyond her Eames chair to the single gallery-framed photograph that graced the wall behind her desk. There hung a portrait of her beautiful family - well-scrubbed children, handsome husband, and the obligatory amiable family dog at a perfect sit in front of their impeccable Weston, Massachusetts home. The young girl would coo and sigh and ask: "Ooh, how did it all happen for you?"

Each and every one of the girls she had helped to the altar wanted to hear her "Story of Romance." They wanted her to tell them a Fairytale.

And Julia could.

She told the story well. She leaned in and confided to this new, bright, hopeful face before her about how her story was almost like, "Well, Cinderella..." Julia had been just a young girl, she didn't have much - believe it or not - and she was struggling to make it big at the world-renowned Plaza Hotel. She and the tall, dark, and handsome Will had met right here in this incredible, majestic building and she had known he was "The One" when she had first shaken his hand that very day in these offices.

She provided glowing details of him sweeping her off her feet - taking her to the best restaurants, the coolest parties, showering her with gifts that couldn't help but turn a young woman's head. And then, finally, Julia would deliver the "piece de resistance" - Will had actually proposed to her on, of all days, Valentine's Day *squeal* but the two of them had kept it quiet until Julia was able to tell her mother in person almost a month later. For that short amazing time in their young lives, the inevitable destiny of their love had been a deeply romantic secret kept just between her husband-to-be and her.

The story always ended in a deep mutual sigh. It really did have it all - romance, secrets, beautiful clothes, youth, rags, riches, and an obviously satisfying conclusion, if the evidence planted on that wall in Julia Santos Rosa's office was any indication.

It was the story that young Julia had breathlessly told their friends when she had originally planned their tiny wedding. It was the story that, as the years went on, she continued to share with new colleagues, acquaintances when the subject came up. It was the same one she had told their children when they were old enough to ask and young enough to care. And it was the very one that Julia had concocted for her mother on that early Sunday morning when she had finally slipped a large sparkling engagement ring onto her hand and accepted the seemingly sage advice of a late night - and possibly, imaginary - conversation between her and a Massachusetts State Trooper on Route Six.

It's funny how memory actually becomes almost like mythology. One wouldn't necessarily tell your children or your mother, or the beautiful young client who sits in front of you in the Wedding and Events Offices at the Plaza Hotel the story of how the two of you met if that story actually involves nothing more than a celebratory bottle of tequila and the intended distraction of a one night stand. And so instead, to veil those less than romantic or inspiring intentions, the story becomes this miraculous myth - a gorgeous origin story utilizing the bits and pieces of the truth to create a new memory about how the two of you fell in love at first sight and have been together ever since.

That myth is then frequently retold and emotional content is imagined and included from the context of the relationship that had developed since that unexpected, and yet fateful, Patron-filled night. The myth shifts, and expands, and grows until it becomes The Only Memory, or at least, a mask that the Memory can wear.

And unless other information - like the Truth - comes and disturbs the mnemonic picture of how your love began, that myth becomes the Story of Your Life.

Your Fairytale. You believe in your own Fairytale.

But the Truth has a way of making itself known, whether you want it to or not. And then the stories have to change, and then the myths must be retold, the fairytales re-imagined,

because the real memories are revived. And you remember what really happened.
If you want to.
And you must decide.
Whether you want this story to be about Julia and her Tall, Dark, and Handsome Will.
Or the story of Julia and David.
So that we can be made to remember the deeply buried truth of that particular boy she had known long before Prince Charming had come along. And that boy, now a man - so to speak - who had found her once again after her Prince had ridden off on his white horse, leaving her - a hapless, hardworking Cinderella - standing once more alone amongst the cinders and ashes of what had become her life.

Chapter 2
Plus One

Six to eight weeks before the wedding of Chris Billings (her college sweetheart) and Deidre Diemand (her college roommate), Julia Santos Rosa's classic black Montblanc hovered over the cream linen response card that she herself had helped the bride choose:

MR. & MRS. WILLIAM ROSA
Number of Guests _____

Number of Guests.
That was the question, wasn't it?
A week ago - one week - she would have written a finely scripted "2" without any thought at all, slid the card back into the envelope and popped it into the mail, all within moments of receiving it. *A prompt response was always appreciated by a bride-to-be.*
But today, as she gently pulled apart the heavy weight of the wedding invitation from the multitudinous layers of fine velum, Julia hesitated.
Why?
The well-coiffed hairs on the back of her neck prickled, and her pen just couldn't make contact with the cardstock.
Why can't I write this?
Could it be that for the first time, she wasn't absolutely sure if her husband would be at her side, looking handsome in his suit, attending to her needs, mingling amongst the other guests, being casually but not ostentatiously generous with drinks, gifts, compliments?
Could it be that for the first time he was more interested in talking to their neighbor about hiking the Appalachian Trail - *of all things* - than he was in discussing the final stages of their pool house renovation?
I mean, since when does Will hike? He goes to spinning class instead of riding bikes with the kids. He uses spray tan

instead of sitting out by the pool. The man gets manicures, for chrissakes.

And yet, Julia wasn't naïve. She knew things had become different between them and she knew why. Or, if she was being honest, who: The new neighbor. Their new friend. Ellen, who did yoga, and had crow's feet. Some earthy, free-spirited wisp of a mother of five. *Five kids!* Ellen had ignited some sort of light in Will that Julia - lovely, well-preserved, well-mannered, hard-working Julia - had never seen before. Over sidewalk conversations, kids' play-dates, lingering nights drinking in one another's kitchens. It was as though that woman had introduced Julia to a Will she had never met - a man who hiked, and drank beer with the neighbors, and actually wore jeans on Casual Friday.

It wasn't bad. The changes in him weren't awful, in fact, they made him seem, *I don't know, lighter? I guess.* It was just different. Julia hadn't known that he would have liked any of that, or to do any of those things. Julia and Will both worked, and they had the kids, and when they came home, they talked about their work and the kids.

So what was it, Julia? Who is this man, your automatic Plus One? Do you even know who he is anymore?

She stopped herself.

Yes, yes she did.

She didn't have time to mull this out. He was her husband.

Of course she knew who he was.

She was just being stupid.

She wrote a hurried "2" and stuck the card into the small envelope, grabbed her Louis Vuitton Pont-Neuf and keys, and on her way out, slid the response into the mailbox, lifting the red flag.

The card would be in the mailman's hands at promptly 10 AM, on its way to Deidre in a matter of hours. As she pulled out her driveway and slowly accelerated past her house, Julia stared down her black and white mailbox, daring the committing correspondence within that lay so obviously oblivious to her glaringly misplaced anger - *You will not make a liar out of me.*

Chapter 3
Save The Date

Less than a year prior to the wedding of Chris Billings (her beloved) to our very own Deidre Diemand, Chris had had the idea to call *her*.

Dee didn't want to, but as she stared up longingly at the sun-bleached shingles of the sprawling beach-side hotel, with its large sweeping white porches flanked on one side by the beach and the other a huge swath of unearthly green lawn, dotted by berms of razor sharp salt marsh grasses and fragrant sea roses, she knew she was going to have to.

Chris and Dee had been vacationing. They spent their precious two weeks at her oldest sister Joan's house to save some money. Joan had had a summer home on Nantucket since her brother David had been twelve and Dee had been ten.

On that first visit so long ago, David had made up some rhyme about a guy named Dick. Dee had remembered the rhyme so well that she had proudly recited it to her mom and dad in their den one night after dinner, which had earned her a very early bedtime and David more than one smack across the face. Her big brother didn't speak to her for about a week after that.

Dee was approaching forty years old and, for the first time, she was in love - actually in it, not merely the spectator to other people's affairs as she had been slogging her way through in college, med school, her fellowship, and her residency. Why had it taken her so long? Two reasons: One, the lab coats of the pediatric endocrinologists were not as sexy as one might initially believe. And two, Chris and she? Well, they had history.

But here she was, with a gorgeous ring on her finger and planning to marry a man she truly, truly loved. "Head over heels type shit," her once dirty-limericking big brother had said into his beer as he staggered over the deck of his boat when she had reluctantly told him the big news. David had then burped his congratulations to his sister and his best friend and unceremoniously passed out.

Chris Billings, *the* Chris Billings - the man she had longed for since David had brought him to their family's large ten room house for that Christmas vacation from his fateful freshman year at college - had finally asked her to marry him.

David had actually driven his pathetic ass up the coast to get them at the port in Hyannis and take them across the Bay on his S.S. Midlife Crisis. He pulled into a slip that he claimed was owned by a guy he used to work for at the firm in Boston and "Nah, of course he wouldn't mind." It was right on the dock of the Nantucket Plaza by the Sea; Dee had taken one look at the classic Massachusetts island vista before her and known that this was it.

This had to be the place.

She had run inside before the ropes had even been securely tied to the cleats, asking to speak to one of the managers and questioning - hope against hope - if there was space available for a wedding this coming summer, but as her Intended had predicted, the place was booked three years out. Chris had shrugged a meaty shoulder, coming up behind her at the gently burnished white pine desk, "Maybe we could call Julia."

Dee had frowned automatically at the sound of her college roommate's name coming out of her fiancé's mouth, but when the manager perked up, "Julia? Julia Rosa?" Dee had gained a little confidence.

"Um, yes. A dear, dear friend of mine. She actually suggested I come down and speak to you about next, let's say, August."

"I am so sorry," the manager had said, a bit flabbergasted. "She hadn't called me about you, I apologize. Please let me show you the two ballrooms. I'm sure we can make some sort of accommodation."

And so, dizzying delight mixed with just a twist of dread, Dee's fate, and the fate of those around her, was sealed. She looked back at the hotel from the deck of the boat as David had called them back. He had been ordered to vacate what turned out to be his ex-boss' slip, and Dee knew deep down that, yes, she was going to have to call her college roommate, whom she knew best as, Chris' ex-girlfriend.

CHAPTER 4
Someone Blue

The Nantucket Plaza By The Sea glowed from within, lit not only by the gentle flickering of hundreds of candles and a thousand twinkling fairy lights, but the lilt and glimmer of celebratory music and the sparkle and shine champagne gives to happy conversations. The hotel's wedding season was in full swing and Julia had traded out her two Boston events for the three on the island so that she could be here when her dear old friend Deidre would come.

Three weddings, on this of all weeks. Julia had burned through the first two on a heady combination of caffeine and a slow boiling rage. But right now, Julia had less than a half an hour before she was off the clock and she wasn't sure if she had enough strength to make it.

It was 11 PM and this bride – this cute little breathless twenty-seven year old darling – just, JUST swept by in her second gown of the evening, Julia's hands had been shaking so much that she could barely slip the tiny silk-covered buttons into the unnecessarily miniscule button holes in this second - SECOND! - dress.

Who needs two wedding dresses? Why is that now a thing? she seethed to herself. Julia resolved that she would do everything in her power and influence to discourage that trend from gaining any more speed.

She crossed her arms in front of her, her fingers tapping her TRX-trained biceps. *Stay frosty, Julia. Stay cool.*

The bride was a young brunette from the Back Bay. At the onset of their planning, Julia had discreetly arranged for her to meet with a trainer and nutritionist and get her figure dieted down to perfect size 4. Her hair had been coiffed under the expert hands of Marsetta – one of Boston and New York's premiere event dressers – who had swept, powdered, and sprayed the girl into a passable imitation of the Duchess of York.

The redheaded groom who himself had been tailored and groomed to within an inch of his life - under Julia's careful and practiced tutelage, of course - just stared in wonder at his bride's glowing marvelousness. That glow came courtesy of both Julia's exclusive dermatologist's vigorous bi-weekly applications of a bucketful of GlamGlow along with this morning's grueling two hour session of contouring, highlighting, shading, and setting.

The two were joined together dancing under an enormous pergola of camellias, white sea roses, purple lavender flowers, and boxwood that Julia had spent most of last night and this early morning constructing. Their equally manicured hands clasped together with their pre-emptively Botox'ed palms to prevent clamminess, and they stood there looking into one another's eyes - made picture perfect - Julia signaled the photographer in - *and dear God, didn't they just look so fucking happy.*

Julia knew it wouldn't look good if the wedding planner stuck her own well-manicured finger down her throat.

Instead, she took an enormous gulp of air and breathed it out slowly. In through the nose, out through the mouth.

Two dresses!

Okay, breathe. Breathe. This darling little bride was just living out her fantasy - *operative term: fantasy.* One without any bearing on any reality of actual married life. Promises, vows, goals, cakes, rings. Fantasy, illusion, unsustainable perfection, irresponsibly high expectations.

Happily ever after.

Such bullshit.

On Tuesday night - yes, this Tuesday night - her very own Tall, Dark, and Handsome William had walked into their stunning gourmet kitchen - remodeled finally last May - leaned against the exquisite Carrera marble island almost knocking a ceramic fruit bowl onto the lovingly and carefully chosen scraped hardwood floor and announced that he was leaving her.

Her.

He was leaving her.

Prince Charming was leaving Cinderella.

The beautiful peasant princess who had taken on the life of the palace, made it her own, worked harder and had done it better than anyone had before, all while maintaining a home, a family, a full time job, and the same goddamned size she had been in when he met her.

She had braced herself on the porcelain lip of the farmhouse sink as his words hit her back, just below the shoulder blades.

But Cinderella didn't turn around.

She wished she were able to say she was surprised. She wished that somehow she could have the luxury of being deeply wounded by his unilateral decision about their lives together, to show that somehow she would be, could be emotionally affected by the fact that her Prince Charming had just told her he was leaving her for Ellen down the street. He would be moving out and heading straight to her house and that he would take the kids on Saturday.

So instead of raging at him, screaming and crying in defiance, begging him to reconsider their love, their lives together, all the things a normal wife in this scenario would possibly do, Julia merely pointed out the inconvenience, "You couldn't have waited one more week, William?"

"What?" he said.

"The *wedding*."

He sighed, "There's always a wedding."

He was right. There was. But this one was different. Important. Important to her. "I'm talking about my friends' wedding, Will."

"Who?"

"Deidre Diemand and Chris Billings, from college, they're getting married next weekend in Nantucket. We're spending a week on the island..." She looked over her shoulder and saw his blank stare. "You completely forgot."

"Had things on my mind, Julia."

"Oh, I'm so sorry." She faced him, the taste of sarcasm was in her mouth – salty, good, and not as bitter as one might expect. "Yes, things like leaving your wife."

He blinked, "Just cancel."

"I can't. It's at the Plaza. Plus, she's one of my oldest friends."

"That you haven't heard from in how many years?" He added, "And isn't he your ex-boyfriend?"

"William. Please." She steadied her voice. But her "Please" was less of an entreaty and more of a warning.

"What do you want me to tell you?"

"We've been planning this for a year..."

"You've been planning it for a year, Julia. Not me. I didn't have anything to do with it."

"By who's choice, William?"

"Both of ours." He mumbled.

"What?" She asked.

He just shook his head, "What do you want me to say?"

She stared at him. *I don't know, that you've been kidding all this time with Ellen? That you don't really want to leave?* "You couldn't have waited one more week to leave me, William, really? I mean, you're already fucking her."

He had winced. Winced at her knowledge? Or winced at her use of *that* word?

Well, let's see. "So what is the big *fucking* hurry?" She took a little perverse pleasure in the twist in his mouth, it made him look ugly.

"I couldn't put my happiness on hold any longer. Not for you, not for our friends..."

"My friends, actually." She narrowed her eyes, replying territorially.

"Yes, I guess you're right." Will had said. "Maybe that was the problem to begin with..."

She watched him leave, and carefully slid the fruit bowl back two inches, to its appropriate spot on the countertop. "My happiness," she sneered, mocking Prince Charming, to no other of his subjects, but herself.

Julia, now calming, looked down at the bride and had to admit the wedding was, to this point, flawless. Of course it was. Julia's staff was an elite team whose execution of timelines would have made the Navy Seals proud - always on hand, practically invisible and ready to take any trouble out with silent, and just short-of-deadly force, if necessary. Julia had been working with Amy and José for over six years, and their team was one of the reasons why a Plaza Wedding was considered the Nuptials Gold Standard.

Julia's personal record was spotless, in the nineteen years of her career, she had attended every single one of her events - gracious, polite, accommodating. Without exception, she was there. At. Every. Single. One.

Weddings, despite their forced and sentimental indulgences, were Serious Business. And Julia had always treated it as such. Cavanaugh, the senior event manager for all of the Northeast hotels, had reminded her department over and over again, that weddings were a sixty billion dollar a year kind of Serious, recession-proof, cash business-type of Serious. *Happy brides pay their bills; we will have happy brides.*

Julia's particular expertise was to handle the emotional stuff. Perpetually unruffled, no other manager at the hotel was as good at the strategic manipulation of the high-running emotions of weddings. Every wedding contained within it the seeds of familial drama and Julia approached every single one with a sharp sensitivity, an astute coolness, a sympathetic detachment.

In fact, one of her first conversations with a committed bride and groom began in her splendid office, with Julia in her most mannerly, but assuring, tone asking gently, but firmly, "Just so that I can be aware, and to ensure that your special day is about the two of you, the joy of your families coming together, are there any, let's say, issues that could possibly come up during your wedding day?"

It usually took a moment or two, Julia at first would dutifully note the initial listings of allergies, or food sensitivities that they would start with, but it was usually not more than five minutes before one of the intendeds blurted out something about how their drunk uncle had habitually and notoriously dropped trou at every family event and how their second cousin had had a sex change, and then had another one and changed back, and their fifteen year old brother - the beloved baby of the family - could possibly try to feel up every single one of the bridesmaids.

Julia would nod and keep her face perfectly impassive, sympathetic as she rapidly noted the list of potential dangers. There were always the tricky troubles that she wasn't made aware of as well - stuff even too sensitive for the soul-confessional her office had become - such as the plethora of scandalous information available in, say, your average Best Man's speech. Oh God, Julia's deep sleep anxiety dreams usually contained a tuxedoed young man holding a cocktail and a microphone.

With so many years under her belt, Julia could, without bragging, say that she knew more family secrets than your thousand-dollar-an-hour Boston family psychiatrist. Will told her that someday she could write a book - Julia could make them millions, he told her.
Back when he seemed to care about her work.
Or was it the millions?

Julia, Billy, and Annie had spent that first night alone huddled together on her giant king-sized bed. Not completely alone. She had broken a long-standing household rule of Will's and allowed the family's Golden Retriever to cuddle up with the two kids. The four bodies lay there, not saying much about what was going on, but even her thirteen year old boy took reluctant comfort in the closeness of his mom, his little sister, and his big, fluffy dog.
The kids had spent Wednesday and Thursday nights in there too, instead of their own rooms, while Julia hunched over work details: from the champagne, flip-flops, and custom robes in the traveler's baskets in the hotel rooms to the very last beach rock candy favors poured into tiny metal sand buckets, tied up in tiny crafting sailing rope with scented sprigs of rosemary, mint, and lavender flowers.
The mindless minutiae of the Nantucket weddings - work that could have easily been handled by Amy's assistants, or José's workers - helped Julia. It gave her something for her hands to do. Despite her calm, cool, and collected exterior, Julia had found her hands to be twitchy, restless over the past few days, like two birds no longer soothed under the weight of that singular metal ring.
She just kept telling herself that it was okay. She could do this. She had easily handled hundreds of weddings before this. She would maintain her flawless record. Her brain kept steady, her breathing regular by the painstaking, repetitive details, so that the plans – the new plans she would have to make about the house, the car, the kids, her life - were left just at bay.
Plans could wait until later. After.
She hadn't told anyone at work yet about William moving out. She hadn't breathed a word to anyone, outside of immediate necessity. Thankfully, her boss wasn't interested in

her personal life, just the Plaza's particular slice of that sixty billion dollar Serious Business.

"Well done, Mrs. Rosa," he had commented, surveying the Nantucket location. "You've outdone yourself yet again." He gazed at the looping photo slideshow of the entire family's wedding pictures interspersed with the bride and groom's childhood photos, "Almost makes you believe in love, doesn't it?"

She *almost* choked, "Almost, Mr. Cavanaugh."

"The Plaza once again provides a magical beginning to two young lives." He had put his hand on her arm and looked sentimentally into her eyes.

She tucked her left hand into the crook of her elbow. *If Cavanaugh tries to hug me, I'm going to lose it.*

Mercifully, he didn't. "Yes. Magical," she had replied trying to hide the general unease welling up in her stomach, glancing down on his hand on her arm "So. Very. Magical." He smiled and squeezed and told her he would see her the Monday after next when she returned from her "working vacation," back in the office, bright and early.

The band struck up the first few lines of Sister Sledge's "We Are Family," *here we go*, she breathed deeply, trying to make a continuous circle with her breath, containing her anxiety trapped in that small manageable space beneath her ribcage. Julia looked over at the wedding guests, happy, smiling, swaying either to the music or the aftereffects of Open Bar.

Julia needed something to do. She needed something to occupy her brain – a catering issue, an electrical blowout – anything that could save her from just standing here, helpless against all this singularly ironic L.O.V(omit).E.

And the Universe delivered her one for the book.

"Excuse me, Miss?" clipped a British accent standing to her left. She looked over and recognized the father of the bride, Mr. Brighton, was at her elbow. "You are the manager, aren't you?"

"Ah yes, sir. Julia, the wedding manager, what can I do to help you?" She gathered a small polite smile to her lips.

"Yes, well, I was told you would be the one to speak to about a… a matter."

"Of course, sir."

"Well, you see, it's a bit sticky."

"I am sure we can fix it," she assured him.

"All right then, you see my wife - excuse me, ex-wife - has just announced to me, that she has asked the minister to renew her vows to her new husband."

Julia nodded, keeping her features under control, not exactly sure how to respond yet, but patient, attentive. *Was he asking for sympathy? Assurance?*

Mr. Brighton continued his clipped syllables. "Here."

What?

"Tonight."

Wow.

"When the bride and groom are having their final dance."

Julia nodded, biting her lips back slightly.

"In front of everyone."

Oh boy.

"I don't care what the cost, just please," he gazed at her earnestly, "make it not happen."

The mother of the bride can be an X-factor in a wedding, the bride and groom can be sideswiped by the emotional parental overload. Their child is getting married, and so, much like the Best Men, there can be the element of surprise to their maternal antics.

Julia got it. She didn't agree with it, but she got it. Up to this point in their lives, the mother is the contact person for the family - typically in charge of schedules, holiday events, parties. The mother is the Chief Operating Officer, so to speak.

And a wedding is usually the first time that the daughter is the one at the center of the events of the day. The bride has to step in to become COO and it can make a mother nervous.

Or maybe, a little jealous.

And attention-starved.

And in the worst cases, flat-out batshit crazy.

Julia's anxiety converted directly into adrenaline-fueled energy, her brain shifted into professional overdrive. Julia flipped through her mental file folder of what she knew about the relationship between the mother and father of the bride: Yes, theirs had been a sticking point in their initial conversations; yes, there was the issue of the bride's new stepfather not being terribly welcomed into the family circle; yes, Mr. Brighton was the name on the very large checks; and then - most importantly to Julia - yes, that sweet little bride would be mortified. Devastated.

The day was sweet little Hers, not her Mother's.

Julia admonished herself a bit; the mother had exhibited the classic high maintenance signs at their earlier meetings - seating issues, unhappiness with cake design, disdain at the color of the groomsmen's ties. Julia should have taken additional steps to ensure that the mother of the bride had felt adequately honored.

"I see the dilemma," Julia drew in a large breath, buying herself some thinking time, then smiled and took his arm, "Please go and enjoy yourself, Mr. Brighton, I will send Piero over with another? Manhattan, is it? I promise this little issue will, of course, work out for everyone."

He left her at the bar and she turned. Like a fighter about to go into the ring, like a ninja poised to attack, like a Starfleet captain on an important diplomatic mission, Julia was ready. *No one was going to upstage her bride.* Not on her watch.

With a calm professional detachment, the Plaza Hotel's premier wedding manager swung into action. A text immediately drew Amy to the front of the ballroom and José from the kitchen. They had looked down at their phones and had looked up, making eye contact, and on Julia's signal:

Amy sidled close to her hip, "Julia, I can take this."

Julia thought for a moment, her assistant was wonderful at handling many of the detail work that needed to be done for each one of the weddings, but she had yet to tackle a larger onsite issue.

"I appreciate that, Amy."

"I really can, Julia, I know you've had a tough week."

Julia spun on her, "Wha-at?" her voice cracked the word into two pieces. *What did she know? How did she know?*

Amy looked at her slightly startled. "I mean, you've been busy. The three weddings…"

"Oh," Julia nodded. "Yes, very busy."

"And I thought…"

"No," Julia interrupted, "No need, dear, I've got it." Julia's regained composure had a slightly rougher edge than she had intended. She couldn't let Amy see, so she softened her voice deliberately, "You're very sweet to think of me. But I've got it." She looked down at her phone, "José says Piero's got the kitchen cleared. Let's go."

They walked out of the ballroom together. They would meet in the kitchen, and plan, confirm, and execute the Charm Offensive. With Julia, ready, poised, confident at the helm.

Within twenty minutes, the impending wedding-ruining vow renewal apocalyptic disaster Mother Lode had been thwarted.

And the great part about it was the mother never realized that she had been thwarted.

After a brief conversation with the New York office, Julia had skillfully taken the mother and new stepfather into a sumptuous private office just off the main ballroom. Julia fed her a drink and some caviar canapés. Julia knew that people ate caviar canapés regardless of whether or not they liked fish eggs, because simply, everyone - from every walk of life - liked to say they ate caviar. And with the utmost tact, and careful grace, Julia convinced the Mother of the Bride that a three night stay at the New York Plaza would make a much more adventurous and auspicious vow renewal event.

The handsome, and fabulous, catering manager José had entered with another tray of avocado lobster rolls with a spicy cilantro dipping sauce and offered a modest dinner for fifty with the flowers of their choosing. And ever-efficient Amy, Julia's timeline manager, her second hand, delivered the final masterstroke, assuring that she had two Broadway theater tickets for their stay, just name the date.

The new stepfather shrugged and thanked them, and the Mother of The Bride beamed. "You all are spoiling us. Thank you!"

Thank your ex-husband. "How many years will you to be married?" Julia smiled into her question.

"Five years."

"That's wonderful. And you know, renewing your vows is such a special occasion and it would seem a shame to just throw it onto the end of your daughter's wedding. I think that you should give such, such a milestone the attention it deserves."

The Mother of the Bride nodded hypnotically at Julia's Jedi Mind Trick, "Yes, the attention it deserves. Exactly. It is special."

The wedding manager encouraged them to take advantage of the new upgraded suite available to them for the night and watched as they wandered back into the ballroom, excitedly holding hands and making new plans for their stay in New York sometime around New Year's Eve.

Julia sighed out her thanks to her team. She gave them leave on the earlier ferry. Amy protested, ever careful about the timeline, but Julia assured her finally that the place was shutting down. She could handle the rest of the night.

Julia sidled quietly up to Mr. Brighton who was watching his daughter and her new husband enjoying their last moments of their evening in the ballroom of the Nantucket Plaza by the Sea. He turned to her, motioning toward the band, "I think they're quite good actually."

"Ah, yes. The wedding band."

"You're not a fan."

"On the contrary." She turned to see the father's face smiling at her. The visage was pleasant enough, handsome even. She had guessed at their first meeting early fifties, too early to be considered a Silver Fox, too old to be in his prime - that odd bloated age, before a man becomes craggily handsome, as only men can do in those later years of life. "I just wanted to let you know that the former Mrs. Brighton has reconsidered her renewal. For this evening, anyway."

"Yes, I see that." He saw his ex-wife and her husband dancing among the crowd on the floor. "Thank you."

"Of course, sir. The Plaza is always happy to help." She added gracefully, "And any extras will be itemized for you."

He looked at her, still smiling easily, to convey his gratitude, but his eyes looked into hers a little more deeply than she expected. And then, she watched his eyes flick over her entirety - it was quick, but noticeable. Julia knew that he wasn't looking at her as a helpful employee of the hotel. She was startled out of her professional authoritative role by his unexpected appreciative gaze.

To be honest, on any other weekend of her life, Julia would have found him somewhat attractive. She may have even flirted with him mildly. Because honestly, a good English accent is hard to pass over. But that was the occasional meaningless friendly word or two from behind the airtight barrier her wedding ring had always provided her. But tonight, there was no wedding ring. *Not tonight. Not today. Not right now. Maybe not ever again.* Looking down at her hand, she felt suddenly and embarrassingly naked.

"I don't really care, Miss... Rosa? It is Miss, isn't it?" he looked pointedly at her hand, she looked down at her empty ring finger, the pale skin dented and circled under her knuckle,

Oh God. She didn't know what to say - she was a Miss. No, she was Mrs. Julia Rosa. Her married name, that was her name. But what about now? With the ring gone, did that mean her name was gone now too? What was she supposed to say? Ring meant "Mrs. Julia Rosa." No ring would then mean "Ms. Julia Santos."

Her identity was tied up in a ring. A ring she wasn't wearing.

What do I do?

She felt like she was being forced to make a big decision right now, with no one to discuss it with - no committee of two to convene. Was this how the rest of her life was going to be, making these decisions, *like what do I call myself, all by myself?* No need to stick her finger down her throat, she felt legitimately ill. She managed out, "Well, actually, it's Ms. Julia Santos."

She saw his glad acknowledgement. She saw him hand her his business card, she read *Richard Brighton*. "I work in the financial district, Summer Street. So perhaps we shall see one another again, *Ms. Julia Santos.*"

Her maiden name called her out. She saw it in the air hanging there in front of her. It was like getting caught by an old acquaintance you knew at the grocery store, but you had ducked down the aisles to avoid talking to. *I don't want to see Julia Santos. I don't even know her anymore. What would we have to talk about?*

"Perhaps," with a smile that she hoped was friendly, but not overly so. Julia had made enough major life decisions for the last five minutes.

With the crisis averted both professionally, and then personally, Julia had hoped that the automatic routines of the breakdown would calm her mind, soothe her hands, keep her occupied. But she found that the reset of the ballroom did little to occupy her mind and her little knot of anxiety re-established itself to just between her lungs, pressing down on them, trying its best to expand its living space.

Piero had given her one surprised look and assured her that he could handle the bar and the wait staff - she looked a little green around the gills. She whispered out a thanks and barreled out of the ballroom.

I've got to get out of here.
I can't.
Yes, I can.
Julia could leave now.
Right now.

She had a couple of days. The kids were at her brother Kevin's place on Martha's Vineyard just across the Bay, she could grab them and pull them to the ferry and she could arrange for Amy, or even Gary, to take the helm for Deidre Diemand and her wedding.

Julia Rosa - sorry, Santos, no, ROSA - *oh my God,* she was suddenly schizophrenic! - skip out on a wedding?

No.

Why the hell not?

She could text her friend, let her know what had happened and plead with her that she was sorry but it would be too hard, right now. Julia breathed out. She could do that.

Dee would understand.

But, would everyone else?

What would her boss say? What would that awful Emily Raffia at the New York office say? And what about all of those people at the wedding - would everyone else see her absence at Dee and Chris' wedding as some weird jealous statement about Dee marrying Julia's old college boyfriend?

What would it look like?

Should I care? Julia thought. *I've got Billy and Annie and the house...What do I do with the house? And work? How* am I going to fit in hours? There are twelve more weddings this summer alone!

How is this all going to happen?

She stopped in the middle of the doorway, her hands splayed out in front of her - *Dee's wedding? Chris? William? The children? The house? Santos? Rosa? Who's going to see? Who do I have to tell? What does everyone need to know?* And then. *What do I do now? What do I do now? What do I do now?*

And then he knocked her right off of her Louboutins.

She was hit by what seemed to be a moving wall, and her sheath-dress-covered ass skittered along with her anxiety-ridden thoughts across the polished pine and her first thought was, *What the f...*

She looked up.

It first looked as though she had been attacked by a giant grey wool fisherman's sweater, but as she took the huge, rough hand that was offered to her, she noticed that the sweater had a shaggy mane of dirty blond hair and a moustache. The dumbest, old-timey-est moustache she had ever seen.

"Fine place for you to be," the sweatermanmoustache growled at her as he straightened her up by her arm.

"Excuse me?" She yelped back indignantly, pulling her elbow out of his strong grip.

He looked like something out of Moby Dick. "You're excused." He hoisted his canvas bag farther back on his shoulder and walked right around her to the front desk.

She was dumbstruck, her mouth open, she stared at the back of his shaggy head indignantly, she put her hands out in front of her *of all the rude... This is a resort town. These aren't the streets of Boston for chrissakes. Who did this idiot think he was - a fricking pirate?*

He looked back at her standing there, as she turned this way and that, unable to fully express her frustration, her incredible irritation, and she swore that under that stupid-looking caterpillar that was sleeping on his upper lip, he smiled at her.

Smiled.

Ugh! And for the first time in years, somewhere out of that cool, even professional woman Julia had become, the specter of the tough girl she had once been blinked her eyes. Something in that smile was infuriating. She snarled, actually snarled, in his direction, which only seemed to make the caterpillar curve upwards further.

"Stop being a dick, David," called out a familiar voice, as Julia felt an arm slide around her waist. "Don't let big bad brother bother you, Jules."

Julia turned, acknowledged her friend and slid into the embrace, "Dee!" as they hugged. The arms of her friend felt surprisingly good, comforting, soothing. She exclaimed without thought, "I'm so glad to see you!"

"You too," her old roommate shouted out, almost surprisingly.

"Wait," Julia came to a slow realization of Dee's previous attentions, "that's Dave?"

The big sweater, now made somewhat recognizable, ambled up, and imitated their screaming, waving his hands in front of him, "Aaaahhhh! Aren't you all a little too old to be screaming like little schoolgirls?

"That is Dave," Dee sighed as her brother stood in front of the two of them, arms about one another's waist, "he looks like a moron, doesn't he?"

"Show some respect, Deidre," Julia, smugly. "*Captain* Moron," Julia saluted primly, and Dee took the pirate stance. The girls fell into giggles.

"We're in Nantucket, aren't we? Home of Mariner Literature. It's a statement."

"What kind of statement? 'I'm not interested in being attractive anymore?'" Dee sassed her brother.

He sighed and shook his head, and moved around the wall of women. "At least Captain Moron knows not to stand in a doorway like the Village Idiot," as he passed Julia's side, and headed down the driveway of the hotel toward the dock.

Julia's blood heated rapidly, her coolly professional adult mind was steeped in some deeply adolescent physical urge to rip Dee's stupid, troublemaking brother to shreds. Here she was, caught by Deidre, her husband off fucking their neighbor, and like nothing had ever happened, like no time had passed - Dee's brother was giving her shit, trying to be funny. It was late, she was in the middle of a perfectly appropriate anxiety attack, her boss and her colleagues were gone, and it felt like this big fluffy one had just knocked all her years of carefully practiced decorum right out from underneath her.

In the vernacular of her beloved sci-fi, she went from cool, collected Spock to rage-filled, bloodthirsty Klingon in about twenty seconds flat.

She spun out of her friend's embrace, "Charming, David." She stomped after him. "You haven't seen me in - how many years? Four? Five? - and this is how you say 'hello' to me?"

Dee called after her brother, "Shave off that stupid moustache, David! This is *my* wedding David, not some Village People Convention!" She watched her friend stride after her brother. "Jules, we need to talk about the florist!"

"Be there in a second!"

Shaggy David didn't look back at his sister or her as he headed down the private dock of the hotel, he said straight ahead, "Oh yeah, hello Julia, or should I say, 'Hey Jude.'"

"Really?" she stopped, "That's the best you've got?" shaking her head.

He strode down, unfolding some of the contents of their long history along behind him on the rough wooden planks of the landing. He obviously noted that she slowed pace because he shouted back so she could hear him, "It's such a good song!"

"Would have loved to have heard the whole thing," she shouted back, feet planted on the edge where the pavement met the wood.

"I know, a live performance too, seems such a shame to have missed it," he provoked up the long wooden pier.

It jumpstarted her tirade, and she lunged - well as much as one can lunge - down the wooden dock in a form-fitting but modest dress, "You're bringing back a twenty year old argument, Dave," her black shoes clattered down the gangplank. David had stopped next to a large white boat and stepped aboard ducking into the cabin.

The tap, smack, tap of Julia's red-soled heels slowed as she couldn't help but admire the vessel. The rays of the Nantucket moon skimmed across the surface of the water and stopped on the long teak railings, making them glow and shimmer with pale light.

Her breath caught a little, *did David Diemand just step inside this boat?* She ducked a little to see if she could spot him moving around, "And uh, you still haven't quite figured out how to talk to girls yet, have you?" she called down to him.

His great dirty blond mane of mess popped up, the stupid moustache, the dumb mariner outfit, he looked right at her, "No," he admitted, but added, smiling devilishly, "but I can still get them to follow me."

That stopped her.

Her friend's big brother stopped her in her tracks, foot on the rim, hands grabbing the ropes, about to attack, and that one little joke from when she was just a kid rocked her weight back onto her off foot on the dock. She laughed at herself. She had to. *What was she eighteen again?* She looked down at her shoe, and shook her head.

He watched her retreat, straighten up, smooth out the front of her dress, press her hands to her hips, and take a large cleansing breath.

She looked over at him, pulling herself together. "Hello, David," she conceded.

"Hi Julia." He smiled, the corners of his eyes lifted above that moustache. "Now, you're here to help me with my bags?"

Julia just turned on her heel and walked down the dock back to the hotel front door. "I'll see you later, David."

Spock returned.

"Yeah, probably." He watched her walk away for just a minute.

Maybe two.

CHAPTER 5
To Have And To Hold

Oh shit.

He pulled his sweater over his head and flung it back into the cabin of his impressive 35 foot convertible Viking.

He had a few minutes to go through his onshore routine, clearing out the cabin he'd been living in for the past six months, make a list of supplies, and see what needed repair.

This is not what I need.

David leaned over and checked the cleats and stepped onto the planks. He had been hoping that when Mrs. Julia Santos Rosa had shown up that she would have somehow become horribly disfigured in the past few years, struck in her prime with some form of elephantitis, or alopecia.

Or both would have been good.

Okay, so maybe he didn't really wish her an oversized arm or hairlessness, he just didn't want to have to look at her for the next week laughing and joking with that…husband… while he sat at the goddamned Singles table.

He could have asked someone… who? Jessica? Kirsten? What the hell was her name? The preppy blonde… Who the hell was he kidding? They were all preppy blondes. But then he would have had to be trapped with the same girl for all of the Wedding Hells' Bells that his sister had somehow roped him into.

There he would be, six months Laura-less. *Not a level playing field.* He almost wished Laura were here just for this goddamned wedding - not that his ex-fiancée had called him. Or spoken to him. Or acknowledged in any way the significance of their ten-year relationship. She didn't seem to care if he was still alive. But still, Laura would have been a buffer at least, to have her there. *For just as long as Mr. and Mrs. William Rosa were around.*

He leaned down and grabbed his gas cans and headed down the dock; he had to check with the harbormaster and fill up.

Get a grip, Diemand, he reprimanded himself. He paid the kid at the pumps and filled up first one, then the other of the bright red plastic containers, *you haven't spent any significant*

time with Julia for a while, twisting the caps, *you haven't given her a second thought...*
He stopped himself.
Well now, that's just a lie, you fucking moron. He headed back to the boat, and stowed the fuel. He had given her second, third, fourth, fifth - he could go on - for, well, as long as he had known her. *Jesus, he was a moron.*
A Captain Moron. He grinned. Although he didn't want to.
Such a smart ass.
He straightened up. A Very. Smart. Ass.
He was glad he had avoided the arrivals for his sister's guest thingy. But of course - of course! - on his last trip in to secure things with the manager, he had almost crushed Juju as she stood there in the doorway like some distracted driver. She still had those slim hips, those long legs, the big eyes, that funny little nose, smirky mouth and that fabulous, fabulous ass.
He sniffed at the pits of his dirty white t-shirt, and rubbed his hand over the moustache that he had worn for the past six months, much to his family's fury.
He sighed deeply. Interaction with *her – that one* - was going to be inevitable. And boy, he'd gotten into so much trouble because of her over the years.
Inevitable. Trouble. His eyebrows flicked up at the words, a little grin turned up the corners of his hair-covered mouth.
Inevitable trouble?
Inevitable trouble.
He might as well make it fun.

CHAPTER 6
Until Death

So there it was.
And here she was.
Solo.
Days of preparations, fittings, assembly, rehearsals, mixed with a sundry of destination wedding events. *Unless.* Unless she wanted to confess what had happened, make it news, say it to the world, *give it some finality.*
Make it real.
"Will has left me. We're getting a divorce."
That would get her out of this wedding for damned sure.
Out of a wedding.
Unthinkable.
But it would.
But then I'd have to go home. And think about the next steps.
Steps.
You have to take steps in a divorce right? You know, steps, like what happens when someone in your family dies. Is that what divorce is like? A funeral?
A divorce. A funeral. *Grief for a loss of some kind.*
You're sad, and you cry, and then you have to make arrangements. They have to be made. Because no one really cares how sad you are, not really. Sadness is assumed, a foregone conclusion. You can't just stop, call into work right away, pull the kids out of school, and then do nothing. You have to take steps. Go to meetings with your family. And there are strange appointments to be made and met, almost immediately. No pause to take it in. To think, to understand. There is odd vocabulary to be learned and used as though you understood it all along. And other people, not important people - not like your kids, or your brother, or sister - but estranged cousins, and out of touch aunts who come and call within hours of the news to console you, but you end up consoling them, helping them deal, helping them to understand what happened. You're easing their pain.

And that is what is supposed to comfort us? People asking about the mess the other had left behind. Whether it is death or a divorce, it is a mess. And you have to explain your mess to everyone.

How does that comfort anyone? How do the procedures of death or divorce help anyone understand what they've just lost?

I need to learn about lawyers, and mediators, and PRCs and division of assets. All unfamiliar and uncomfortable things and words and phrases she had heard about from people who were going through it. People she had pitied. "Pitied" was the word she had actually used, as she had almost gloated some bit of gossip to her husband. A gleeful kind of pity. *Thank God, it's not us right?*

Can you imagine the glee in those people's eyes when they hear "Julia and William Rosa are..." what?

And here she was, if she was going to tell them, and stay here, that is exactly what she would be. She was going to be pitied.

I don't want to be pitied. I was pitied; I used to be pitied. I grew up in the continual state of being pitied, no matter where we moved, or what we wore, or where we went to school. I will not be pitied again.

So, what do I do?

Wasn't that the big question?

I just need a couple of days. A week. To just adjust. To look at this and see what has to happen. Have time to logically think it all out.

That's fair. Isn't it?

She felt vaguely nauseous again.

She dialed her son's cell.

"Hey Billy-Budd," she breathed into the receiver.

"Hey Mom," his newly deep voice answered. That adolescent voice, now closer to his dad's than to the little boy he was a year or two ago, was a little disconcerting.

"Hey kiddo."

"What's up?"

"You and Annie good at Uncle Kevin's?"

"It's fine."

"You sure?"

"Yeah, it's fine."

His aloof tone was annoying. He sounded just like his father had in their private conversations over the past couple of days, whispering into her cell phone about *the logistics of this week* and *his move*.

The progression of their separation seemed detached from the familial elements of their life together. *This could have ended with a big fighting meltdown. A screaming match. But that was not them.* No. Because they had never fought like that. Will and Julia discussed things. Will and Julia behaved like mature partners. Negotiations, compromises, deals, not fights.

Billy is not his dad, and she needed to remember that. She felt tears rising under her lower lids, so she projected, "Are you okay?"

"Yeah, I'm good," he paused.

"How about your sister?"

"I don't know."

"Billy, how is your sister?"

"Okay, I guess."

"I need to know if she's okay. Please give me a real answer."

He was clearly uncomfortable about telling her anything, he sighed audibly, "She's fine, I guess. I mean, she's cried a couple of times since you left. But then, she's eating ice cream and laughing with Uncle Lothar."

Julia didn't know what to do, "She might be kind of confused, Billy, you've got to be nice to her."

"I know," he sighed again, as though he, as a teenager knew all the things that were supposed to happen and how everyone was supposed to handle everything in their parents' separation. Somewhere inside her, Julia felt an urge to scream. But then he asked, "Hey, are we going to Ellen's tomorrow night?"

And her son's question shoved the air from her lungs. *Oh Lord, her house.* Julia was sending her children to *her* house. This would be the first of many of these conversations with her children.

She breathed shallowly, "Not until Sunday night, I think. Your dad is getting you from the ferry and I would imagine he would take you there."

"I wasn't sure how it was going to work,"

"What do you mean?"

"Well, I mean, like, if you're not there, does that mean Dad can go to the house and stay there with us?"

"Well, I don't really think..."

"Because he could just bring Ellen and James and the little kids to our..."

"No!" She half-shouted out, the urge bubbling to the surface, but caught herself, saying more quietly, with more control. "No, I don't think that's how it's going to work out, Billy."

"Oh, okay."

"Okay," she constrained her voice. "Hey, I have some time Sunday morning, so why don't I pick you up then, we'll go to the beach here, picnic, we'll get boogie boards, you guys will have fun."

"That's fine."

"Fine," was going to be as good as she was getting. "Good," she said, "Put your sister on, okay?

"Okay,"

"I love you."

"Yeah."

"Billy."

"What?"

"Say it."

"Say what?"

"Say 'I love you' to your Mom."

She heard again the weary sound of the teenage boy, "Love you. Mom."

"Thank you."

"Yep, here's Annie."

"I'll see you Sunday. Don't stay up all night playing Xbox..." But she knew he had already handed off the phone to his little sister.

"Hi Annie, what do you think about a beach day?"

"Yes!" Her nine year old enthused.

"Sunday?"

"Yay!"

"Good, I'll tell Uncle Kev, I'll pick you up at the 8:20. And tell Uncle Lothar no more ice cream!"

She giggled, "Okay, I love you Mommy!"

"I love you too, baby."
"I'm not a baby, Mom."
"Just my baby."
"Mo-oom."
"Okay, okay." She conceded, she couldn't have the two of them annoyed with her, not tonight anyway. "Night, love."
"Night."
After a brief conversation with Kevin, her brother, who's simple and well-meaning question, "You doing okay?" almost choked her, Julia swallowed deeply, opening up her throat and blurted out her Sunday plans, surreptitiously sniffed a goodbye and made it up to her room. She hung up her clothes and busied herself with the huge gift basket that Deidre had created for each one of the rooms of the wedding party.

As Julia had advised, the basket was complete with a Diemand/Billings Destination Wedding Itinerary. This was the first time she had seen Dee's magnum opus. She unfolded the pages. And then, unfolded it some more. And then, unfolded more. And more.

A five page long itinerary? Holy smokes.

Deidre had been thorough, scientist-thorough, documenting every event, all arrangements, every contingency detail.

She noted the flowers on the stationary. *Oh, Dee had asked about the florist!* Julia pulled out her phone and texted her friend.

A few minutes later, BUZZ. Julia looked down to see the reply: 'D's ? can be answrd w/ booze. CU@ bar – Chris.'

Text-speak, Chris? Really? We're not twenty years old.

She shook her head. She looked at her swollen eyes in the bathroom mirror, and wiped the mascara that had rain-guttered into these odd bags that had formed under her lids over the past couple of days. Julia was usually meticulous with the maintenance, but she couldn't just not sleep a steady eight hours and think her forty year old face was going to let her get away with it. She pulled out the caffeinated eye roller from her bag of tricks and saw the sparkle of her diamond platinum wedding band tucked amongst the MAC lip stain and the Nars mascara.

Dee had seen her, but she hadn't seen William. Could she just pretend that her fella was upstairs? Sick, unable to come down, *but wishing you all well!*

No, after a week of him being in a hotel room, people might start to think that was, maybe, homicidal? Should she just pull off the Band-Aid all at once and just tell the Diemands and the Billings that yes, William had left her, yes, this week, and yes, she was okay and no, she certainly did not want to meet your single cousin, Fred?

Yeah, because she had handled herself so well with Mr. Brighton.

What do I do?

She could pretend that he had some sort of sudden business engagement. That seemed easy enough. She dug down deep into her makeup bag and pulled out her wedding ring, slid it onto her finger. The ghost of her husband's presence suddenly hung about her, an expectation that any second he could just show up at her side and she could feel again at ease.

There. No other explanation necessary.

CHAPTER 7
Knots

There they were, Dee and Chris, the intendeds. Julia sighed and smiled. Her college roommate and her college boyfriend had found one another at Mary Ann's wedding years ago and had been, more or less, together ever since. Julia felt a unique sense of satisfaction about this relationship, as she had been the one to, more or less, push them together.

Ex-girlfriend hooks up ex-boyfriend to ex-roommate. Old friendships have a way of becoming almost incestuous.

Julia remembered there had been some snipe-y gossip among the college crowd at that wedding - something between Mary Ann, her little sister Hannah, Jacob, George - all people Julia would be seeing *this* week. *What was it?* Oh yeah, Mary Ann had fiercely whispered to Hannah at the reception that Julia was going to freak out about Chris talking to Dee, and Mary Ann had seethed that she wouldn't have Julia freaking out at *her* wedding.

I know right, Julia had said to an eye-rolling Hannah as she gestured over her then very pregnant stomach, *how dare the boy I broke up with waaaay back in college look at another woman in front of me as I sit here with my husband. Oh, and especially while I'm pregnant with my second child!*

She doesn't get it, Hannah had laughed.

She's getting married today, she probably should start to try, Julia hadn't been able to keep the smugness from her voice. She had been married the longest out of all of them. *Amateurs,* she had grinned over to her handsome Will.

Big-bellied Julia had been the only sober one among them all at Mary Ann's wedding, and had prodded Chris, when he had had enough liquid courage, to finally ask Dee to dance.

And from there, it was destined to be.

Eventually.

So now, Dee squealed at her approach and Julia gave both of them a proud hug and smooch.

"Just don't go grabbing her ass out of habit, Chris," Dee warned, attempting to be playful.

Chris put his hands up, "Spoilsport."

"Please, people." Julia shook her head. "He wouldn't recognize it back there anyway, after twenty years and two kids, whole new topography."

"You're talking crazy," Dee frowned.

"Motherhood's been good to you, Jules, trust me," Chris said into his wine glass.

Just not marriage. She took a deep breath, "William couldn't make it this weekend. Crazy work. He sends his…uh, apologies."

"Oh, Julia, just you?" Dee tilted her head.

Julia avoided her look, and just nodded, "My apologies to the bride, I am without my Plus One." She turned to Chris, "Oh, I know you guys had your day and I can still take Jackson. The kids are still coming though, so I was thinking, the beach?"

"Sounds good." Chris said.

Dee looked at her - examined her, really - and furrowed her brow.

Julia could feel her old friend's scrutinizing gaze. Dee wasn't falling for the conversation deflection to Chris. "So, we are here to celebrate and celebrate we will," Julia announced grandly.

Chris responded with a "Whoo!"

"Whoo!" Julia repeated, a little stiffly. "So who's here?"

"Um, sisters Joan, Helen, Paula will be here tomorrow. Jason, Mike and Mark will be here for the final fitting."

"Dee's family is practically the whole wedding party."

"College-y friends, most will be here early," Dee continued, "Um, Hannah and Jacob posted that they'd be here in a day or so - she's so pregnant! They're taking a babymoon! And Mary Ann and George just called and should be down in a minute, and you already saw our best man."

"Ah, yes, David," Julia nodded. "What has he been doing?"

"Not much of anything."

"What else is new?" Julia actually smiled at the thought.

Her friend complained, "He's a forty-two year old still acting like some dumbass kid. Homeless, jobless, directionless."

"He's on that boat? Not working?"

Chris defended, "Um, he's been working, you know, here and there."

Dee jumped on him, "He's a fricking burnout, Chris, ever since he dumped Laura, he's been roving around..."

"I still can't believe he dumped her..." Julia shook her head.

"I know! She was so sweet." Dee looked down at her hands in her lap, "I almost invited her to the wedding."

"But you didn't." Chris warned. Dee didn't respond.

Julia looked over at them, "I always expected they would get married."

"But you forget he's my stupid brother," Dee stated simply. Mary Ann and George wandered in, saw them, and waved, "Here they are!"

Chris defended his friend to the end, "It just didn't work out." George and Chris shook hands and they took their place at the bar.

Dee didn't stop her tirade against her older sibling even as she hugged and kissed Mary Ann and George hello, "They're together for a decade - a decade! - he's got his accounting job, she's working, they live in a beautiful condo, BUT never an engagement ring. Never."

"Did she want one?"

"Of course she wanted one!" Dee exclaimed, "And he goes off and buys some used yacht. A yacht. He had a midlife crisis without actually having a life! After that, I'm surprised *she* didn't dump *him*. He's just sailing up and down the coast, this sailor Jack Kerouac, I've-gotta-be-free shit. And he looks like absolute..."

"And here he comes!" Chris shouted. He then warned as David came into the bar. "These two have been ragging on you for like five minutes!"

"Shocking," David yelled back.

Julia turned to David, expecting to see the hairy monster she had chased down the gangway, but instead, she found herself surprisingly happy to actually see the face that was coming toward her. In the short time from his assault in the lobby, he had pretty much gotten rid of all of the shagginess - his hair clipped close, his face clean shaven. He strode easily toward them, his old swimmer's legs moving out from the pinions of his hipbones, his movement loose, his long, lean arms swaying slightly from the broad rack of his shoulders. He had always been so skinny as a kid, thought Julia, mentally shrugging at the odd memory, but now she could make out some musculature under his blue dress shirt.

That explains the moving wall in the lobby.

"Thank God!" Dee exclaimed at his appearance.

His cheeks had hollowed out a bit since Julia had last seen him, accentuating high cheekbones she had forgotten he had, and his usually pale skin was freckled brown, which made his smile almost dazzlingly white.

Huh.

She had never thought of David as better looking than Chris - ever - but seeing them here together after all this time, Dave had definitely aged much, much better. The whole stupid sailor thing maybe worked for him, his ash-colored hair bleached out a bit by the sun, his jaw made more square by Gravity's notoriously unfair love of men, and his eyes crinkled a bit at the corners.

The whole effect was, *ahem,* Julia thought, *pleasing.* So pleasing in fact that she found herself, needing to suppress a smile at his oncoming approach.

Thank goodness she caught herself.

Because there was no way on God's Green Earth that she was going to let him think she was happy to see him, never mind let him know she thought he looked good. Not after the way he had treated her out in the lobby, at his boat, made her feel like some dumb kid again.

But she would take the high road. She turned graciously in his direction and said coolly, but politely, "How are you, David?"

But he would have none of that. "I am doing rather well, Julia," his tone mocked her formality.

But she couldn't stop herself from reacting to his scornful expression. He was like wet sand in her shoe. *Immediately irritating.*

"What?"

"Don't you think we skipped the polite hello, been so long, good to see you niceties when you practically knocked me down in the lobby?"

"You knocked him down?" Chris laughed.

"I did not," Julia defended, her mouth open at the blatant injustice, "He knocked me down."

"I would never do such a thing," David teased.

"You just did."

"Liar," he spoke out of the side of his mouth.

Her voice raised an octave by the end of her "I am not."

"Why would you just lie like that?"

"What are you talking about?"

"To my family? To our friends?"

"Are we in a playground?" Julia looked around, disbelieving, unsettled. "Are you going to pull my ponytails? David, I am not lying and you know it."

"I can't say that I know anything…" David started.

"That's for damned sure," Julia interrupted.

Dee harrumphed her agreement.

David ignored his sister, "But I do know when I've been assaulted…"

Julia shot back, "Assaulted?" turning from him to tattle to his sister, "He walked smack right into me, knocked me off my shoes."

"I love those shoes."

"Thanks."

"It's not like I didn't I help her up." David complained to Chris, "She wouldn't help me with my bags."

Dee looked over at him, "I'm just glad you shaved."

Julia said, "Everyone should be."

David made a face at her. And before she could stop herself, she stuck out her tongue.

"Playground, Julia," he tsk'ed.

She ignored him.

They settled in at the corner of the bar, the girls on one side, the boys on the other. George turned to Chris, and to Dave, and Dee started with Julia and Mary Ann and with such a fantastic jumping off point provided by David and Julia, the old bickering began.

And for a few minutes, just sitting there, Julia felt, well, normal.

Well, not normal. How could it be normal?

But it was. But bot normal as in - life with a husband and children and a house and a dog and a career and responsibilities.

Normal for the current audience. The college crew. Just buddies hanging around. Suddenly, she was transported to a time where these people never left her room. And as she gazed around at all of them, even with the irritation, and the worry, and the current shitstorm of her life swirling around in the background of her mind, she thought to herself, *Thank you, Mr. Scott.*

She had been lifted from that unsteady world she was currently inhabiting and she was sent down into this old, familiar place of easy conversation, and sharply pointed barbs intended only to make the whole crowd laugh, and a feeling of deep connection that can only occur through shared experiences, where a constant smile was just waiting at the corner of your lips. In the middle of the most insanely crappy time she could remember in the history of her life - and considering her history that was saying something - she was there right now, back into a place she had almost forgotten had existed.

Or maybe wanted to forget.

But why would she have wanted to forget it?

It was all so long ago.

Most of those memories had been sweet. And right here, these people had been at the heart of all that had been good about those days.

And perhaps most importantly, right now, the Ghost of her Husband Just Past didn't linger in the spaces between Dee and David and Chris and Julia.

So for a few brief moments, she was back – that young girl with her life ahead of her, with big ideas and bigger plans. The difference was, instead of drinking cheap beers, and smoking weed on crappy futon couches talking about politics and late night skit comedy, they all now sat on worn Italian leather barstools and sipped expensive wine and various call liquors, talking about their jobs and their children.

"Look at us, all grown up." Dee smiled.

"Well, most of us anyway," Julia turned toward David.

"Just because I've managed to avoid a messy divorce makes me not a grown up?" he said right to her.

It made her breath catch in her throat. *Why would he say that? Why would David say that, right now to me?*

When she looked up, she saw him punching Chris' arm.

Chris, he's talking about Chris. Her heart started back up. "Easy to avoid when you don't get married," Julia breathed out.

"Technicalities," Dave smiled.

"Are you gay?" Dee queried

"Because I'm not married? What state do you live in?" Turning his attention on Julia, "and you're one to talk. You were the first one married out of all of us and what'll it be? Fifty years?

"Seventeen," Julia answered quietly.

"Mhm," Dave harrumphed.

"And the first to have kids," Dee noted

Julia shook her head, "I know. Crazy."

"Could've told you that," Chris took a swig of his Scotch.

"Did you know William is thirteen, and Annie is going to be ten?"

"Pictures!" the Mary Ann requested, and Julia obliged, pulling out her phone.

"Well, Jackson is getting up there, too," Chris said.

"Come on, show him."

Dee added, "He's upstairs with my sisters' kids."

As they went on chatting about the progeny and how Jackson and Dee had been bonding over swimming together at the Y, David had gone uncharacteristically quiet. Julia had noticed that he looked over the photos, but barely said a word.

A flood of the older Diemand siblings entered the bar. *The Blonde Brigade*, Julia used to call them. The group had always intimidated her; they just looked so different from the people she had grown up around, or had gone to grade school with. With their Polo shirts and khaki shorts, the family had always looked like they just stepped off the golf course or out of the yacht club. In their pinks and greens and oranges and sky blues, the entire Diemand clan was often hard to tell apart.

That wasn't completely true.

David always had stood a little bit apart.

Julia had always appreciated his more haphazard sense of style - if you could call what he wore "a style." In college, Julia and David had both pretended they could care less about what they wore - one because he was too cool to care, one because she was too pretty to worry; one because he was making a deliberate jab at the preppy perfection of his moneyed family, one because she couldn't afford anything more extravagant than the clearance rack at the Gap outlet at the mall.

But Julia was a grown up now, she had to remind herself, with clothes and a car and a house equal to, if not nicer than, any one of them. She knew that for a fact. She had entered their world, made it her home, and inhabited it with style and an amount of grace, all the while never losing appreciation for the things that she had worked so hard to achieve.

And you know what? Despite this Tuesday, she was still the significant Julia Rosa - if only for a little while more - and she could do this. She squared her shoulders and could meet them head on with discussion of this year's elections, who wore what at the summer Boston weddings, and the features on their latest cars.

And ah yes, the booze. The memory of the Diemand family dysfunction refreshed suddenly in her mind, arriving with the next round of really, really strong drinks. The gap in age between David and Dee and his brothers and sisters had not created the close relationship that the youngest two had shared. And at family events, Julia remembered, every single one of them all liked to pretend that the eight of them had been grown up as the bestest of friends all along.

Except for David.

Julia sighed, longing to go back to the ease of those first few moments, with those few people who knew her in that past life - her hungry years, those tricky times she had publicly prided herself on, but sometimes, privately felt ashamed of. Yet, she knew that sweet comfort was gone in a wave of immaculately kept well-wishers.

Dee and Chris went off to mingle with the family. Mary Ann headed off to find a table. Julia found herself seated at the bar about four empty chairs over from where David and George were making small talk.

And suddenly, she wished for the comfort of that rat of a husband of hers.

William was good in a crowd.

William was his absolute best with an audience. And this crowd would have been his perfect audience.

"Julia!" David called over to her, "I just heard..." he spoke carefully, "...your fella isn't here."

George went off to find his wife.

"Oh," she straightened up, pulling herself out of her head, "Heard you were flying solo, too."

"Safer that way," David moved over to her chair.

"How so?"

His eyebrows went up, "Would you subject a date to the Peanut Gallery?"

A smile gathered at her lips as the memories floated up to the surface, "Oh God, the Almighty Peanut Gallery. I hadn't thought about that, whooo..." she breathed out. She put up her hand automatically, paused and stuck her thumb straight up, David did the same, and they turned their wrists simultaneously down. "How many boyfriends and girlfriends were fed to the lions after a viewing?"

"Too many to count."

He squinted at her, accusingly, "You never brought William by until well after you were married."

"You know, it was different then, David," she said offhandedly, trying to keep it impersonal.

"I think you must have been nervous to bring him even now. Knew I'd be here, alone," he smirked at her.

But impersonal with David was clearly going to be hard. "I think you've given that too much thought," she rolled her eyes.

He leaned in, and she could just feel his breath on her ear, "I think I'm right."

She pushed him away. "Not a surprise."

He grinned at her, a devilish look in his eyes. It was friendly, but only because it was familiar, she could see the vestiges of the Big Bad Wolf in its offered intent, but David wasn't threatening in any way, shape, or form. *No, this wolf could be quite easily tamed, even if he did threaten to bite.* Not like that Mr. Brighton. *Yikes.* She found herself grinning back and shaking her head at her friend's exasperating big brother.

But then, Mr. Richard Brighton happened into the hotel bar, and, just for Little Red alone, all hell broke loose.

Ooh, boy, she smoothed down the front of her dress.

David noticed, and then followed her gaze towards the man at the door, his interest piqued, "Who's that?"

"Oh, no one," the lilt in her tone, casual.

"He looked right at you when he came in."

"It's no one, David."

"No one?"

"He just recognized me from working the wedding tonight."

"And he's continuing to look at you now…"

"I'm not responsible for his actions." She tried being coy. She knew that given the opportunity, David would most definitely flirt with her. And flirting would distract him from questions about this man. Questions she wasn't ready to answer to anyone, questions that could possibly make her head explode. "Maybe he just thinks I'm pretty."

"You are." He took note, but *goddammit,* he wouldn't let that sweet, little, kittenish tone throw him off - he knew her better than that. "But you know who he is."

"Well, yes, he was the father of the bride."

"What's his name?"

"Something Brighton."

"'Something Brighton,' really?" He didn't let up. He narrowed his gaze at her, pinpointed.

She squirmed slightly under his gaze, just a shift in her seat, just the tiniest little bit. "Richard Brighton, I think it was." She was trying hard to maintain casual.

"Hmm," David's suspicion was high, he moved behind her, sliding from one shoulder to her next.

"Hmm, what?" She turned in the chair on him, resting her hand on the back of her seat.

His eyes looked down.

She followed his gaze to the hand on the finely carved wood and her eyes widened. *Oh crap,* and before she could snatch it away, he caught her left hand between the warm, rough palms of both of his large, flat hands. He watched her face as he rubbed gently, his callouses scratching up the paint of her weekly maintenance. She was startled by his familiar contact - this sudden closeness with a man who was most decidedly not her husband, but still claimed some long lost familiarity to her person - but she would be damned if she was going to give off a tell to David Diemand. She stared back at him, her honey brown eyes unblinking up at his gray green.

After a smug few seconds, he broke the challenging stare by examining the evidence he held in his hands. He looked down at his own thick, insistent fingers as he rolled her slim ring finger with his large calloused thumb, moving her platinum band back away from her knuckle.

She finally pulled her hand back, he released it from his firm grasp. She glared at his face, interpreting expressions that she was realizing were recognizable - *goddammit, what did he see? What did he know?*

His eyebrows lifted up. "Interesting," he murmured.

He did know. Didn't he? Oh God, he did. How did that sonofbitch know?

She grabbed the front of his shirt and hissed, "You, with me, now."

"Yes, ma'am," David agreed. He let himself be led out of the bar to the lobby. As he passed the table where Mr. Brighton had seated himself, he smirked over to the man's watchful gaze, chucking his chin and flicking his eyebrows suggestively in the man's direction, to Mr. Brighton's many unhappy returns.

She dragged him across the lobby, into the now empty ballroom where she had just spoken with that Mr. Brighton not hours before, clicking the double doors shut behind them.

She didn't let go of David's shirt. "Hey! You think you know something, then spill it!"

His hands deep in his pockets, he had a slight smile on his face, rocking back onto his heels, it was clear that David was enjoying himself. "It's not always elementary, my dear Watson."

Enjoying my misery. "Tell me what you think you know, David Diemand or I will kick your smarmy ass!"

"Alright, alright." He chuckled and then grabbed her left hand, pulled it from his shirt and held it up to her own face, explaining, "I didn't notice right away, but seeing it there now, made me realize that I didn't see it on your hand earlier when you were down by the boat."

"What?"

"You straightened your dress when you were yelling at me down at the boat - no ring. You straightened your dress just now - ring."

"So?"

"Husband's not in attendance..."

"He's busy..."

"At a destination wedding in which you will be gone for, wow, more than a solid week."

"And..."

"What idiot would be away from you for a week?" He slid his head towards her. "And well, just all of those circumstances add up to the idea that you could be up to something unmentionable," he shrugged a shoulder, "which it just so happens I am in a position - many positions, really -" he smiled to himself, "to accommod ..."

She was standing there listening to him, listening to him attempt to cajole her, albeit jokingly, into admitting that something was amiss in her marriage. Like it was *her fault*. Like she had done something wrong. She couldn't take it anymore, she wasn't the one, she wasn't the one to cause this, she was not taking the blame for this one. "*I'm* not cheating, David!" she shouted.

He stopped.

She heard herself, "I'm not the cheater!"

She saw that he had stopped and she tried to gather herself back up.

Her words, her helpless expression had hit him suddenly just below the sternum - her furrowed brow, her pained eyes, her bottom lip between her teeth. *Oh.* He hadn't meant to hurt her, "Juju," he said softly.

A tide of salt water suddenly rose up, stinging behind her eyes. *No one had called her Juju in ages.*

She sighed deeply. "Dave, it's just...." She couldn't finish. She looked up at his face, his eyebrows pushed down, the corners of his mouth tucked in, and realized, she had just given it all up - her big secret, the one thing she had to keep to herself to make it though this whole thing - to David.

Not the first time...

He looked at her and wanted to do something, help, somehow, fix what he had done. He glanced over and then sidestepped quickly to a table, where fresh linens had been set for the morning. He grabbed a folded cloth napkin and handed it to her. "Are you okay?"

"Of course I am," she said sternly, standing herself straight, wiping the corner of her eyes with it. She gestured with the linen, "You do know I have to have Piero replace that setting now." But really, her frustration at him was pointless - his face was twisted in concern for her - she couldn't be upset. *Well, not with him.* And not right now anyway, when he was trying to be his version of nice. "I'm sorry, David. I just I don't know, he's gone and the kids, the kids don't know what to make of him moving out yet. That's the worst part."

"That's the worst part?"

"Yeah. He left Tuesday."

"Tuesday? This Tuesday?" his eyebrows shot up, his eyes widened, and he pointed down at the floor as to emphasize that particular day of the week's immediacy. "And you came to do this wedding?"

"Yes. I don't know. I had three weddings this weekend I had to cover so Dee could have the spot and I don't know what I am supposed to do, David. I couldn't deal and I couldn't make it weird because of, well, you know, your sister and…"

"And Chris. Gotcha," he finished for her, nodding in realization. "So no one knows."

"No one here," she turned on him, "and they're not going to find out."

He shrugged, "Fine."

"Fine?" she repeated, almost surprised.

"Not my place."

She looked up at him. He was looking at her in complete earnest, his intentions clear in his eyes and she could see that he was being serious. Actually serious. For her. She had the sudden childish urge to leap on him and hug him hard.

But no, that would not do, she would remain reservedly grateful. "I appreciate that. Really. You will tell no one?"

"No one," he repeated, vowing.

"Because this weekend is not about Marriage, it's about The Wedding." She pointed out each word, emphasizing the practical credo of her entire profession: The marriage could fall apart on the airplane to the honeymoon, but you made fucking sure that the wedding itself was nothing short of Everywoman's Romantic Fantasy Perfection.

David let his shoulders drop in annoyance, "The excruciating, endless wedding."

Julia actually stopped at his description, and laughed. Out Loud. A legitimate LOL. *Oh God, textspeak.* She shouldn't have laughed, but she did, yelping out involuntarily, "Oh my God, yes!" She put her hands to her head and huffed out, "Did you see that itinerary? I've never seen anything like it. And I've done a Kennedy!"

David looked up to the ceiling, his hands pressed together, "Please let it be Ted, please let it be Ted, please let it be Ted..."

"No, it was one of the young ones..." But finally getting his meaning, and she huffed out a laugh, "No! A wedding! A Kennedy wedding!" She punched his arm.

"Hey!" He punched her arm back.

"Ow!" She half-yelled.

"Ow yourself!" He rubbed his arm, "You weren't kidding about the asskicking. You've still got mean little knuckles."

She laughed, "You actually hurt me."

"I did?"

"Yes."

"I'm sorry, I'll kiss it better," he took her elbow and rubbing the sore spot, he pulled it towards his lips.

She pulled her arm from his grasp. "It'll be fine, Dave."

"So what do we have to do first?" And he ticked off a ridiculous, and only slightly exaggerated, litany of events, "The guest reception, the breakfast, the luncheon, the afternoon tea, the dinner, the supper, the rehearsal, the rehearsal dinner guest reception night out..."

"I know!" she shouted, guffawing, "David! Alone. We're the Singles! Do you know how awful these things are without a Plus One? I do! I've borne witness thousands of times! This is going to be torture!"

He laughed with her, the two of them in the same boat. "Like Waterboarding Wednesday at Gitmo." *His boat.*

They looked at one another and grinned through their giggles, but he watched as the corners of her mouth and her eyes started to turn down, and their incredulous laughter dissipated into the empty air of the deserted ballroom. They quieted together, and she turned her glance to the floor.

After a minute, she murmured, "David?"

"Yes?"

She pleaded, "Stop making this funny, please."

"Sorry." He kicked at her foot, trying to get her attention, trying to bring back the old tune he just recognized from the notes in her laugh, but he could only force her gaze up as far as his chest.

"I wrinkled your good shirt," she noticed.

"Don't worry about it."

"Probably your only one."

"I'm not that pathetic."

"I'll have it ironed." She said to the ballroom, out where their shared joy had filtered out only moments before.

He shrugged a shoulder, "It's not that bad."

She suggested, seemingly to his shoes, "Can I buy you a drink at least?"

He straightened his shoulders, and ran his hand along his jawline, exaggerating his thinking process, "You're going to buy me several drinks," he assured her, "You are going to buy me several drinks to keep me quiet."

Her eyes shot up to his, and she saw that Satan himself was reflecting back to her from his flashing irises. "Are you kidding me?" she stared him down, threatening.

There she was again. "Relax," he cackled, "Just sounded villainous, kinda cool."

She tilted her head, "Milking my misery for booze? Yeah, cool."

"I don't know, I vaguely remember someone yelling in my face," he imitated "'Hey Jude, you owe me some alcohol!'"

She let herself remember for just a second, but she wasn't going that easy on him, "This is not a joke, David." She opened the door.

He opened the other, as they left the ballroom, "A Diemand does not joke about alcohol."

She ducked into the kitchen to catch some waiter about the missing napkin on the place setting. And he pretended to head back into the bar.

But, how does a man feel when he suddenly finds out that the Greatest Lay of His Life is suddenly available?

Not just available, but *Vulnerable and Available?*

No! Not just Vulnerable and Available, but Vulnerable, Available, and currently Beholden to Him.

He feels like the Universe had finally realized itself and found a little something to pay back all of the fucking misery it had doled out to him over the past year and a half.

And that man takes a moment in the men's room to at least, "Ha-HAAAAAAAAAAAAAA!"

"Your boyfriend's gone." David whispered to her over his beer as he passed her from his quick, but triumphant, trip to the restroom. After scanning the room for a now absent Mr. Brighton, he found her mingling amongst their friends.

She glared at him again. *She had signed a pact with the devil.* "So, here's a question."

"Yes?" He stopped.

"Mary Ann, George, have you seen his boat?"

"Yes, I was on it the night of the engagement dinner, it's just so amazing."

"It looks really lovely. But David, here's the question I need you to answer."

"Yes?"

"I've heard that you live, by yourself, on this boat. Just out there sailing all over the place…"

"Doesn't that seem so romantic, Julia?" Mary Ann interjected.

She stopped herself from actually frowning.

David said to Julia, "Mostly around here, but I've gone down the coast a couple of times."

"You must get lonely," Mary Ann asked, "out there on the sea," she touched his arm, "all by yourself."

"Not always all by myself, Mar."

Mary Ann's perpetual one-sided flirtation with David had been a running gag for years, so Julia just continued, "But when you are all by yourself, do you ever…"

"Yes," he interrupted.

"You don't know what I was going to ask."

"I had an idea."

"Ew," she realized. "Just stay with me."

"Okay."

"Have you ever, I don't know, thought about the fact that you could just die out there all by yourself and no one would know…"

"Julia," Mary Ann admonished on the sidelines.

But David's head slid back on his neck, "Hmmm."

"I mean if you die, somehow," she pressed, "you'd probably be out there for a really long time before anyone would notice."

"People would notice," Mar countered.

"I don't know, he goes off for days…"

He agreed, "Weeks actually."

"At a time," Julia nodded at him.

He actually considered her comment, "That's true."

"I mean, eventually someone would come looking for you, or at some point, float upon your creepy ghost boat just bobbing out there on the waves."

"Jules…" Mary Ann started.

"I'm just saying…" Julia shrugged.

But David wasn't put off, "I think an important detail is: how do I die? Are we thinking Jaws, I fight off a big great white and get bitten in half below the waist like Quint says when he's telling about the guy bobbing up…"

"David!" Mary Ann seemed disgusted both by the comment and the fact that the two of them seemed to be carrying on this conversation for no one but themselves.

"No," Julia added thoughtfully, "I was thinking more along the lines of you were eating dinner out of a can or something and you choked on your baked beans or creamed corn."

"Who would choke on creamed corn?"

"It could happen." She watched the delight in David's eyes. She had forgotten that, despite his tendencies toward irritating, he had always been easier to talk to than most people. *Half the time when he spoke you just wanted him to shut up,* but this sort of weird conversation could always just happen with him, she never knew why. She could go off on some strange tangent and he would just eat it up, playing off of her and pushing her on. It made the corners of her mouth start to twitch up – this fast back and forth between them.

"I'd say, baked beans."

"Good with it."

"Oh, ho, yes I am eating out of a can…"

"Like a dirty, smelly hobo…"

"And I stagger out onto the deck…" he built on.

"And try to give yourself the Heimlich over the railing," she took it further.

"But it doesn't work and so I'm dead out there on the deck, choked to death on a singular baked bean."

"In mere minutes. Asphyxiation. Dead."

"Left out there, for days at a time."

"Possibly weeks."

"My rotting corpse just baking in the hot, hot sun," he delighted in the gory imagery.

"That's completely horrible!" Mary Ann yelled, aghast, at the two of them. Her husband George just shrugged, amused at the gross out tennis match between the two of them.

Julia fed into the disgust, pushing on the destructive description, "Your skin and muscles and organs being picked apart by sea gulls."

"Ah huh."

"Until there's nothing left of you but sun-bleached bones," she nodded.

"Yeah!" But then turned considering, "Okay, so, how are you going to die?"

"Hit by a bus," Julia waved a hand delicately.

"Guts spread all over the pavement?" he considered this deeply, but the corners of his mouth kept pulling up, and his eyes were dancing.

"Brains," she answered, matter-of-factly.

He couldn't help it - he snorted, which sent her into peals of laughter, and which made his smile unable to leave his mouth.

Mary Ann shook her head at the two sharing what couldn't be called a joke, "What is wrong with you two?" completely perplexed and slightly peeved. She took her husband's sleeve and left them alone, where they seemed to be anyway.

It was getting late and Julia had had enough. She had done her best, struck out alone amongst the sea of "other" (meaning not David, not Dee) Diemands and put on the show - the small talk, the polite laughter, the questions, she had handled it all out there on her own. *Acting as though, yes, here she was - everything was fine! Husband, kids, family? Perfect! Intact! Of course, why shouldn't they be?*
She had chatted with Dee's family about her kids and their kids - "Oh! It's been so long!" and "We should get together!" and "Dee has missed you!" It was totally, and thoroughly, exhausting. At this point, her mind, her body, her soul was begging her to just leave, *get out, go home...*
To what, Julia?
But she couldn't answer that question. Her mouth grew tight.
Nope.
Not now.
She summoned a last bit of strength.
She chose a moment, took a deep breath, decided to bid a general goodnight to everyone at the bar. She kissed Chris and Dee and made her way toward the lobby.
David caught up with her at the elevator and stood to her side. He spoke, but to the closed mirrored doors, "You think you're soooo funny."
"What?" she shot back, trying not to get annoyed at the very playfulness she had only just encouraged earlier. She wouldn't let him see how much this night had taken out of her. But it was hard, she was so tired. So she did not look his way, replying sarcastically instead, "Fantasizing about your death?"
"Didn't talk to my sisters about getting picked apart by seagulls."
"Didn't come up."
He chuckled.
"Plus," she spoke in front of her. "Dead men…"
"…tell no tales," he finished for her. "I know. Sleep tight, Juju." But he made no motion to go, he just stood at her side while she waited for the elevator.

"You too," when he hadn't moved, she added, "Captain Moron." The elevator dinged and the doors slid open.

"Ugh, just go," he pushed her gently inside, feigning his own irritation. She turned herself around and watched him wave his hands dismissively at her. He stalked off back toward the bar, toward the crowd, and the doors reunited in the middle, reflecting back the distorted image of her reaction to his pretended indignation. She noticed that there was a shadow of just a slight smile on her face.

She made it.

At least, she thought she did.

It took a few minutes, but after tonight - *no* - after *days* of keeping it together, for work, for the children, for her husband, for her clients, for her team, for her boss, for herself, poised, professional, perfect Julia just fucking lost it.

She was fine as she stood there alone, when, at the next floor, a young couple entered Julia's elevator. The tall, handsome, young man held the petite little redhead's hand and they stood close to one another. Julia gave both of them a small smile of acknowledgement and returned her gaze to her own reflection in the doors as they rode upstairs.

It only took a moment, but then Julia realized that as the young woman nestled into the crook of her young man's shoulder, his attention seemed to divert from the women he entered the elevator with. In the mirrored doors, she saw him giving Julia a thorough visual examination.

Her brows drew down, and she watched her own face become a naked stream of emotion, as he not so furtively seemed to appreciate every angle and curve of her figure.

She should have let it go.

It's not like it hadn't happened before. *Christ,* she was a forty year old woman. If she didn't know how to handle the unwanted gazes of men at this point, she really should have turned in all rights and privileges of being a woman.

But today, the fact that this man had a beautiful girl just under his arm, and he was giving his full-on attention to someone else, well that *just churned her goddamned butter.*

He turned his glance away and whispered in his girl's ear, almost tenderly, who then looked up to his face, with loving adoration, and snuggled herself further into his crook.

And after a second or two more, his eyes came back to rest on the reflected Julia. She stared at him and he winked.

Winked.

At her.

With a girl under his arm, he winked at Julia.

And she could not contain herself.

"Hey, buddy," she heard herself mumble, "Eyes on your own paper."

The two snapped to her attention. He, unfortunately, was the one to react, "Um, excuse me?" the lecherous one cleared his throat.

"I think you heard me," Julia warned.

"No, I'm afraid I didn't."

"Well, let me put it to you this way," she barked. "How about you try and love the one you're with, buddy?!"

"I'm sorry," he stammered. "I don't know what you're talking about."

"Oh ho, please. Yes, yes, you do, *sir.*" *As though, sir, made it better.* Julia, the consummate professional when it came to matters of the hotel and their guests, had no idea where these angry, brazen words were coming from, but if she had just looked in the mirrored doors as she spat out her tirade against every cheating male's black-hearted, attention-seeking, selfish bullshit, she might have recognized it.

She went deeper, "And you," she spun on the girl, "you're just standing there. Too in love, or *something you think is love*, to see what is going on right in front of you. Oblivious, because he's so tall and he's so handsome and aren't you just so lucky?" Julia gestured vehemently at the man, waving her hand at the fetching figure he cut in the elevator. "Well, no, I'll tell you something – you're not lucky. You're not lucky at all. You, my darling girl, you're a fool." All the fury, all the frustration, all the hate she felt right now for her circumstance, her husband, his mistress, herself, flung itself desperately out of her soul, through her vocal cords and into the words that she spat at the poor little girl, "A FOOL!"

Those words thrown out there into the small space of the elevator had no choice but to hit the girl, hard and fast, one by one. And then the young girl burst into tears, and the thought-to-be lech of a young man turned to comfort his young companion and told Julia, quietly, "I just said to her that I thought you looked just like my aunt."

The old spirit that has somehow briefly inhabited her and forced her to spill her stupid, angry, pained, bitter guts all over the inside of this elevator suddenly abandoned her.

Aunt.
His.
Aunt.

Julia's face in the reflection went blank, stunned at the realization of what she had done. And what the term "aunt" conjured up - sweet, kindly, old women who would hug you and bake you cookies and come to your school plays with your mom. Hot embarrassment bleached her face of color and she held her own hands tightly clasped in front of her as she tried to gather herself up again. The young woman whimpered in her man's secure, loving arms.

Thankfully, mercifully, the bell rang for Julia's floor. She stepped out and then, thinking the better of it, she held the door and turned fully to the young couple.

"I'm sorry," she whispered out.

Which just sent the young girl into wails.

"Just go," said the man, angrily.

"But, I didn..."

"Please, ma'am!" as he saw her try to speak again.

Ma'am. Aunt. The words chased Julia down the hall as she ran tap, smack, tap down the long hallway to her room, fumbling with her keys in a desperate race with her own crazy, runaway emotions to just get into the safety of her room so she could break the hell down in private.

Chapter 8

Or Poorer

Julie had tried to go to bed after talking with Billy and Annie, thinking that after she had spoken to her babies she would be able to sleep. Their excited voices on the phone had cheered her temporarily, as they both rushed to tell her that Uncle Kevin was letting them stay up and watch a movie as long as they were quiet. "He said if he and Uncle Loth can't hear us, we can stay up as late as we want," Annie bragged to her mom

Julia chuckled, "That was the rule when he and I and Auntie Charlotte were kids, on our sleepovers, as long as the parents didn't hear us, we were okay."

She remembered bringing Dee home one weekend from college to her mom's "latest and greatest" find - a tiny two bedroom apartment that was a few blocks from the train station in the city. The two eighteen year olds had stayed up for the entire night, watching Julia's mom's TV on low volume and whispering together like middle schoolers. Julia smiled to herself when she remembered their blundered attempts at making pancakes in her mama's scraped up cheap aluminum pans for the following morning's breakfast.

Julia saw that Dee had tried not to let the shock of her roommate's home register on her face. Everywhere Julia's family had lived had been pretty much the same - one or two bedrooms when they were lucky, a living room, a bath and a kitchenette. Julia's college classmates didn't have homes with kitchenettes; they had eat-ins and butler pantries and sometimes, actual butlers. Seeing this place through Dee's eyes, Julia had felt a twinge of shame at the unexpected lack of space, the suddenly shabby furnishings, the now noticeable absence of a view. She knew that this place could have been in a different universe from the one that her college friends had known, but she had brought Dee home because she wanted her roommate to know more about her and who she was - *and how far she was going to go,* Julia then thought proudly. And Dee had been so sweet and told Julia's mother that she had loved coming. And Julia's mother had cocked her head at her daughter's new friend's amazement that there wasn't a drop of alcohol in the place.

The kids were anxious to get to their movie and Julia bid her little ones kisses and sweet dreams, and reluctantly clicked off her cell.

But sleep wasn't coming. Again. *Aftershock, I guess.* She had no choice but to stay up and at least be productive - making lists, writing emails to the florist with Dee's request, and trolling for ideas for her coming work on the wedding blogs.

It was about two in the morning when she finally got up and stretched, rubbing her eyes. She peeked at the view from her window. She was on what was considered the "offside" of the hotel, so instead of the unfettered view of the sandy beach and the ocean, Jules looked down on the dock. Despite the less desirable room proffered to the help, Julia couldn't deny that this scene was still pretty. *Even after all these years, I appreciate any view at all.* She saw a single twinkling light among the black, sparkling night, and wasn't sure if that was, or possibly could be, a light from David's boat.

Guessing from where she was standing, and how far she had gone, it might have been him, still sitting there, awake and alone, the light still on his little cabin, afloat at sea.

Just like her.

CHAPTER 9
For Richer

Julia was showered and dressed long before she was scheduled to meet up with Dee for breakfast previous to their appointment where Dee's dress was awaiting its final inspection.

They sat at a table on the front porch that overlooked the bluest ocean Dee had ever seen. "The colors are almost unreal here."

"It is amazing, isn't it? According to the weather," she glanced at her phone, "we should be able to get some great shots on the beach."

"Is this where you and Will got married?"

Julia almost choked on her eggs at the mention of her husband from her unknowing companion, it was a topic she had hoped to avoid, but hadn't really figured out how. "Um, no. We had a little ceremony in the Public Gardens. A JP, nothing big." She said, "Now about Chris' tuxedo…"

"I think about it now, Julia," Dee continued, expressing softly, looking up at her, full in the face, "and I wish I had come."

Julia shrugged, "We had a little dinner, my mom, his family, his partners. You didn't miss much."

"I don't mean the reception." Dee looked down at her coffee. "I mean, the wedding, to be there, for you."

"That's really sweet," Julia wanted to just avoid any discussion that had to do with Will, but she then realized that particular aversion would eliminate about seventeen years of conversational material, "but don't worry about it. Can we talk about when the favors are expected to arrive?"

"No, Julia, you don't understand," but Dee wouldn't let it go, "we've been seeing a lot of each other over the past few months, and we've been talking. And I don't know - you've been so wonderful to help me with this wedding. And it makes me realize that I just… we just stopped, you know? We just stopped talking before. It's been years…"

Julia considered, and replied, evenly, soothingly, "Well, you were busy with school and your research and I was busy with kids and…" she swallowed, "…Will, and it happens you know. Life gets really busy. Time passes."

"But we live twenty minutes from one another..." Dee was beginning to get teary. "And there's something..."

"No buts, Deidre," Julia had to stop her. "We're fine. It's fine. We're friends. We've been friends for years and no amount of time will change that. And you and I, we're here now, right?" Julia finished off a bite of melon from her plate.

"Yes, we're here now." Dee struggled.

"Exactly," she assured as her friend smiled meekly over her eggs. "So there, we're good. I love you and you love me."

Dee nodded silently.

"Alright then, dry your eyes, sweetie," Julia added matter-of-factly, "and let's talk about your fucking wedding."

Dee couldn't help but laugh with surprise through an intended whimper, "Such a bitch."

Julia corrected, "I'm authoritative."

"Same thing."

"Yeah, well, a girl from my side of the tracks doesn't grow up to get shoes like this without a big ole healthy dose of bitch in her."

Dee wiped her eyes and cocked her head, down at her friend's shoes, "They are great."

"Thanks."

Dee regarded Julia. "I never looked at you as 'from the wrong side of the tracks.'"

"Oh yeah?"

"You had such drive."

"I guess."

"You guess?" Dee shook her head. "No one could stop you. You did whatever you wanted." The waitress came by with the check.

"Well, that's not true. I did what I had to do."

"Bullshit, Julia."

"It is not!" Julia laughed and signed her name to the bill.

"You put your mind to something and you just made it happen. With school, with work..." Dee, gathering her bag, looked up at her from under her eyebrows, adding, "...with men."

Julia replied, almost to herself, "I can't even begin to tell you how wrong that is..."

"I just never thought that you had anything but success ahead of you. And look at you now, you couldn't be further 'from the tracks.'"

"I could end up back there at any second."

"Please." Dee scoffed.

"I don't know, Dee," Julia regarded her, "I used to think that if I was determined and if I worked hard enough I could change everything. I could make anything go my way. I could control it."

"Of course you can control it."

Julia stood up. "No, see. You don't understand. I grew up in a different place than this, than you. When you don't have things, when you don't have support, when you don't have... resources? I guess... it's hard to make things happen for yourself."

"That's not true. You could have done anything you wanted."

"No, Dee. No I couldn't," Julia shook her head slowly, "You could. But not a poor girl from East Boston. We didn't make things happen; things happened to us - my mom, my brother, and me. Bad and good. That scholarship changed me. I got it. It felt like it was a miracle. It made me think that finally I was in control. Me. I could work for something and I could keep it. I made something happen and I wasn't going to stop. Not for anyone, or anything."

"Well, that is something I always admired about you."

"I'm not sure now if it is something to admire."

"How can you say that? You have a beautiful home, children, husband. You have everything I have ever wanted."

Julia looked at her friend, her breathing growing shallow, and more than anything at this moment, she wished she could tell her the truth, to confess to her that she was on the brink of losing everything she had worked for because... because, why?

Well, that was the question wasn't it?

Because she hadn't stopped for anything? *Or anyone? Not letting emotions get in the way.*

But she couldn't say that to Dee. Dee was about to be joined to the Man of Her Dreams. Dee was about to Embark on the Journey of Her Lifetime. Dee was about to be a Bride. Julia couldn't say such things to a Bride.

Not even if that Bride was her friend.

Especially if that Bride was her friend.

Julia considered the circumstances and just said, "And you are about to have all of that, aren't you?"

Dee looked at her friend for a second and a smile broke out onto her face, "I am."

Julia agreed, "So let's get this woman to the bridal shop!"

As Julia got her keys from the valet, Dee texted Chris for him and David to meet them out front. The boys stumbled up together from the dock and slid themselves in the back seat of Julia's BMW. Yet another realization came over her, *how much longer will I have my car? My car? Is this even my car?* The knot of anxiety sat at its regular table just behind her left set of ribs.

Distract yourself. Breathe and distract. She looked at the rearview mirror and saw a sleepy David, his almost-rectangular blond head lolling about in her back seat. "You awake, Diemand?"

Chris elbowed him.

David didn't open his eyes, his heavy brows, relaxed, "Mhm, comfy."

Dee looked back at her brother, "Best bed he's been in in months."

"My bed's fine," David protested, eyes still closed.

"Then why don't you ever sleep in it?"

"I sleep."

"Not much," Dee admonished, "You keep your loose change in those eye bags?"

He shot back, "You keep your laundry in yours?"

"Kids..." Julia warned.

"I know, right?" Chris lightly punched the back of her seat in Parent Solidarity.

"So, was that your light on down at the dock late last night?"

"You spying on me, Juju?" David grinned sleepily, slowly, at the thought.

"No, I just was up, you know, working." She caught his open eyes in the rearview, light gray in the morning light.

He nodded at her, the snarky smile gone from his mouth and his eyes, and she could see that he had a full understanding of what she was just beginning to experience - how long the nights could be. Einstein touched upon something like that in his Theory of Relativity - in the deep wells, time moves more slowly. "Yeah, I'm usually just up, can't sleep too much, so I read."

"Such a scholar."

And surprisingly, he scoffed at that, "Yes, I'm sooo smart," closing his eyes again. Julia could hear the sarcasm, but she wondered if the other two had heard that single note of bitterness in the deep rasping sound of David's gruff morning voice. She wanted to signal to him somehow that she knew, to look into the rearview and let her old friend know that she got it, that she could feel it too, but he didn't open his eyes again. And he said nothing more until they got their destination.

Dee's dress was gorgeous.

Under the yellow and pink soft lighting of the bridal shop, Julia had finished buttoning Dee up in the exquisite Raimon Bundo couture gown and pushed out the bustled train. The two women looked satisfied at the image in the mirror for about a minute, but then turned on the critical eyes - one professional, one personal. They had seen this beauty several times. They poked and prodded at a gap that appeared along the bustline, a wrinkle over the waist.

The seamstress left to grab some pins and Julia took the opportunity to run through their W-Day timeline. "The photographer will be here at 8 am, Marsetta will be there to start hair and makeup probably around 8:30."

Dee, in her dress, looked horrified, "Oh God, pictures before makeup?"

Julia looked down at her phone, "I can have the photog come later if you want."

"Yes, please. Need something professional to handle this first," Dee circled her own face with her finger. "Lately, I look in the mirror and I think you know, hey, I look pretty good, and then I see a picture of myself from that same time and I can't believe how awful I look."

"Is it our age?" Julia chuckled in understanding, "I always think I'm looking great, but photographic evidence tells me different too. Double chin, or my hair's like this..." She pushed a clump of it up over the back of her head, while typing out a quick schedule change.

"Yes! I know! What is that?" Dee concurred but then she thought, "I think David has some sort of weird poetic theory about something like that."

"He does?" Julia looked up.

"He calls it Door... something...Gray. Christian Grey? No. It starts with a D, Delor..." Dee thought out loud. "Is that what it's called, David?" She yelled over the peach silk wall partition that separated the dressing rooms.

"Huh?" Her brother appeared at the opening, still in his T-shirt and jeans, but Julia noticed he was barefoot on the beige carpet. He had just been starting to get changed.

Huh.

She could see a slight bulge at the hem of his short sleeves, his biceps just visible over ropy forearms. He had leaned out considerably since she had seen him last - heavier and happier with his lovely Laura. Now his jeans hung loosely over taut hipbones. Her mind was difficult to control lately, and it wandered back, unsupervised, into a deep pool in her memory, stirring up things along the bottom long enough to let a thought bob gently to the surface, which then made her wonder, *I wonder if everything would look different now...*

Julia shook herself slightly. *Stop, just stop. What the hell is the matter with you?*

He pointed at his sister's dress, "Hey, that's pretty."

Dee nodded a thanks, but wanted to know, "The Delorean Gray Effect?"

"S'not 'Back to the Future,' Dee," he shook his head.

"The Delorean was not gray..." Julia added. The brother and sister looked over at her. "It was stainless steel."

David cocked an eyebrow in her direction. "It's not wrong for me to know that," Julia said offhandedly.

David looked at her for a second more and then continued, "The Dorian Gray Effect, you know, from 'A Picture of Dorian Gray?'"

He was greeted with blank stares from the two women.

"Famous short story? By Oscar Wilde?"

Again, nothing.

He phrased his explanation to offer as much chance of recognition as possible, "Portrait of this conceited guy - sells his soul to stay young and good-looking - his picture takes on all his sins - it gets old and decrepit instead of him - made into a film, 1945?" the stops and starts of his probing questions making his voice melodic.

But still, nope.

"Ugh, a scientist," he pointed at his sister, "and a business manager" he pointed at Julia, "I couldn't light a match with the spark of humanity from both of you."

Dee rolled her eyes, "English majors are just bitchy because they know they just paid $125,000 for an education that only qualifies them to work at Starbucks." She frowned, "So, the Dorian Gray Effect?"

Despite the disdain, he jumped back at the continued interest - an opportunity to teach his idea, "Oh yeah, it's sort of when you see someone that you've known for a while and you care about, you don't really see them, you *see* what you *think* of them - their beauty is all you see."

He watched the women ruminate over his explanation, and then offered an illustrative example to his audience. "Think about Dee and Chris, they've known one another forever. When our Deidre sees her husband to be, she doesn't see his big beer gut, she remembers his athletic shoulders from back in his football days. She doesn't stop and notice the bald spot on the back of his head..."

Deidre shrugged and turned back to the mirror.

"Hey..." They heard Chris, hurt, from the next changing area, just muttering, barely audible, "I don't have a bald spot." They heard a rustling as Chris was turning his head this way and that in the triple mirror, "Do I?"

"Don't come in here!" the two girls yelled over the partition.

David continued, "She sees his lustrous black mane from when he had a ponytail."

"He had a ponytail?" Julia mouthed at David.

He nodded. Julia drew her lips back in dismay. He widened his eyes in agreement and they caught each other in a silent, shared laugh - a quick connection from across the room. He smiled at her as he went on, "Her eyes gloss over the flaws and she sees the best of him, despite the fact that he has let himself go to forty-two year old shit."

"Forty-two year old shit who could still beat your skinny ass!"

"You'd have to catch me first, Fattie!"

"Love, true love." Julie commented on their manly exchange of idiocy.

"Deidre!" A whine came over the partition. "The suit you picked doesn't fit!"

David came slightly closer to Julia, murmuring just to her, on a quiet aside. "You might be an X-factor in my theory though."

"And how's that?" She questioned.

"You told me a forty!" Dee yelled back to her groom.

"I am a forty!" Chris yelled over again. "This doesn't fit!"

"Hold on, I'm coming!" Dee hollered over the peach silk screened partition, gathering her dress.

"Wait..." Julia held up her finger to Dee.

David explained his theoretical shortcomings to a distracted Julia, his voice soft, "I would say that just by looking at you, that you seem more beautiful now than you ever were before," he paused.

"Come on, David..." she sighed.

He made his tone more gruff, "...but I'm not really sure if I like you all that much, anymore."

Her brows lowered, "Hey," and her voice arose in involuntary dismay. Julia turned to the bullshit artist who had just the hint of a smile at the corners of his eyes, he was looking at her, barely able to await her inevitable indignant reaction, and there he was, back again. The teasing, silly, inappropriately flirtatious David had replaced the one who actually felt emotions. Julia spoke to his sister, as she frowned at him, "No, Dee, you are in your dress, and he cannot see you in it. I will go." She tore her eyes from his maddeningly playful ones and stood up.

Dee paused and then nodded at her.

Julia yelled over the partition, "Are you decent?"

Chris yelled back, "It's not like you haven't seen me naked before, Juju."

Dee glanced furtively at her old roommate.

Julia rolled her eyes. "Oh for chrissakes," she yelled back, "I just am not sure if Dorian Gray will help you out in my case, Chris!"

There was a twitch of a smile on Dee's lips.

After a second, "I'm good." Chris yelled back. "Pants on and everything."

Julia stood up, and smoothed down her dress, "Well," she said to David, still waiting for her to react either to his words or to his look, "I can explain your X-factor very easily, Mr. Diemand, and not through some dumb Irish metaphysical poet theory," she challenged.

"Metaphysical poet?" he nodded, impressed. "Tell me." He stood straighter.

She looked right in his face. "Your advanced age is affecting your vision..."

"Ouch."

"And, you just haven't spent enough time with me to remember how fantastic I really am."

His eyebrows shot up, and he thought about her analysis for a moment before he replied, "I should withhold ruling out my theory as invalid then."

"Good idea" she offered to him, just as she passed his shoulder, "Handsome."

Ho-ho, she just took that theory and ran with it. *Right at me.*

He watched her walk behind the partition.

'Handsome' means she's attracted, right?

*Or wait...*there was a flaw in his theory, after all.

Does it mean that she isn't?

Julia found her old college boyfriend trapped in the stockade of a too-small black dinner jacket, he shouted at the mirror, "Why the hell do we have to wear fricking penguin suits anyway?"

Julia saw his frustrated fidgeting and selected another jacket off of the rack, a larger size, "Wrong cut for you," she said diplomatically, "try this one." She helped him pull his ex-football player's physique out of the straining seams of the evening wear.

David, still sorting out the practical application of his theory, followed Julia back through the opening, leaving his sister with the returned seamstress, catching the two exes in earnest conversation.

Chris, annoyed, "I just don't see why I have to wear a tuxedo."

"Well, Dee wanted a traditional ceremony, and traditional is usually formal." Julia offered him first one sleeve and then the other.

Dee yelled over the wall, "Quit bitching, Chris!"

"Love, true love," David repeated Julia's words.

Chris turned around to look in the mirror. He spoke to Julia's reflection. "We're on an island, what is wrong with a shirt and tie or something? Isn't that formal enough?"

Julia shook her head, to his reflection, "How about: it will make your wife happy to see you in that tuxedo."

"I didn't want to do this black and white shit from the beginning, how about what makes me happy?"

"You might want to start with: making her happy can make you feel happy," David offered quietly.

Julia glanced in his direction, but he was looking at his buddy.

"I don't need your bullshit, too, dude," Chris laughed.

They heard a groan of frustration from over the peach wall and a rustle of Dee leaving the room. "I'm going to the bathroom!"

Julia turned to the groom, "Let me put it to you this way, Chris," Julia tugged on the sleeve, and straightened the shoulders of the black jacket, then grabbed Chris' bulky arms and forced him to look in her eyes. David watched her as she explained slowly to the intended groom, "Tuxedo is to woman," nodding with each of her words for emphasis, "what lingerie is to man."

Chris thought it out, for a good long while, and then a slow realization came over his face, breaking with a smile. "Ohhhhhh."

"Uh-hmmm." Julia let his meaty arms go.

She turned away and looked over at David, widening her eyes again in disbelief, and nodding, he chuckled.

The day was exhausting, which should have been a good thing.

The rest of the wedding party arrived as scheduled and Julia spent most of the rest of the day with the seamstress, conferring with Amy on the timeline, and running through the schedule with José. She confirmed her assistants' arrival on the appropriate morning and then fell exhausted on her bed. Chris kept insisting that she go to dinner with them, but it was all too much. Julia lay fully clothed, grateful to have made it through this without more than a mention of her William and she fell into a fitful sleep on the couch in her room.

But she didn't really make it. Julia found herself, wide awake, at approximately 2:45 am.

She didn't have much to do in the way of work. She didn't need to update her blogs. And a few more emails time-stamped at two or three AM and people would start to think something was seriously wrong. There was only one thing for her to do. The one thing that could soothe her tired mind. The only thing that over the years could make her brain stop running in endless circles, as she lay awake at night, running down lists and schedules and hopes and dreams and What Ifs.

"Help me, Obi-Wan Kenobi," she mumbled to her hotel room remote, "You're my only hope."

The SyFy Channel original movie, "Megashark VS Crocosaurs" appeared bright and CGI'd on her darkened screen.

Ah, science fiction. The only thing to soothe the savage beast of her brain. It didn't matter if it was Lucas, Roddenberry, Whedon, Bradbury, Serling, or Newman, Webber and Wilson, or even some B movie cheese-fest. Time travel or space travel, vampires or werewolves, dystopian exploration or creature features, Julia didn't care. She sat under a blanket from the bed and let herself get drawn into the terrible graphics, the horrific storyline, and the atrocious acting of the late night monster fest.

At home, Will was The Princess and the Pea - anything could and would disturb his light sleep. He would come looking for her downstairs at the computer or at the TV and she would have to click off before he saw the photon torpedoes or the Tardis materializing.

So to just sit here, alone in a hotel, as the guy who was Erkel tried to explain to the Army commanders how the Megashark was going to wreak destruction, was like an odd, marvelous little self-indulgent treat.

At three o'clock in the morning, she got a text.

She looked quizzically at her phone, she didn't recognize the number.

'Lights on. How come?'

'Who's this?'

'Your Handsome Secret Keeper.'

David. 'Where are you?'

'Boat.' She went to the window of her room, and saw a faint light from a boat down the dock. 'Still up?'

'Nope sound asleep. I sleep-text now.'

'Such a brat.'

'You're a brat. Go back to your hammock or something.'

'Don't sleep in a hammock.'

'Assumed.'

'Wise ass-umption.'

'Terrible.'

'I know.'

'Good night, David.'

'Night.'

She put down her phone and pointedly closed her drapes. She fussed around the room for a minute - looking at her dress for the wedding, checking up on an Emily Post formality, straightening the blanket. She may have even Googled Richard Brighton, just out of sheer curiosity. But then, on the screen was the option - Google Earth. And she typed in an address.

And there it was. Ellen's house. Where her husband was right now. In *Ellen's* house. In *Ellen's* bed. Kissing her lips, touching her breasts, pushing himself into... *let's not go* - Julia blew out a breath - *there.*

She zoomed in closer on the aerial view, Julia could make out a red and black bicycle thrown haphazardly on the front lawn. Just two blocks down the street from where she lived. Julia checked at the date on the photo.

Last Updated.

At the time this satellite picture was taken, Julia and her husband had been happily married.
Happily?
Really?
Her phone buzzed. His voice was on the other end.
No, not the adulterous Prince Charming's.
His.
"You feel like coming out to play?"
"No, David," she said, exasperatedly.
"How come?"
"It's late."
"And?"
"I should be asleep."
"And so should I. You are free, love. No one to answer to. Start to enjoy that freedom little."
"I am. By myself."
"You don't have to be."
"You must be used to it."
"What?"
"Being alone."
"Nah. I don't think you ever really get used to it."
"How about the not-sleeping thing?"
"You can get used to that."
"How long have you gotten used to that?"
"A year?"
"Oh my God."
"It's not that bad."
"How do you do it?"
"I told you I read."
"You don't have a huge..." she lingered, "...place for a library." She smiled broadly at her unintended joke.
"What?" he tried to sound disgusted, upset, furious. He wasn't convincing.
"You heard me."
"I don't know what to say, or how to react... Wait a minute," he asked in mock horror, "Should I be insulted, or turned on, or something..."
"No, I just figured the boat, you and your large... number of books?"
He gasped.

"Please!" She retorted to his overreaction, "We've been friends for so long... Oh wait, no, that's wrong. I forgot your jury's out on whether you like me anymore or not."

"They're ready to come back with a verdict, I'll tell you." he shot back. "'Please' yourself - in the past, like day and a half, you've called me a moron, you've wrecked my shirt..."

"I didn't wreck your shirt..."

He corrected, "You wrinkled my shirt, threatened to kick my ass, expressed a desire to see me choke to death..."

"What do you want? Sweet nothings?" she laughed.

He considered, "It'd make up for the shirt, at least, if you're offering..."

"I'm not."

"Fine." He conceded and then, after a second, he remarked, "Those two, you know, from the bridal shop, they have a lot to learn, don't you think?"

"Chris and Dee? Oh God, I know! They don't know what's coming at them."

"Not in the least." She heard a deep rumble of laughter from his throat.

Julia, "They're still in that idealistic stage of love that they think honesty is the best policy."

He added on, "Or that both of their opinions are equally important and must be heard and acknowledged as valid each and every time."

"And that being right means you shouldn't have to apologize."

He laughed ruefully, "But who are the two of us to talk? The Lonesome Losers, right?"

That stopped her, and he heard it in her voice, over the airwaves, "I don't know. I'd still like to think I know a little something about relationships."

He added, gently, "Well, yeah, seventeen years is nothing to sneeze at."

"Yes, seventeen years." She said, more softly, "But that's where my expertise runs out, I guess."

"Hey," he started, making his gruff voice equally soft, but thought the better of it. He cleared his throat, "How about I forgo the sweet nothings. How about just talking dirty? That would negate any and all obligations you may..."

She interrupted him, "Didn't I already say, 'good night, David'?"

"Technically, you texted it."

"So I'm saying it now."

"No, first, I need to clear something up," he added, "I do have a large... number of books. A very impressive... library."

"You don't have enough room on that boat."

"S'all digital."

"Battery-powered," she started to giggle.

"Now, don't start..."

"I understand..."

"Heeey..."

"Well, men getting older..."

"I said, don't start..."

"...you've got to make concessions for these sort of functionality problems..."

"There are NO functionality issues with my LIBRARY..."

"...It happens when you get older, Dave. Nothing to be ashamed of."

He guffawed, and then chuckled, admiringly, "Shut up, Santos."

"Gladly."

She hung up, annoyed with both her moment of pained vulnerability as well as his reflexive, pain in the ass ability to make her snap out of it.

CHAPTER 10
Getting Half-Hitched

Jules had left early to grab the kids in the morning. As she had volunteered to take Chris' son Jackson with her children to the beach for the day, the bride and groom could go along with members of the bridal party for preparations for the Rehearsal Dinner. Julia had offered to help but Dee had wanted to handle that particular night on her own. Julia was a little glad to be free from having to spend the day with all of those Diamond Diemands, far easier to be with the kids.

Hannah had arrived with little Jackson just after Julia had come back to the hotel with her two in tow. Annie had bounced on the big king-sized bed her mom had originally reserved for her and her husband. Neither one of them had slept a full night in it yet. Billy had flung himself in the chair by the window.

"Dee said I should come down," Hanna proffered, "see what this kid thing is all about."

They embraced at the door.

"Don't let us scare you, Hannah" Jules laughed as she handed out the boogie boards, the picnic basket, and the towels to the thirteen, ten, and nine and a half year old respectively and ordered them to march. She shouldered the beach chairs, their umbrella, beach ball, and her bag of supplies - talcum powder, sunscreen, and water bottles.

"Can I carry anything?" Hannah asked.

She pointed to her friend's burgeoning belly, "I think you've got enough there."

Hannah grabbed the beach ball, "Stick this under your cover up and we'll look like twins."

Julia could see the three of the kids negotiating for which spot on the beach was best, but Julia's assessment of the tide determined where they would lay out their provisions for the day on the warm sand. She read them each an individual riot act and sprayed them with yet another layer of sunscreen.

"Coming Mom?" Billy queried, although he already knew the answer.

"No, honey, I don't want to mess up the new pedi." She saw a fleeting look of disappointment, and she frowned at herself. "Go, have fun."

She pulled her cover up over her head, a navy blue bikini clung to her hips and lifted up her breasts. She slid her Gucci sunglasses down over her eyes and settled herself down next to Hannah.

Hannah was happy to doze in her chair, shifting every twenty minutes or so to try and keep the circulation going. Julia was glad for the quiet, running tacitly through the details of the wedding brunch's menu with José on the phone. About an hour later, three wet, smiling kids accidentally dripped poor Hannah awake.

Julia was up and ordering, "Dry off, more 'screen, and then you can head back in, okay guys?" The kids grabbed their towels and chatted about the height of the waves and how far Billy could throw them in the water.

Hannah looked over at her, "Okay, so, tell me the truth."
"What?" Julia froze.
"You look... good."
"Um... thanks."
"So, you have to tell me."
"What, Han?"
"First, what changes after kids?"
"What do you mean?"
"You know - the body. What happens?"
"Oh, um," Jules shrugged, "Do you want the truth?"
"Straight."
"You're not going to be able to unhear this."
"Give it to me."
"My ass traveled two inches south."
"What?"
"One inch for each kid."
"Are you kidding me?"

She grabbed a significant portion of her round backside and hoisted, "Used to be here," she let it fall, "now it's here."
"Oh."

"And this, not too bad," she poked at a small bulge of skin at her lower abdomen, "but, I am doing at least 8 hours a week at the gym - TRX, Insanity, CrossFit, Zumba, jogging, spinning and no matter what, Han, I can't make it go away."

"Really?"

"Does not go away," Julia repeated.

Hannah blanched.

"And these," Julia grabbed her boobs, "Well, the nipples…"

"Okay, okay, please stop."

"I warned you." She narrowed her eyes, "See these tiger stripes right here? Those are attractive right? And this?" pointing to small purple veins over the tops of her thigh.

"Julia!" Hannah shouted, "Please!"

"Fine," Julia shrugged and lay down on the towel next to her friend, "Forties don't help either."

"So I'm getting a double whammy."

"You've still got a couple of years." Julia offered. "So has everyone touched you yet?" pointing to her friend's ample stomach.

"Yes, what is that?!"

"You're like the Buddha."

"I know."

"It used to drive me nuts!"

"Total strangers come up to me all the time, sometimes they don't even ask, they just touch the belly. I have thought about punching people."

"I got to the point where I just want to tell people I'm not pregnant, you're just rubbing fat."

"I'm going to do that!"

"I don't think you can deny that though, Han Solo." She looked over at her friend's belly, she started out with her hand, "I have to admit, I can barely help myself!"

Hannah cocked her head at her, "You want another one?"

Julia thought, "The clock is winding down, Hannah, plus, well. Will…" she trailed, "seems to have made that decision pretty clear," picking her words carefully.

"Yeah, okay, but if you could…"

"…but if I could, I'd do it again. That whole first year, where all you do is hold them. And even when they get older and their little tantrums, and then just watching them learn… It's so ridiculously hard…"

"Greeaat."

"No, it's so - I guess the best word for it would be - wonderful." Julia whispered out of the corner of her mouth, "Even with the assalanche."

Hannah laughed. "You look fabulous."

"Well, I do always need to 'present well.'"

"Huh?"

"Part of my job is that I, as a representative of the Plaza's management, must maintain a level of 'appropriate presentation.'"

"Are you kidding me?"

"Nope. I deal with high-end weddings for a world class business, I have to be part of the product I sell."

"Is that legal?"

"Well, yes and no. They can't fire me if I gain a little weight or anything. But if I am not dressed, or appropriately manicured, or my hair is too long, or too short – I'm serious, it's in my contract! - I would not be helping to promote the Plaza Wedding brand, which would put my job in jeopardy."

"That's crazy."

"Well, you know, attention to detail, good presentation, classic but up-to-date, that's what these big deal weddings are all about. And there are huge perks to working with the Plaza. I could point you to all the best hairdressers, designers, shop owners, caterers, nutritionists, jewelers, dermatologists on the East Coast."

"How about…" Hannah glanced quickly down at the sand and then back up to Julia, "plastic surgeons?"

"Oh yeah," Julia laughed, "you should have seen the old nose on my last bride…"

"So, would you ever have a little…?"

"What?" Julia looked at her friend.

Hannah pointed to her face.

"What?"

"You know…"

"Hannah, are you asking if I've had work done?" Julia unhinged her jaw. "Oh my God."

"I'm just wondering!"

"Han!"

"I was asking because you look so good!"

"No you're asking because I look like I need to sleep for about a month!"

"Not at all!"

"You are such a liar."

"I'm sorry."

"I have never, ever had a single procedure done to my person. Ever."

"Fine."

"Fine."

"Good for you."

"Yes, good for me," Julia agreed adamantly.

Hannah pressed. "No Botox."

"No." Julia answered.

"No collagen filler?"

"No!"

"Bee venom?"

"I said, 'No! I have not had anything done!" Julia yelled, but then broke into giggles, "But I have my first appointment scheduled for next month."

"You bitch!" Hannah laughed. "For what?"

"The Almighty Bo."

"Ah-ha!"

"Yeah, well, honestly, I'm going to have to cancel it anyway..." Julia then noticed Billy looking at something on the horizon.

"Cool boat," she heard him breathe out, as he stared toward the water line. Julie followed his gaze at a large white boat slowly approaching the beach side of the harbor. It chugged along as swimmers noticed and gave it wide berth. It dropped anchor about twenty feet off shore.

She saw her son start to walk out to the yacht, zombie-like, inexplicably drawn, "Billy, stop!" she called after him, "That kid," she muttered to her friend.

"Rethinking another assalanche?"

"Ugh," Julia got up and jogged to her son wading into the water, while directing her daughter and little Jackson to stay with Hannah.

Without commemorating the fact that this was the first time her swimsuit had actually gotten wet, she had caught up to Billy when he was about waist high in the water, "Billy, what the heck do you think you're doing?"

"Just looking Mom, geez," he told her, annoyed. He yelled up, "Ahoy!"

"Don't 'geez' me, kiddo," she warned.

"Ahoy!" yelled back a familiar voice.

Oh, God. She had spent so much time concentrating on her son mesmerized by the beautiful, gleaming white man-toy that she failed to realize that she had spent the wee hours of the morning on the phone chatting with its captain. "Aren't you supposed to be doing wedding stuff?" she yelled up.

"I could say the same about you." The voice rang down, and a scruffy head appeared over the railing. David, wearing a ripped up pair of olive green cargo shorts, a faded black t-shirt and deck shoes, slipped down and plopped into the water with them.

"I've got the kids," she excused herself. "Dee's going to kill you."

"No she's noooooot," he dragged out the words, like he was the teenage boy denying responsibility. "Just couldn't take..." and then his brain sort of faded out of his sentence. Signals were not reaching his mouth from that brain because there was some sort of temporary recircuiting of blood flow. David finally got a good look at Julia's half-naked body, there in the water, right in front of him. And the only coherent thought floating around in there was *Whooaaa.* Well, half-coherent. The water was lapping up against her bare honey-colored skin, her hair pulled back from her eyes, her fine jawline, and firm cheeks, and that dark suit that just hugged her nicely toned frame. *That goddamned lucky water.* But he had to tear his eyes from the wet, bikini'd Julia because he then somehow noticed the tall boy next to her. Periphery returned to his tunnel vision and he had to recover and quickly assess - *her face, Will's hair*. It wasn't until then that he was able to finally finish his sentence, "...you know, another day, of preparations."

She didn't seem to notice the long pause of his vaguely pornographic mental journey, "I see."

He turned to the kid, "Hi, I'm Dave, Dave Diemand," he held out his hand to her son.

The boy, who had been confused by the conversation between the guy with the cool boat and his mom, made sure to do as his dad had taught him, grasping the hand firmly and looking the man in the eye. "Hello, sir, Bill Rosa."

Bill? Julia furrowed her brow.

"How do you know my mom?" said her suddenly very direct young man.

"We knew each other from college." Dave answered him, equally directly.

Billy looked at her for confirmation, "Dee's big brother. Mr. Diemand is here for the wedding," she confirmed.

Hannah had Annie and Jackson by the hand and was wading out to the three of them by the boat but her belly was not providing enough flotation for them all.

"It's a great boat, Mr. Diemand."

"Dave, please."

"Dave."

"It is, isn't it?"

"Hi Han."

"Hi Dave," Hannah shook her head at him.

"I was just chugging along and I heard you guys were out here with my soon-to-be-nephew and I thought I'd ask if you wanted to come on out."

Billy's face lit up from within; he reverted quickly back to a kid with a fast Can We Mom? hop in the water.

"I love your boat, Dave!" Jackson chimed in, Dave went up to Hannah and took the now swimming little guy in his arms.

"This will be your third or fourth time as my first mate, Jack?"

The little boy counted it out, "Fourth!" he beamed

Julia asked, "Hannah, are you going to come?"

"Goodness no - the motion. I could barely make it on the ferry. But don't let me stop you. I am very happy here on the beach under the umbrella."

He said to Julia, "We can troll over and get lunch at Galley Beach if you want, the kids can swim right off the deck, it's great."

"Mo-oomm."

"We can fish, see some seals maybe, give the kids the whole Nantucket experience. Far more important than stupid wedding stuff."

"Seals!" Annie squealed.

Julia looked around her, the three faces - nope, make that four - beaming with hope, "If I say no…"

"You'll be Shanghai'ed," David said.

"I've got stuff on the beach."

"Well, then let's go get your stuff, Juju," David smiled.

"Juju?" Billy asked his mom.

"Yes, Juju is something like 'magic,'" David explained. "There was Good Juju, and Baaaad Juju."

She gave him a warning glance over her shoulder.

"That right there," he pointed at her, looking at Billy, "was Bad Juju."

She just shook her head.

They carried the towels and bags over their heads, and left an already snoozing Hannah with a full picnic basket under the beach umbrella. David carried Jackson on his shoulders and hoisted him onto the deck from the half-submerged swim ladder.

He lifted up a smiling Annie who introduced herself mid-hoist, "Pleased to meet you, Annie," and offered a hand to both Billy and Julia. He got the kids life vests and helped Julia buckle them in. He showed them the boat and then offered them a spot to sit, while he fired up the engines and moved them slowly back out to the open sea.

Dave took them out to the Sound, cut the engines, and came down, "Who's up for a swim?"

"Right here?"

"Seems as good a spot as any."

Annie asked, "With the seals?"

David said, "I'm not sure if there are any out there now. But maybe some will happen on us."

Billy jumped up to be the first to go in, "You coming, Mom?" he asked.

She deflected, "Um, you going in guys?"

"Yes!"

"I don't know," Annie started.

"Wuss!" Billy teased his sister.

"Am not! I'm waiting for the seals."

"Seals bring sharks, Annie."

"Sharks?"

"Billy!"

"They do!"

Dave offered, "We'll sit up here on the gunwale..."

"I don't see any guns."

"That's just what this is called, you and I can watch for the seals."

Billy leapt off the starboard side into the dark blue water. "Come on Juju, or are you afraid of sharks?"

"I'm sorry, young man, but did you just call me - your mother - 'Juju?'" She looked at her son, *suddenly the teenage wise-ass?*

"She won't come in," her son mocked, "she'll mess up her mani or her Keratin treatment," he imitated a high female voice.

"Is that supposed to be me?"

"Maybe?" he tried to look serious, but a grin was creeping up on the corners of his mouth.

"You are playing with fire, young Bill," Dave laughed.

"I'll muss up my pedicure!"

"I don't say that!"

"You just said it!"

"I didn't say 'muss'!" She half-shouted at him, her hands on her hips, looking down at his more man-than-boy face bobbing up at her from the water, "Well, you know, at least, I'm not as bad as your father," she mimicked, "'I can't go out on the bike ride with you guys, I have spinning class today!' right?!" She chuckled, but she found herself looking at the two fallen faces of her children, and then she found herself trailing off her mocking tone, her silly mimicry, what she meant to be a little joke at their dad's expense.

And before last Tuesday, it would have been.

This would have been nothing more to this situation than her gentle teasing of their serious dad and the kids would have understood the humorous harmless intention. They would have even gone back to their father, biting back their lips, and telling him of their mom's joke, and he would have pretended offense. But now, the words coming out of her mouth made her accurate observation sharp, their current separation made her humor bitter, and Julia saw that Billy and Annie's faces were torn in half, between old familial habits and a new unintentional division of loyalties.

David politely busied himself with Jackson's life vest.

And Julia knew that she had to so something.

She couldn't do this to her kids, intentionally or not. She couldn't put her kids in the middle of what was happening with her and their father.

She had to diffuse the bomb she had set and she had to do it quick. Nothing was coming. Should she apologize? Explain that isn't what she meant? Try to reason with two little kids whose faces so clearly showed fresh pain?

She did the only thing she could think of.

"Oh wow, kid. You know what? You're just going to get it." She yelled, "Megashark Vs. Crocosaurs!" And she leapt out, into the water, executing a giant cannonball into the ocean right next to where her boy was floating. The wave of water was so tremendous that it slapped up over his head and down into his wide-eyed face and his open mouth.

She surfaced, next to him, unsure of what he would say or do next. She looked up at her daughter, who was staring at her big brother's utterly shocked expression. She looked over at him, floating next to her, wiping his nose with one hand and pushing back his wet hair with the other.

Julia found herself holding her breath above the water.

And then, slowly, gratefully, Annie began to giggle. The little girl couldn't help herself. The scene they had just witnessed - their beautiful, perfect mom had just cannonballed into the ocean off the side of a big, white boat! It was like nothing she had ever seen before. And the laughter fell from her like the little drops of water.

At first, one, then another, and then her brother caught those same little droplets and he started to chuckle, as the gush of giggles sprung from Annie, shaking her life vest. Jackson heard the laughter and peered over the side of the boat. And David watched Billy push his hand over the surface of the sea and douse his mother, who laughed right out, thankful, at her two wonderful children.

"Come on Jackson! Annie!" Julia shouted up at them, "The water is incredible!" Jackson leapt into her arms and the two of them went under, Jackson's life vest and all. They came back up to screams and giggles.

David could see Annie wanted to go in and join the splashes and yells, he watched her face working out the problem. She reached her toes toward the ladder, "You going?"

The girl nodded, a determined set in her jaw, *like her mom.*

"Jules!" David called.

"Mommy!"

Julia surfaced again.

"Who's Megashark?" Annie asked nervously.

"Me honey," Julia offered. "Nothing's going to get you."

Her face turned upward, Dave could see as she looked up at her daughter that the lines of her mouth softened, the eleven between her brows smoothed out, she looked relaxed for the first time since he saw her in the hotel lobby.

Julia asked, "You want to come in, baby girl?"

Annie nodded down at her over the life vest.

"Dave?"

He had been watching Julia again, and was caught off-guard by her request, and jumped up extra fast to cover, "'Course." He took the little hands in his and lowered her down the ladder to Jules, her arms upstretched to catch Annie. They were connected by the length of a kid, their eyes met, gray green to honey brown and there it was, a warmth sparking and soaring along the paths of his veins. *There was the face all the boys fell for.*

All of them? Or just you, you idiot?

She looked away to smile at the wiggly daughter in her arms, kicking her feet, keeping both of them afloat, "See? We're like dolphins in this big ocean," she told her girl softly.

"Or Crocosaurs!" Dave shouted as he leapt fully clothed into the water, next to them, flopping painfully with a giant slap on the water, sending nothing short of a tidal wave over their heads, and his deck shoes shot off into the waves. They laughed so much, they were hiccupping sea water.

Julia watched as Dave and Billy were setting up Annie on the fishing chair, "We're strapping you in so you don't get pulled out to sea by some giant Megashark," Billy explained to his sister.

"Coooool," Jackson sighed, never far from the heels of Dave or Big Boy Billy. "Me next?"

"Sure." Dave agreed.

It was interesting to watch David fishing with all of the kids. He showed Annie how to cast, helped Jackson pull in a fish, much to the delighted screams of the girls, and Billy, he treated like, well, like he was a guy. Direct requests, grosser jokes than Julia was particularly happy with, but also with an expectation that Billy knew what he was doing - on the boat, fishing, swimming with little ones. He treated him like he was the kid in charge.

"Sunscreen while I have you wiggly ones strapped in," Julia ordered.

A collective groan from the kids. She sprayed and slathered them quickly - a little more gently with the little ones, a little faster with the big one, whom she could sense just barely tolerated the attention.

She glanced over at David, who was developing a fine layer of pink over his well-freckled tan. "Don't think you're not getting 'screened too, my friend."

"What?"

She came on him with the bottle before he could protest, "Hold your breath," she sprayed his neck, pulling his shirt away from the collar, "You should be putting this on every few hours."

"Huh?" he said, and as she sprayed, as he inhaled, "jes..." he stuck out his tongue and spat, "Gah!"

"Hey white boy, no arguments, you're going to get skin cancer out in all this sun." She squirted a big glob onto her hands and smushed it all over his forehead, face, she ran her hands over his nose, cheeks, and down his neck, like he was one of her charges.

He scrunched up his face at her not-so-gentle handling, muttering, "This could be a lot sexier."

"Close your mouth." She rubbed her hands over his mouth and chin. "Oh-kaaay." She smeared the lines along his hairline back into his newly shortened hair, smoothing it back and over to the side, flattening the sides and back with her palms.

"Huh." She stopped and admired her work. "Wear it like that, kinda David Beckham-ish."

He frowned at her and Billy smiled to himself, his mom noticed and the teenage face went blank. David mussed up his own hair again and the kid's smile instantly reappeared.

It was interesting to see her son in this light. The boy who couldn't stop teasing his little sister, whom she had to badger to unload the dishwasher, and still wanted his mom to tie his cleats before a game, "because I can't do it tight enough," she could see out here Billy was capable, thoughtful, serious when needed and ready to jump up to help.

So, is this a guy thing? He is thirteen, he's going to be turning into a man. How am I supposed to navigate guy things?

They had docked and gone ashore for lunch at a beachside bistro. The kids mowed down hot dog after hot dog and cardboard box after box of French fries. They wanted to take the boards out into the water again, "S'posed to wait twenty minutes," but she conceded at their discouraged faces. "Alright go," she pointed with her chin. "But stay where I can see you".

"We can watch from here," Dave assured her.

"Billy, you make sure everyone's good," she tried this putting him in charge thing.

"I will." He nodded and ordered his two followers to the shore. They ran off, boogie boards under their arms.

So now that they were alone - well, as alone as one could be at a beachside restaurant on Nantucket in the summer on a beautiful day - she turned to her boating companion. "No kids, huh." She wasn't asking, she was stating. They sat at the small table overlooking the small beach yard.

"Nope."

"Surprised."

"Really?"

"Well, yeah. I always assumed."

"Assumed what exactly?"

"You seemed like you were on that road." She put her elbows on the table. "You and Laura."

He sat back, "To what?"

"You know…"

"Getting married? Settling down?" He looked out over the water as he spoke, only glancing in her direction. "Nah."

Julia pressed on, "Laura?"

He looked at her from the corner of his eye. "Takes two to tango, right?"

She shrugged, "Just funny. The kids - it's too bad, because seeing you, with them, you've got the touch." She thought, "But you did study to be a teacher."

"Yep, English." He nodded in her direction.

"But you didn't stay…"

"…never finished my masters degree and you know, there's not enough money in it."

"But, a better schedule than accountant." She leaned back into her chair.

He looked her full in the face now, grinning, "Nothing's better than what I've got now."

"No schedule."

"No job."

"Ah, no job, no house, no car, no kids."

"Pretty sweet," he said self-deprecatingly.

"You, my friend, are a catch!" she pointed at him.

"I don't know," he shrugged, looking down, almost shyly. But then, his eyes flashed from underneath his heavy brows and he grinned, impishly, "I've reeled quite a few in."

"Oh, quite a few," she rolled her eyes.

"Yep."

"Yes. Let me see, they flopped around your deck for awhile, gasping for air and then when you were done, you tossed them back in?" she teased.

"Catch and release," he went along.

"Doesn't really sound like you."

"Oh man, you think you know all about me."

Their eyes lingered on the others across the small table, slight smiles on both their faces. It was easy, friendly.

Julia was the first to look away, to take her elbows off the table and break off that odd current between them, conversational impulses. "I didn't say that."

"How about you? How are you going to handle it?" He paused, leaning forward, his stubbled chin still in his big rough hand, that little grin still in the corners of his mouth. He was trying to tempt her back into their own small little circle of two at the table, "Will Mr. Brighton be your first foray back out into the world of... fishing?"

"Oh, geez." She put her hand to her forehead, "It's too soon to even think about, David. Dating? Do you even know the last time I dated anyone?"

"Pretty sure."

"Okay," she conceded. "That was a long time ago. And David, I don't even know him, I wouldn't know what to do. I'm not a...fisherman anymore." She shook her head, "You know, I can't stand listening to myself: I'm a broken record – what do I do? That's all I can say – what do I do?"

"I couldn't tell you."

"I thought we were the tenured professors."

They looked at one another again. A little more serious.

Just sitting there, just looking at him, she felt an oddly familiar warmth, something, she didn't know what. *Let's change the subject.* Julia, once again, broke ranks. She had to. "You do know you are going to get in trouble on my behalf?"

"Won't be the first time," he waved it off, finally leaning back into his seat, "Why the hell would I want to spend a day inside some cheesy ballroom..."

"Hey, that ballroom is not cheesy. It is a premier location at a Five Star hotel..."

"Sorry, no, you're right. Why would I want to be inside that uh, lavish, stunning ballroom..."

"Thank you."

"...or whatever when I could be out here on the boat?"

"What was Dee going to have you do?"

"I don't know, I don't keep track of that stuff. That's your job."

"Still..."

"Boat? Ocean? Fishing? Sun? There's no contest. You and the kids are nothing but an excuse." He shrugged, "Plus, you're going to buy me lunch."

"With drinks, I'm sure."

"Just one. Can't have you trying to get me drunk again. Like that other night. One might start thinking you were trying to take advantage of my innocent nature."

She snorted.

"Bad juju."

They talked - just talked - for hours. The kids, at first so happy with their partially unsupervised freedom, came and went, taking full advantage of the two adults engrossed in one another, but after a very long while, they came up, complaining that they were all starting to get tired. Julia and David looked up at them, surprised, glancing unbelieving at their watches and phones.

The time had floated by on just the easy flow of the conversation. They hadn't discussed anything in particular - no more treading on heavy subjects of love and loss - although Julia was still dying to ask what really happened with Laura. They had just talked and laughed and agreed and argued about what happened to be around them, what the kids were doing, what movies they had watched, that girl's giant boobs, how sand makes glass, a new book he had read, that guy's hair-sweater at the beach, how nice a day it was, and God, they were getting so damned old.

The sun was starting to set in the Western skies and so they agreed with the little ones that it was indeed time to head back. Billy started out sitting on the stern deck in the nest of towels and blankets his mom had created for them, from what she had found inside the cabin. He lay there with his sister and little Jackson, their muscles made loose and heavy by the hours of sand and sun.

Julia had snuggled up next to her girl, and dug her nose into the crease at her daughter's neck, salty and warm. She giggled sleepily, Jackson snored gently. Billy's dark curls had been blown up by the wind and surf, his freckles pushing out over the bridge of his nose. He lay on the towels, his growing feet casually thrown across his mother's in front of him. She wanted so badly to hold onto this precious moment of contact, but Julia could see that her son kept glancing upwards towards the top deck amidships where Dave steered them back to harbor.

He saw her son look up at him, she nudged, "Go ahead," she yelled over the sea spray and the roar of the engine. She watched as he climbed, and saw Dave clap the kid on the shoulder once in greeting and the two stood watching over the bow, silhouetted in orange sunlight, occasionally turning their head to talk only to one another in some maddeningly unheard conversation.

They rolled into the dock and left David on the boat, to deal with the dozen or so text messages on his phone when they came back into range, each one more furious than the one before.

"Thanks, Dave, they loved it." She shouldered a sleeping Jackson and grabbed Annie's hand.

"Yeah, thanks Dave," Billy shook his hand.

"No problem." Dave turned to her, "You've got to bring that one up to the suite. You got him? He's heavy."

"Yes. Hopefully, Chris will be the only one there."

"Bah." He waved off any worries about his sister's wrath.

"Nice to spend the day with them."

"It is."

"See you soon,"

"According to the schedule…"

"So," Billy turned to her in the hallway up to the room, after leaving Jackson with Chris, he said tentatively, "is Dave your boyfriend?"

"Oh my God!" she shouted out, startled. "What gave you that idea?"

"I just thought Dad had a girlfriend now, so Mr. Diemand must be your boyfriend."

"Billy, no," she admonished. "Just because Dad has a girlfriend…"

"It's not a big deal," Billy interrupted, "Mrs. Shaffer is dating my biology teacher I think."

What sort of crazy swinging world is my son being exposed to? "No, no honey. It's too… Oh my God, I can't believe I'm talking about dating." *Again.* She took a big breath, "Honey, that's not how it's supposed to work with a marriage. It's not just done the day someone decides to leave." *At least it shouldn't be, right?*

"So, Dad's coming back?"

She thought, "I don't know, sweetie. I don't really know how this works anymore than you do."

"Do you want him to come back?"

Oy vey, she busied herself with the key card, "Do you?"

"Yeah, I guess so." He wandered in through the hotel room door, calling back to her, "Just be easier."

She sighed, and despite her better logic, despite her hard-earned knowledge, her first thought was *he's right, it would be.*

CHAPTER 11
Someday My Prince Will Come Back

Julia got a text: 'I think we should talk.'

Prince Charming. He possessed a Magic Mirror. BUZZ: 'Can I come out to see you when I get the kids tonight?'

She held her phone in her hand, staring down at the screen. The knot of anxiety breeding like a goddamned rabbit in her ribcage, pushing out her breath. *Oh my God, Will wants to come to get them, to the island. Where everyone will see him. Ask him why he's not here. Ask 'how's the business deal?' Ask about... well, everything or anything.*

She sent back: 'I'll come across with the kids.'

BUZZ: 'See you at the landing.'

She clicked off. But wait, what does Will want to talk about?

Maybe...

Nope. She couldn't go down that road.

But.

Maybe her husband has come to a realization. Maybe he's spent enough nights in that Ellen's crazy, messy house and her insane five kids. And maybe he considered that they would be taking their two once in a while - *God, seven of them!* - and he couldn't stand the idea.

It would make sense, he was always so proper, so neat, so perfect all the time - all of that haphazard, earthy, fly by night, let's go on an adventure crap may have worn on him already.

It had on Julia anyway. Her shoulders pulled down under what seemed to be an unearthly amount of weight.

Maybe he will come and we can talk and he can come back and the kids can go back to Kevin's and we can be alone and finally talk together. We can be grateful for one another again, we can make changes, we can make this work, we can go on hikes if that's what he wants, we can finish the house, we can sell it for all I fucking care, just please...

Put everything back to where it was.

I don't want to think about this anymore. I just want to go back to the original plan of Happily Ever After.

And what the hell is wrong with that?

Nothing.

It all hinges on this conversation, doesn't it? Julia thought. It all stems from what he needs to talk to me about. *Should I push it now? Text and ask? Call him on his cell or just wait and see this out face to face?*

No, face to face, he can see me. Face to face, he will see what I look like. I present well.

Face to face, he will know what he is leaving behind.

If in fact, he's leaving me behind at all. Julia let herself smile at the thought.

But just for a second.

"Wow, Mommy, you look really pretty." Annie remarked at Julia's sundress, the skinny straps over her shoulders, the silken fabric just brushing over her breasts, her behind, and flowing easily around her knees. The lilac color of the dress set off her tan and worked perfectly paired with gold strappy Ferragamo sandals. Julia's brown hair was pulled back and off of her face - the ponytail facelift, she smirked at herself - but also, a smart move for a ferry ride across the Sound. She kept her makeup simple, just a light, summery shimmer over her eyes, cheeks, and lips. She looked in the mirror, approvingly. She looked young, pretty. Prince Charming would approve.

Screw that. Any man would approve.

"Thanks, baby girl." She gave one last glance in the mirror. "You ready to go meet Daddy?"

The three of them headed from the hotel on the shuttle. They settled in for the forty minute trip across the water on a deck with a bar and snacks. Julia didn't drink a drop - she needed a clear head, but the kids had one Coca-Cola each and a box of mozzarella sticks. Her stomach growled at the marvelously greasy smell of the fried cheese, but she would be damned if she was going to meet her husband with a bloated stomach and no Spanx with a big fat oil stain down the front of her dress.

She would have been at the dinner Dee had planned for all of the friends who were finally arriving that night - a kind of reunion. Julia had texted Dee that something had come up with the kids and she would need to take them over. Dee had texted back a frown-y *(textspeak!)* face, but then assured her that it wasn't a problem and they would catch up tomorrow morning.

Julia ended up being especially glad she didn't eat when the big ferry turned into the harbor, her stomach was doing flip flops and it wasn't from motion sickness. Will had texted that he would meet them at the dock and that they could talk there. Julia grabbed Billy and Annie's hands and squeezed them nervously as they walked in line down the gangplank, looking for Will's dark head of hair to be there above everyone else's.

And there he was.

In his dress blue shirt and khaki pants Julia knew he had just thrown on, he took her breath from her lungs. Will was - without any doubt, without any bias - a truly magnificent-looking man.

He pushed through the crowd, or more exactly - when the crowd saw Prince Charming heading toward the beautiful woman and her lovely children - they moved out of his way.

"Hi," she said, smiling, breathless.

"Hi," he smiled back at her, all straight white teeth, "You look," he glanced appreciatively, "great."

"Thanks," she said.

He hugged the kids. A beautiful reunion of a beautiful family.

Together again at last, Julia sighed gratefully.

And then, she noticed the dog.

"What's, um, Star, doing here?" She watched Billy go and scratch their big fluffy Golden Retriever behind the ears and Annie tried to give him a hug, Star's tail wagged slowly.

"Well," Will started, "that's what I needed to talk to you about..."

Julia felt like someone had punched all the air right out of her lungs, "You needed to meet me to talk about the dog."

"Yes, well I know..."

"The dog..." she said flatly.

"Yes, the dog. I have the dog and..."

"Are you kidding me?" A flash of heat reddened her cheeks.

"I know, Ellen said I shouldn't bother you ..."

"Oh she did, did she?" Julia crossed her arms in front of her, a breastplate of armor.

"I know it's not really fair for me to ask this..."

"It's not really fair for you to ask much of anything, William," Julia interrupted sharply. People close by turned to look.

Will noticed, he tilted his head closer to her. "Julia, we promised we wouldn't do this kind of stuff in front of the kids..." he reminded.

"Well, then why are we?" She retorted.

"I would owe you, big time."

'Stuff?' 'Kids?' 'Big Time?' Who was she talking to? "Owe me what exactly?"

"Well, Ellen is allergic to the dog. We figured we could at least try to keep him at the house so the kids wouldn't feel the transition so..."

"'The' house?" *'The' house means our house. He doesn't mean 'our' house.* "You mean, Ellen's house?"

"Yes. Ellen's house. Well, our house, now, my name's on the mortgage." He coughed, "Already."

"Oh, I see. Wow. Yes, real estate agents work fast, huh?"

"Yes, so," he sputtered slightly, "the dog - we wanted to try for the week while you were working, but E's been miserable......"

He called her "E?" "Oh well," she pulled in her lips, biting them between her teeth, "I feel so bad for her."

"Julia," he pleaded. "You know he got sick at our kennel last time."

"You're saying you want me to take the dog, back with me, to the hotel?"

"It's pet friendly, I looked it up."

"I know it's pet friendly, I work for them!"

"I know that."

They stood there, squared off. Will was attempting to be calm, but Julia could see his exasperation. The kids were attempting to busy themselves with the dog, but were caught up in watching the tense exchange.

Julia looked at their faces.

And she knew what she had to do, again. "Well," she took in a huge breath, she will be the bigger person. If not for herself, but for the children, "the kids are going to miss you, Star," she took the leash of her dog, "but you're with me."

"Thank you, Jules," Will looked relieved. "We really appreciate it."

We. She ignored him, albeit politely, and turned to her son and daughter, "Okay, I will be home on Sunday night. Be good for your Dad and Ellen. I love you so much." She hugged and kissed them hard.

Will grabbed their bags and said, "Call me when you get back to the house, I'll walk them right over."

'The' house. Whose house? My house? Will it still be my house?

"Yes, please," Julia replied. He moved to hug her, but she put her leashed hand up. He took the signal and nodded. He headed back to the car, his arm around his children, their faces turned back to her, "Love you, Mom."

"Had fun, Mom," Billy called back to her.

She waved.

And then, Julia took her dog back up the gangplank of the ferry. She sat alone on the aft deck, cold in the night ocean air, shivering, the only warmth was that of the soft fur of her good-natured dog leaning on her left leg, sitting as close to her as he could possibly get.

She had gotten back in plenty of time for the dessert portion of the reunion dinner, but she chose instead to take Star out onto the beach. They walked together in the sand for about two hours, Julia carrying her expensive sandals, and Star carrying his leash. He was subdued, just walking next to her, his lovely feathered legs steady on the sand and surf. He listened to the vocal cues from his mom as she struggled step after step with the thoughts that went through her brain and out of her mouth. He heard a few familiar words, "billy, annie, daddy, walk, bad" but the rest was just superfluous human gibberish.

She watched Star hop up on the giant bed, turn himself into the middle and flop down straight out to sleep. "New trick, old dog," she said, raising an eyebrow.

And then Julia hit the minifridge. Hard.

Her phone buzzed about an hour later, she picked it up: 'Hey, where were you?' She sighed. *Thank God, it's David.*

'Ferry. Had to take the kids back.' She texted back.

'Got booze?'

'Waaay ahead of you.'

'Sneak out of your dorm.'

'Can't.'

'YNot?'

'Don't text-speak, David, you're too old for that shit. You were an English teacher for chrissakes.'

'Point taken. Why not?'

'Got a boy in my room.'

'Oh.' Then, 'Sorry.'

She typed: 'My dog, dumbass. I've got my dog.'

'You have a dog?'

'Yes. Husband's woman is allergic, so I had to take my dog.'

'What's his name?'

'Will.'

'No, dumbass, your dog.'

'Starbuck.'

'You named your dog after coffee?'

'Will thinks so. But no, favorite character on Battlestar Galatica.'

He was typing '*Moby Dick?*' when he was interrupted by her text: 'and 1st mate in Moby Dick – you should know that, Mr. Chips.'

He chuckled. 'There is some humanity in you.'

'Somewhere.'

'Come down.'

'What about Star?'

'Let sleeping dogs…'

'K.'

'Textspeak, really?' David replied.

'FU.'

She opened up the tiny refrigerator, scooping up the proportionally tiny vodkas, rums, gins, and bourbons and shoving them in her purse. She gathered her card key and her sandals, pet her snoring golden lump on the bed and slowly closed the door behind her. Her heart was beating fast, like she was doing something wrong.

It made her giggle.

Out in the brightly lit hallway, she tiptoed past the other silent doors, worried that for some reason they might hear her. It did feel like when she and Dee used to sneak down to the boys' room on the senior floor. But she knew that the plastic bottles in her bag wouldn't make any clinking noises, and she affirmed that she was a grown up. Even still, it was vaguely suspicious to be a forty year old woman, wandering the hallways at three in the morning, clutching her shoes and a large purse.

Who was on her floor? Julia blearily flipped through the file folder in her mind: *Most of the major players should be up here* - yeah, this floor would be lousy with Diemands.

She was passing the door of Dee's suite just in front of the elevator, and as she pushed the call button, the suite door opened and Chris stepped out.

Her first instinct was to duck down the stairwell. *Well, that would be dumb.* Why should she hide? She had no reason to feel ashamed, she wasn't nineteen and she also wasn't smuggling pot down to the second floor of the dorm. *Get it together, Santos.* She straightened up her posture and boldly claimed. "Excuse me sir, what are you doing - visiting the bride before your wedding?"

He was completely startled, looking almost sheepish, then he saw it was her. "You scared the shit out of me, Juju. I thought it was one of Dee's weird cousins or something."

"I asked you a question sir," Julia ordered.

"Well, I might as the same of you, where are you coming from? Or where are you going?"

"Going. Down to the dock. Dave wants booze."

"Oh yeah?"

"Yeah," she said, "Wanna come? I've got tons."

"Iiiii shouldn't."

"Yeah, you shouldn't." She opened up her bag and showed him the booty, tempting him. "Dave's going to meet us, go get your girl and come on..."

"We're not teenagers, Jules," he laughed.

"Whatevs," she mocked.

"We've got an early morning."

"You're sure?" she pulled out an ounce of bourbon, shaking it gently in front of him.

"You are such a bad influence."

"I am not," she said indignantly.

"Always were."

"You're getting me mixed up with your best buddy, Dave, there, my friend. I was hardworking, driven." She added, "Your wife even said so!"

"Yeah, driven to do what you wanted. 'Bad Juju,' Dave used to call you."

"Like I said, he's one to talk. Come on, wake up Dee, let's go," she cocked her head to the side, "the four of us. Be fun."

"Nah, she'll want to sleep. Me too. Big coupla days."

"Yes, biiig, looooonnng days," she tried not to smirk.

The elevator doors opened up, "Night, Jules."

"Night, Chris."

The late night/early morning air off of the harbor was chilly as she slipped on her Ferragamo sandals and ran down the dock to the only boat with a light on, David was waiting for her on the deck, "Freezing," she said as she hopped over onto the planks.

"Well, okay. You barely have anything on. Wow." He breathed, looked at her, standing there, the woozy beauty in front of him. With her hair back and the little bit of makeup, she looked like a glowingly beautiful twenty year old. He had to pull his gaze away, clear his head up a bit. "Booze'll warm you up. Whadja get?" he pulled out a deck chair for each of them. She opened the purse to reveal the treasure.

He pulled out a couple of vodkas and cracked them open, handing her one, but noting her continuing shivering, said, "Hold up." And he ducked back inside the cabin, he came back with the big ugly grey sweater he was wearing from when he slammed into her in the lobby.

She held the bulky item up for inspection, "I'll be a fancy girl."

"Not what you're used to, huh?" he nodded. "Well, I'm not used to having girls putting on clothes on here."

They clinked, or rather, clunked, the tiny plastic bottles together. He drank.

She gave him a sideways glance, "Didn't realize I was boarding the Pussy Boat," before swigging.

He spat out some of his vodka.

"Come on," she giggled the contents of the bottle down, "You're a sailor, for chrissakes! Get with it, Papa Hemingway."

"Well played," he rasped out, his throat stinging, but he approved of her second literary reference of the evening by, appropriately, drinking.

"I have a whole bonfire of humanity in me." She pulled the huge sweater over her head while David pulled his hibachi out and started to light a small fire.

"Well, then you can light this up," he frowned at her, "Soaked in alcohol, I shouldn't get too close to the flame."

Despite his complaining, he got the little kindling going, and she had settled in. "Saw Chris and asked him to come down, he said no, so just the Lonesome Losers I guess."

"The Lonely Hearts Club Band."

"The Beatles." She murmured softly. She shook her head. "Am I gonna make it, David?"

"I don't know, what do you think?"

"The Rehearsal, the Night Out," she widened her eyes. "So many people, so many questions. Where's Will? Why the dog? What am I going to do?"

David looked at her, "You've got to come up with a defensive strategy."

"Defensive strategy…" she trailed off.

"So?"

"What?"

"What is the story?"

"What story?"

"The story you're giving to everyone."

"Oh, um, business holding him up?" Julia offered. "That's what I told your sister."

"Hmm," David thought, "It's a good thing you have me."

"You don't think it'll be enough."

"Did she buy it?"

"Yes," she thought, "Um, well, I then sorta changed the subject."

"So, no."

"What reason would she have to doubt it?"

"As in all good literature, important truths and convincing lies have lots of details. What sort of business - he's a CPA or something, right?"

"Commercial real estate."

"Okay, then, you need a big business deal in Boston - counteroffers, buyer backpedaling, escrow accounts, zoning problems - so that by the time you are done telling the story, people have already wished you would stop."

"So when people ask, I should just talk and talk and talk?"

"Until their eyes glaze over."

"I can do that."

"And if all else fails, just excuse yourself to take care of the drunk best man."

"A classic," she approved.

"Plan."

"Plan."

"So, in exchange for my wisdom, you must tell me the real story."

"Dave..."

"Come on, no marriage just ends. There's always a story."

"Do I have to?"

He nodded.

She sighed, "You want to know the truth, huh?"

"I am very interested in the demise of your marriage."

"Why would you say something like that?"

"Misery, company."

She sighed, "I don't know." She saw his patient face, knowing he would wait her out and she figured that she had nothing to do but dive in, "I'd like to say how we've been unhappy for a very long while. I'd like to tell you that we both knew it was coming for years. I'd like to confess that I knew we grew apart long ago. But, that's not the truth, David. Not really. I don't think."

His eyebrows raised, "So what is the truth?"

"I don't know. For all intents and purposes, we were a happy family. We just finished remodeling the house. The kids - they're just beautiful..."

"Agreed."

"Thank you," she paused and took in a deep breath. "Will was working and I was working. Perfectly normal. Nothing was out of the ordinary for us really. I mean even the sex was…"

He interrupted, abruptly. "I DO NOT want to hear about you having sex with him."

"Please."

"You heard me."

"I have two children, David."

"I just said I do not want to hear about you having sex with him."

"Why don't you like him?" she started. "I always thought if you just gave him a shot, the two of you would get along. You never gave him a chance."

"Really? You're defending him now?"

She saw the irony and sighed, "Seventeen years of habit."

"So…" he encouraged.

"Okay, well, all I can say is. It happened. To him."

"What happened?"

"It."

"What 'It' are you talking about?"

"I can't say it."

"Try."

"It's stupid."

"Just say it, Juju!"

"No!"

"What the hell are you talking about?"

"Love!"

"Love?"

She almost yelled. "Yes! Motherfucking true love."

His eyebrows went up, "Very romantic."

"I wish I were kidding you."

"About love?"

"Yes. True love? It doesn't exist, David. Not really. It's a good lie, right? Stuff of fiction. Lots of details about soul mates and being perfect for one another, and can't live without each other? It's a myth. A legend. You know, like a Sasquatch, or the Loch Ness Monster."

"You are drunk."

"I am." They absently clunked another nip together and drank.

"So Loch Ness Monster..."

"I'm not kidding," she insisted. "Head over heels, true love, love at first site, meant to be, soul mates... bullshit. All of this stuff - the wedding stuff I've been selling for years. And I am the Merchant of Love. It's what I do. The Manager of Romantic Fantasy. You don't get better than me when it comes to weddings. I know I sound like a conceited ass, but it is what I do. And that? That's the epitome, isn't it? The Wedding! That's what it's supposed to be - the End All, Be All of True Love. And they all live Happily Ever After. Such. Complete. Crap."

"You think so."

"I know so," she nodded, "At least, I thought I did." She looked at the tiny bottle in her hand, adding softly, "I'll tell you right now, I don't think I've ever *really* believed it. The whole True thing." She stopped, not looking at him. "But there it was."

"Hmm."

She paused, her hands grasping at something in front of her, the little bottle jostling with her gestures. And she turned to him, "It was really weird, like watching the plot of every romantic, like Nicholas Sparks tearjerker you've ever seen. It was just like, these two people, one day, turned to each other, looked deeply into one another's eyes and that was pretty much it." She sat up on the edge of her own chair, and turned right to him.

"Uh-huh," he watched her carefully.

"I was there the first time their eyes met actually." She shrugged, sardonically. "We were at a pool party for the neighborhood kids. No big deal - Will didn't even want to go. I made him - I requested it. We went and Ellen was there with her five boys - she's got five boys. And for whatever reason, I can't even remember what we were talking about at first and Ellen and he were just in this little world," she whispered out the words, "Like no one else existed." She brought her hands to her chest, confessing, "I didn't even realize that I wasn't saying anything in the conversation for almost an hour. I just sat there and watched them. I was laughing at the things she got him to say. I was wondering at the things he told her. Within minutes of them meeting, she got him to talk about things I never had been able to. And I'm sitting there, watching them," she sat back in her chair, and said out loud, "and I see them," her voice wavered, "and there was no one else in the world for them at that moment and I look from one to the other and I think, 'Oh, shit.'"

She slid herself off of her chair, she needed to move closer to where he was sitting until she was just at his knee. She wanted him to hear her, she wanted more than anything for David to understand. He would understand. Her elbow on his aluminum armrest, at the level of his chest.

She looked right at his face as she told the story. *Julia was a close talker when she was drunk.* And previously, he had always savored that particular quirk of her personality. But the pain in her eyes was a lot to take in, and it was maybe a little too familiar.

She went on, "He was suddenly someone I had never met. That maybe I had wanted to meet. He was so animated, so alive! And I looked at the two of them, and I knew exactly what it was, I recognized it, David. Right there. I knew what it was as we were sitting on those plastic lounge chairs right next to our neighbor's pool."

She stared up in his face, watching David's sympathetic expressions. *He was so good-looking, wasn't he?* Just rough and raw and masculine with his big hands and his broad shoulders and *God, those eyes.* Those incredible eyes, they looked like the sea.

"Like magic, David," she whispered.

He was quiet for a good minute, just looking at her, he pulled himself up a little and leaned in until his face was mere inches from hers. He could feel her warm, alcohol-tinged breath just there, soft against his lips, and he repeated her word back to her, just as softly, "Magic."

"I know!" She almost laughed it out, rocking back onto her heels, breaking the spell of her errant thoughts and drunken attentions, pulling away from him. "Are you kidding me, right? I brushed it off, thinking that's nuts. We're together. We're married. We have a family and a home and a life. But looking at it now, God I was a moron. There was nothing I could do." She stood up, staring out into the water, "I was powerless against it. Like the Dark Side. She lived a couple of streets over, I'd see her when I would walk the dog. She used to wave and smile and then one day, she stopped waving, and she'd go into the house when I'd walk by, and that's when I kinda knew. Knew for sure that what I saw hadn't been an illusion."

She turned, and faced him, but stared off at a point on the deck, "I kept walking by there every single day, I could have changed my route, taken the dog to the park or something, but I didn't. Just kept walking by her house and looking into the yard. Her goddamned mess of a yard."

She turned back to the port gunwale. David just sat and sipped, his eyes following her, but keeping his face impassive.

"A lot of days, I was almost surprised when he came home after work. I wasn't even all that mad, really." She stopped, and laughed ruefully, "And this is the worst part. I wasn't upset that it was happening. Not that it was happening with him and her, but that it wasn't happening *to me*."

She spun around and dropped down to her knees in front of him, "I've seen fantasies, David. I've made them come true for people on a regular basis. The flowers and the music and the love all around," she flung her hands. "But David, I am telling you I've watched a real, live fairytale happen in front of me. A fairytale. And it just made me sad." She looked up, her eyes made golden in the firelight.

"Sad how?" His face was twisted, bitterly in what she assumed was his empathy for her.

"When you finally get to the 'Happily Ever After' in the big fairytale ending and you realize, this one's not written about you."

He squinted at her, long and hard. He didn't know what to say to her, to her confession. His face stung as though she had slapped him, but the feeling was numb, like she had done it years ago and the old pain had resurfaced as only a memory to remind him of her and what she had done. Those words. These words - they hurt in his throat like the horked up vodka.

She leaned back, "He came home Tuesday night after it had happened, I guess the first time, and he was so upset, he was ashamed of himself, and I told him to go."

David had to clear his throat to dispel some of the bitterness, "So there was sex?"

"Pretty sure." She pushed on, "I'd like to make excuses..."

"Jules..." he shook his head.

"I'd like to say, 'You know what? I hated the life we were living.' Our marvelous, beautiful life. Or maybe, it was that the two of us had just become so caught up in... material things, that I wasn't really happy, that I somehow knew I wasn't fulfilled by all of those..." she spat out, "possessions." But she widened her eyes at him, "But I was! I was fulfilled! I loved it! I loved every shoe, every cashmere throw, every diamond earring, every piece of Waterford crystal, every expensive school tuition payment, every over-the-top Look-At-Me luxury vehicle we ever leased. I loved it, David. Because I. WORKED. FOR. THOSE. THINGS. I worked my whole life. To get those things. That was the whole point. And he told me he loved them too. I know he did." She shook her head, "I thought he did. That's what he told me."

She looked down, "He used to whisper to me, at night, in bed, that we were the Joneses - the ones everyone had to keep up with. We had it all - God, why do you think we had to get a dog?"

"Companionship? Teaching the kids' responsibility?"

"Oh for fuck's sake, Dave," she chuckled bitterly, "it was for the fucking Christmas card. Will's in real estate, the way a piece of property looks is everything. Presentation."

"So that's what you were? Property?"

"Don't poeticize it."

"I'm not."

"I don't know."

"What do you know?"

"Honestly?"

He nodded, so she said, "I know I'm scared, more than anything. I always complained that I was too busy, between work and the kids and Will, I just didn't have time for anything. But now, I'm afraid all of that time's going to come back. I'm scared that all the overfullness of life will be replaced with nothing. No more Friday night movies and Sunday pancake breakfasts together and the holidays we'd have to figure out whose in-laws to visit and the high school graduation presents we were going to buy and the college visits we'd have to arrange and the kids' weddings and the retirement we'd planned, and... and the cemetery plots we'd bought - I'm not kidding, that's one of the things I've been thinking about for the last few days. The fucking cemetery plots. Like I'm going to now have to figure out a new place to go when I die. Every thing had been planned, David."

Planned. That old word. He felt this inexplicable dim fury - *was it from her, was it from him, was it old, or was it new?* He couldn't help himself. He felt for all the pain she was expressing right now, but *how can you have that?* Old dead-and-buried anger and shiny-newborn sympathy shouldn't mix. *You know, like beer before liquor.* The plan. Her plan. He had to speak slowly, to prevent the bile from tainting his words, "You're going to have to make new plans, Julia."

"But I already have plans, David," she said stubbornly.

He stared at her, his doubt, pointed, "I don't know what to tell you."

"You know," she turned to him, seating herself back on the gunwale, like she had come to some drunken epiphany, some inebriated knowledge, "Your sister complains about you not getting married David, but I think you had it right. To have nothing to lose, nothing but yourself?" She nodded heavily, "Yeah, it sucks, but no attachments, not as much collateral damage. Just you, suddenly free."

"Free," he repeated softly.

"Free," she said, again, dazed by her own profundity. She shook herself out of the drunken genius of her self-insight, straightened, and looked around, "So, curiosity satisfied?"

He said softly, not looking at her. "All I needed to know."

"Good." She put her feet down and stood, and walked to the chair, bent and took the handles to her purse, ready to spring back up, she said to the side of his face, "Can I go?"

He grabbed her arm closest to him, "No, you're taking the booze with you," and held on.

She was still bent over, but shook her spinning head at him, "I'm tired now."

"I don't care," he held on.

"How old are you?" she protested.

"How old are you?" he challenged.

"Younger than you," she shot back.

"That's still not young," he countered.

"No, it's not," she conceded, still in this bent position, held captive by his strong hand. She looked at his mouth, so close, his eyes troubled, stormy, and an old idea popped into her head. *A delicious old idea.* "Might be fun to pretend, though, wouldn't it?" she bit her lip at the old memory.

He looked down, and she smiled, her face right next to his, her arm still held firm in his grip. He could draw her close, he could pull her in to the warmth of his body, he could gather her into his strong arms. He would hold her and she would form herself to the familiar lines and just let herself go. It wasn't just the booze. She had seen it in his face, the desire, *he still knew.*

And he reached over.

Her breath caught expectantly and her eyes closed in anticipation.

But she didn't feel his hand come around her face, her neck, to hold her chin, or put his hands in her hair like she had expected, he simply pulled a bottle from her purse, and muttered gruffly, "Depends." He let go of her arm, tilted the vodka back, and emptied it down his throat.

She shot up stock straight, her eyes opened wide, her face went hot, embarrassed. She strode across to the railing. She wanted to run, to get out, but she couldn't make herself get off this boat.

And he wouldn't look at her again.

After a couple of minutes, he said softly to the little bottle in his hand, "So when do you think is the next time we'll all see one another, really?"

Her arms wrapped around herself, the words in her mouth felt hot, she looked down and away, "You're the only one left to get married."

"Not anymore. There's you. Again. Right?"

She closed her eyes and nodded, resignedly, "Then it will most likely be at a funeral."

"When I'm finally found dead on the ocean."

"Or when I get hit by the bus."

She turned back to him. *God,* she was an idiot. He had referenced their joke from earlier, but there wasn't a joy, no devilish lilt to his voice. Its usual gruff tones were flat, emotionless, his body slumped, his arms bound against his chest. He did not want her there anymore, but she couldn't bear to leave. He was her only friend at this wedding, maybe her only ally in the whole wide world right now, and whether she would admit it to him or not, she needed him to help her get through the rest of this week. She had to do something, she had to say something to make it better between them, right now.

She put her face in her hands, speaking through her fingers, "We could be wrong, maybe it could just be our current frame of mind, maybe the 'magic'" she used air-quotes and rolled her eyes, "could still happen to one of us."

"Could."

"Oh dear God, are we the Mutants at Table Nine?"

"Yes."

She nodded, gravely, "Dave?"

"Yes?"

"I'm really, really glad you're here."

"I could say the same." He looked at her, finally from under his eyebrows, his eyes squinting over at her.

"David..." she started.

"Go," he waved her off, "...just leave these," indicating the contents of her bag.

"Okay." She nodded, got up to go, taking one vodka and leaving the rest on the planks next to his chair. She hopped up onto the dock, not looking back as she called out, trying a last ditch effort to make her desperately needed friend like her again, "I am glad you shaved off that goddamn moustache. You looked like a dirty sailor porn star."

A laugh escaped his throat without his permission and he shook his head both at her, and the betrayal of his own fucking soul. *How could she still be funny?* He yelled up to her back, "There she goes folks, Up early to do the WALK OF SHAME. She's leaving my boat! In my clothes! Trying to get back to her hotel room before anyone notices!"

"G'Night!" she called back, almost to the hotel drive.

"G' Morning!" he shouted.

She went back up to her room and lay down on the end of the bed, knees bent, her bare feet still on the floor to ensure that the room would stop spinning. Star had awoken, wagged his tail, and gone back to sleep with a groan. She was still in her lilac dress and his giant sweater. She closed her eyes, trying to remember the last time she had seen David - not four years ago, not ten. Just David, David before Laura. *Ah yes, Hannah's graduation, that would have been before he had met her, right?*

Right?

Julia had been twenty-four, he was twenty-six and the entire time, he had barely spoken to her.

Mary Ann's sister Hannah's graduation.

Julia had come with her husband William, married almost a year. She had known that she would see Dave today, after not laying eyes on him or hearing his voice for almost two years. *Since she had left him that morning in the cottage she had rented on the Cape that summer and they had quietly said goodbye, and she had, despite herself and all of the front she had put up for him, cried for the entire two hour ride home.*

Dave had shown up at Hannah's party, a girl Julia didn't recognize on his arm. She was glad, at first, that he had had someone, but when had made his way over to her and William, she could see his eyes, as well as his date's, were bloodshot, and she knew it wasn't from crying.

He had always known that Julia had been a beautiful girl. In college. That summer.

And here she was, two years later, an exquisitely beautiful woman.

He knew he would see her today and hadn't given it too much thought. He was bringing a date, she was bringing her husband. *Big fucking deal, right?* He'd smoke with April in the car and they'd have a good time on her couch later on. Two years since he had seen her. *Whatever.*

What he hadn't planned on was that Julia, the blushing bride, was more beautiful now than she had ever been before. And seeing that, that *guy - that fucking husband of hers -* had brought out something special in her? Well, it twisted a very dull knife that had rusted in a place in his heart a while back.

David had known Juju in black concert tees or olive drab green, and dark eyeliner, prone to wearing a red lipstick that would pale her skin. It had always made her different, it made her stand out. And now, here she was, a woman standing next to her husband in a creamy silk sundress that set off her honey-colored skin, her brown eye makeup bringing out the golden lights in her eyes, her hands and feet manicured to soft perfection, her hair no longer caught in a messy ponytail, but polished into smooth, subtle waves that cascaded down her buttery shoulders.

Julia was no longer striking, she was glowing.

And it hurt his red-rimmed eyes.

"Who are you?" he had ambled over to her, squinting his already narrowed eyes, the devilish look she remembered now just looked unwelcomingly mean.

"Hi Dave," she had tried to smile.

"So, this is Prince Charming, huh?" he had mumbled out to Julia, over his beer. She had nodded and introduced her husband to him and his date, some girl named April he had met at this accounting firm he had started working at.

He informed April that despite being close, *close* friends with William's wife, he hadn't been invited to the wedding.

"It was a small affair, I do weddings for a living," Julia had tried to smile at her, "so I wasn't up for big to-do."

"A small affair," Dave had harrumphed, "You might even call it, 'a little fling.'"

Julia had then glared at him.

April looked excited, "You do weddings?"

"Just starting catering management right now, but hopefully soon, planning and stuff."

"I want a giant wedding," April had popped and snapped.

Dave had laughed out loud and steered his little girlfriend towards the bar.

"I thought marijuana mellowed people out," William had whispered in her ear, she had smiled absentmindedly.

David had spent the next hour avoiding her completely, so obviously that his sister Deidre actually came over to ask her what was up her own brother's drunken ass.

"No idea," Julia had lied.

It was another five years until she saw him again, but truth was, she had put so many memories away in that time, that little lie couldn't have mattered one way or the other.

Julia lay there on the hotel bed and it came to her - shortly after that, maybe months later, she and Will had gotten into an argument over something very stupid, she thought it was some cheap piece of furniture that her mom had given her for their dining room. Yes, it was a little sidebar that her mom had wanted her to have that originally belonged to her mom's sister. Julia remembered because at the heat of that argument, she had mumbled some cutting little jab that she had thought had just come to her mind, "Can't have anything in the castle that doesn't live up to the high standards of our dear *Prince Charming* now can we?"

She had been so proud of the apt description that her brilliant brain had concocted that it had become her go-to name for him in her mind whenever her husband had particularly peeved her.

Holy crap, she sat up, *I got 'Prince Charming' from David.*

He was mad.

Not half-amused, half-infuriated. Actually mad.

Scooping up a bucket of sea water he dumped it over the fire, an angry hiss spat up at him. "Fuck you," he swore at the sound.

If she had been any other woman in the world. With the eyes, and the hair and the dress, and the biting of that tasty lower lip, and the touching, he would have just taken the blatantly obvious opportunity and tapped that glorious ass.

But no.

Because he was a fucking idiot.

He grabbed the diminutive bottles and snapped off the tiny plastic cap of one after the other.

Because he couldn't.

Because what she had said had hurt him.

Hurt.

And he was a pussy, he couldn't just take that moment, that vulnerable and ready moment where she so clearly wanted him to touch her, to kiss her, to sleep with her. Nope, he couldn't because *she had hurt his feelings*.

He pulled his big hand down over his face. *What the hell was wrong with me?*

But how could she be that fucking callous? *"Two people, falling in love, right in front of her, soul mates, love at first sight. Doesn't exist. Loch Ness Monster."*

BULL.

SHIT.

He stalked into his small cabin, slammed the hatch door behind him, spilling the bottles onto the top of the small dresser, kicking his chair out from under the small table. He sat down, his head in his hands.

So, yeah, maybe Julia Santos hadn't *only* been the Greatest Lay of his Life.

She was his Greatest What If.

What If: That one person that you know that you always ask, well, What If? What if things had just shifted slightly, or maybe you two had said something different, or gone somewhere else, if fate had somehow aligned just a little maybe to the right, or to the left, or to the center, would it be you two happily lying in one another's arms on early Sunday mornings, making sleepy love before the kids came in to ask for cartoons and pancake breakfasts?

Occurrences of What If happened during late nights. Or after a particularly bad fight with your significant other. Or even in happy times, when you smiled over at the person across the table at you and you knew that they were not smiling back at you in quite the same way. And the thought would flicker - What If she were here?

And sometimes the thought would be chased away, by an annoyed What Good Does That Do. And sometimes, the thought would linger, and make itself comfortable for an hour, or a day, or a month.

Julia was his What If.

His Only One.

And he wondered in those fleeting moments or those long nights what he would do if his What If ...

But it was so far out of the realm of possibility, when the marriage lasted a year, then five, ten. Hopeful What Ifs tend to have a limited shelf life. You can't take them out of the box very much - they lose value. He had understood that a long time ago.

Until this week.

But now, his What If was right there, denying anything and everything she could about what she knew for a fact was true. From goddamned experience.

Right?

Or.

He hadn't meant anything to her.

That can't be it.

No.

It was just that she never could admit it. Ever. He got up, going through the argument on his own, pacing up to the bed and down to the door along the short length of the cabin of the boat.

He should have just gone ahead and done her. It wasn't like he had never been dick-deep in a desperate woman before.

But he couldn't.

Because it was *her*.

Julia.

And because she couldn't admit it. Not then, so how could she now? SO MANY YEARS LATER.

You know why she couldn't admit it? Because he would have been right? *Yes. He would have been and that would have driven her crazy. She had plans. She still had plans. Her plans came first.*

This is stupid. He sat down again; he had to get a hold of himself. She was drunk, clearly. Why was this making him so mad?

Because I'm an asshole.

It was a long time ago.

And maybe, maybe, she had just... forgotten? After all this time.

How could she have forgotten? he gestured to the empty air of the cabin.

Could she?

Was he that forgettable?

Laura didn't seem to have any trouble just moving on from him. And, Julia had gone on to a life without him without a second glance. His head in his hands, his elbows to his knees, he sat and thought, bent like an anchor, weighed down.

She was coming on to him tonight. *Like. Really.* He should have just pulled the trigger. She was right there and ready. *Oh God, she was ready.*

No, she was drunk. And upset. And vulnerable.
Yes, vulnerable and available and beholden, remember?
And wasn't that what he wanted?
Yes.
No.
If he had done it tonight, he would be nothing to her but a port in a storm.
Nothing more, nothing less.
So?
He wanted more.
Did he?
Or was he just a fucking sap?
Christ, he was losing his edge.
He sat up, breathing deeply. He shouldn't be angry with Julia. It was just dumb. He asked to hear the story; he should have been ready for what was coming.
He should have known, from goddamned experience.
And she did need him. And maybe she would come to him, without having to be drunk and sad and alone, fresh off the boat from seeing another man. *That* other man.
She would come to him, right? Julia would come to *him* because she wanted him. Because she was his What If - that dangerous, precarious built-up memory teetering on the idea of what could have been.
But...
Maybe, just maybe, he was her What If, too.
Maybe.
So it could not be tonight.
No. It wouldn't be right.
But she would come. *Yes.* Because it was there, he could feel it.
Still there.
Not a fool. *I haven't been waiting around for something to show, but I could just happen to be happy to see that same something return.*
Yes.
And what could be a better set up than that?

Chapter 12
To Love, Honor, and... No One Says 'Obey' Anymore, Do They?

He woke to her text: 'Sorry, David. I was an asshole last night. Saw Will, got drunk, not an excuse.'
'Been there plenty of times.'
'Still sorry.'
'No worries.'
'You're too kind.'
'You'll make it up to me.'
'I will. Not sweet nothings. But I will.'
'Figured you'd still be passed out, Megashark.'
'Star needed a walk.'
'You okay?'
'Just trying to make it through this week, David.'
'Can't leave just yet. You'll miss my wedding speech.'
'About how magical love is?'
'You've read it all ready...'
'☺'

The day was Dee's.

Julia barely saw David, but spent a good deal of the time in meetings with his sisters and the bridesmaids, reviewing the final timelines, Skyping with Amy, meeting José's wait staff onsite. It was a nice, busy morning, packed with the most exclusive spa pampering the Plaza could arrange and - most surprising of all for Julia - girl talk.

Julia recounted that for as many weddings as she had planned, she had never actually been in a wedding. And so, she had never gotten to be a part of this aspect of the events - the bonding time. She spent so much time on the periphery, planning these types of things for giggly mothers and daughters and sisters and cousins, but never getting to take part in them, right along with the bridal party. This was different. The Diemands just grabbed her hand and took her with them.

As the day wore on, one by one the Diemand girls begged off to be with their husbands, or go out with their kids, or to spend some time shopping at some of the places Julia had recommended. After such a nice morning together, Julia was actually sad to see Joan, the last one, and the eldest, go. Julia had loved hearing her stories about Dee-Dee and Davey when they were little and their parents would be out for the night and Joanie would force Davey to dance with her in the kitchen. "He's really very good," Joanie confessed in the bright lobby of the hotel, "Strong frame, great hands."

Julia laughed at the apt description, "I don't think I've ever danced with David."

Joan had looked right at her, carefully, and tilted her head, "I think you should."

Julia had just shrugged, and smiled, a little perplexed and a little uncomfortable at the direct order from the big sister. She felt her cheeks flush and she ducked her head. Joanie had hugged them both and left the two friends in the lobby.

The next two days were going to be jam-packed with events, so Dee and Julia toured the island to visit each of the vendors to make final payments. They then went upstairs, ordered dinner and filled up the tip envelopes, unpacked the toasting glasses, cake knife and server and sent them down to José's office, and finally went over the photography schedule and double-checked the programs.

"Julia?" Dee asked.

"What's up?"

"Were you nervous when you were getting married?"

Julia looked over at her, "Truth?"

"Yes."

"I was terrified."

"Really?"

"I kept asking myself, 'Am I doing the right thing?'"

"That's funny."

"Oh yeah?"

"I'm not scared."

"You're not?"

"Is that weird?"

"Well…"

"I'm not nervous. I'm not scared. I'm excited. I can't wait for it to happen." Dee was just shaking her head, her eyes so hopeful. She looked over at her friend, "Am I a freak?"

"You might be."

Dee threw a favor at her. "Hey!"

"Hey yourself, it took a long time to make those." Julia laughed, "You're not a freak, Dee. You guys have been coming to this for a long time. Like a looong time."

Dee nodded, looking down at her lap. "You and Will have been together for a long time."

Julia looked down at her hand, "Yep, me and Will."

They were quiet for minute, Julia broke the silence first, "Hey, try on these shoes."

"Love to."

Julia slipped off her Mahnolo pumps and gave one and then the other to Dee.

Dee laughed, "Pediatric endocrinologists don't wear shoes like this in the lab everyday"

"Well, that's too bad," Julia reached into her shopping bag of tricks and pulled out a large square box and handed it to Dee, "because these would match your lab coat."

Dee's eyes went wide. She pulled open the box, and pulled out the dust bag, extracting first one, then the second, ivory Christian Louboutin peep toe heel with the 'Christian" in gold on the blue interior satin sole. Dee sighed audibly, "Oh my." She turned them over to inspect their trademark fire engine red bottom sole. "Oh Julia, I can't… you don't… you can't be…"

Julia slid over closer to her, "Here is the something blue if you still needed it, but they are not borrowed."

"No, you don't understand." Dee put her hand over her heart and her lip turned down, "I've thought such…"

Julia felt herself tearing up at Dee's emotion, "Please, Dee. You know, I'm the one who deals with all of this, in this business, I deal with all of the emotional stuff - it's what I do. But I have to tell you, this week I haven't been handling it all that well. Not sure why," she laughed, ruefully. "So let's just say, that it's my gift to you, from the business. We always do something for the bride. From the hotel," she offered, "How's that?"

Dee nodded, biting her lips between her teeth, whispering, "Thank you."

"You're welcome," Julia nodded back at her and sucked in a breath. "Okay, so have we gone through the list for the band?"

Julia took Star out and then the two of them flopped on the big hotel bed together. "The only boy allowed," she snuffed into the fur on the top of his head.

Her phone buzzed. She knew who it was: 'TV's on. What are you watching?'

She smiled to herself and typed: 'Porn.'

Several seconds passed. She could almost hear his wheels spinning from here.

'No you're not.' A minute later. 'Are you?'

'No.'

'I'm coming up. Just 2B - sorry, to be sure.'

She looked out of her closed curtains, and there he was trotting down the dock, she couldn't help but let out a little laugh.

"Aw, Buffy?" He checked when he came in. "Dork porn," he put his hand and let the dog who had just barked at his entrance, sniff him. He scratched the fluffy neck.

She feigned nonchalance, and hopped back up onto her bed. "It was just on."

He flopped himself onto the end of her bed. Starbuck jumped around him and settled himself down next to his mom.

"You are still a firmly closeted nerd, aren't you?"

"I'm not closeted. It's just something I do, by myself, in the dark, alone, late at night."

"Watch Sci-Fi."

She nodded.

"Be better if it was porn."

"To each his own."

He got up and opened her fridge. "You didn't let them restock?"

"Sorry." She said from the comfy spot.

He stood up with his hands on his hips, looking around, surveying the situation, "You leave me no choice." He sat at the end of her bed. "I must take you out of here."

"Da-viiiid…"

"Ju-liiiiia…"

"I don't wannnnna."

"Commme onnnnn."

"No." She adjusted her head on the pillows so that she could see past him, "Door, window."

"Ugh." He flopped backwards and looked up at her from the foot of the bed, his hands resting on his chest, "You've been gone all day and I've been bored and you are obligated to entertain me."

She kicked at his shoulder. "I thought I was obligated to buy you alcohol?"

"And?" he caught her foot, and used it to reference the empty minibar.

She pulled it free, "It's the middle of the night."

He rolled over onto his stomach and, elbow over elbow, pulled himself up to her hipbone, where he poked her gently, "I'm up, you're up. Let's go."

"No," She looked down at him, just there, his closeness somehow unusual and familiar, "I'm watching my dork porn."

He rolled his eyes and finally flung himself up level to her and the dog, so that he lay down right next to Star on his coordinating side, facing Julia and the tail-thumping retriever between them on the bed. "Go'way. I just told Starbuck he was the only boy allowed up here." She feigned an impatient annoyance as she watched him, carefully mirroring her pose - adjusting his hands just below his cheek under the pillow, moving his legs, bending them at just the right angle, crossing them at the ankles.

When he was sure that he was her exact mirror image, stretched out next to her and her dog on her king-sized hotel bed, he looked at her from under his eyebrows, and tempted her with the one thing he knew that she was absolutely aching for, "What if I promise to tell you the story?"

She caught her breath in excitement, but merely said, "What story?" trying to pretend she didn't know what he meant, looking back down past his feet towards the vampire love triangle going on onscreen, but curiosity had caught flame inside her.

"THE story." He searched her eyes. "Misery, company story."

"Oh, THE story." Julia feigned indifference, "All right," but she hopped off of her bed with him, as he shot up, clapping his hands and grabbing hers.

"What do we do with Starbuck?"

"He's first mate, isn't he?"

The three of them walked down the hallway, out of the hotel and back down to his boat.

"We've gotta sail out a bit," he pulled the ropes, sliding them off the cleats and pushed away from the slip.

"What?" she put one hand to the railing as she lurched with the tide, the other grabbed the dog's neck as his paws skittered on the teak.

He ran up his ladder and the engine roared up, "'You know,' he imitated, "this place is pretty straight and you are like, the only guy I know who'd have some."

She had to sit as he yanked the steering wheel this way and that to maneuver the big white beauty out of the space, "Shut up, we are not?!"

"Oh yes, yes we are," he yelled back down. As the boat chugged slowly out into the harbor, "I've done my share of smuggling/ I've run my share of grass/ I made enough money to buy Miami/ but I pissed it away so fast."

"You cannot sing, Diemand."

"Never meant to last/ never meant to last."

"I'm going inside." She grabbed the leash and ducked into the cabin and as he screeched, "I have been drunk now for over two weeks/ I've passed out and I've rallied and I've sprung a few leaks…"

"You're just calling the Aqua Pigs to our location you know!" She yelled up.

He stopped, muttering, "Beautiful, and smart."

He cut the engine, dropped anchor, and shut out all of his exterior lights, save the small green to starboard and red to port on his bow. He ducked inside.

He liked seeing her at his table, next to the glow of the lamplight with her dog asleep on his bed.

He pulled a small bag out of a compartment under his sink.

"When was the last time you did this?"

"I couldn't even tell you…"

He threw it down on the table in front of her. "Go to it."

"What?"

"You know what."

"You want me to clean and roll?"

"You always insisted before."

"It's been like twenty years!"

"Like riding a bike."

"You do know this actually makes you forget stuff right?"

"I don't know, in all my years, I haven't forgotten a thing, Juju." He looked over at her and she had to look away, her lascivious actions last night made her warm with embarrassment.

She sighed, "We're not kids anymore, David."

"You were the one who wanted to pretend."

"I don't even know what to pretend, or how. I think I'm just fooling myself, David."

"Isn't that the point of you coming here?"

"I don't know what the point is."

He growled, feigning irritation, "Just stop thinking about it and get to work. Geez."

She smirked, "Don't 'geez' me, kiddo."

Julia looked down at the task in front of her. She's been straight since she started dating Will; he didn't approve of such indulgences *at all*. She had admired that about him, always so adult, always so upright about things. But, as she pulled out a large clump from the bottom of the bag and the odd earthy, peppery smell reached her nostrils, it was as though somehow her hands alone had time-traveled and knew exactly what to do.

Within moments, Julia's nimble, long fingers had cleaned out the stems and seeds and rolled one long thin white joint with the loose leaves and small buds she had collected. She twisted, licking the paper, and sealing it shut, "Stuff's sticky."

"Medicinal."

She thought, "What's your prescription for?"

"Never asked." He lit, sucked, and held, "And you might want to hit this slow, Iron Lung," and he tried to hand it to her.

She put her hand up, "I have drug testing at the Plaza."

"They do not test for this stuff, love."

"Yes, they..." She looked at the joint she had just rolled for him, now burning between his large, calloused finger tips, she looked at it, hesitating for a minute more, and then took it carefully from his fingers, his square, rough tips touching her smooth, oval ones, "Dear lord, well at least I'm keeping glaucoma at bay," hitting slowly, inhaling smoothly.

"And easing anxiety."

"And relieving nausea," she puffed out.

"And helping my symptoms of Adult Onset Attention Deficit Disorder."

They laughed and choked, and sputtered and he handed her his beer.

"This used to be all we did together," Julia giggled out, "wasn't it?"

"Not all we did, love," he waggled his eyebrows at her.

"I mean," she tried to ignore that, "we used to just hang out and drink, or hang out and smoke, and we'd just talk. For like, hours."

"That's not true, we went out, on occasion." He pulled and puffed, "we just didn't have any money."

"You didn't have any money." She inhaled again, croaking out, "I had plenty of money, until I had to keep buying you drinks and food every day."

"I think it was a very good set up."

"You would." She smiled up at him, but those eyes had looked a little too intense for her, she could see that they looked glad, but like they were searching her for, *I don't know.* She quickly looked down at her hands in her lap, and then back up at him, "You promised me a story, so that's what I'm out here in international waters for."

"We're not that far out," he rolled his eyes.

"Open the window, we're getting my dog high."

"Doggy-munchies. We'll go out. Come on."

Before she could protest he grabbed her hand and led her outside, where they climbed up over the gunwale to the bow of the boat. "Right there, lay right there" he pointed to the smooth plastic bow to lie to one side of a small window and he would go on the other.

Why was she just doing what he told her? If this were any other person she would have stopped him on the deck and demanded he tell her what he was doing, now, she just followed his instructions and lay down. She was intensely curious, she did burn to know what had happened between him and Laura, so she was just doing what he said just to get the scoop. That made the most sense out of every other explanation in her pleasantly befuddled brain. She realized as they were laying there together, looking up at the night sky, that they were lying just over his bed, where Star was pleasantly snoring.

It was quiet for a minute, out there on the water, Julia murmured, almost to herself, "S'pretty," at the azure and indigo of the sky above the sea, punctuated by tiny sparkling dots as the water rocked and swayed the boat beneath them.

"Wait, your eyes will adjust and the longer you look, the more you'll see. Soon the sky will almost look white."

He was right, the tiny white polka dots grew in numbers so great she was barely able to distinguish where one began and the other ended. She was lulled, her body felt fluid, her voice quiet, "Where did you get the boat, Dave?"

"Hmm?"

She spoke slowly, "I don't remember you having a particular love of boats before."

"Ah, you think you know all about me."

"I think I did," she grinned. "But I don't."

"It's easier out here, Juju."

"How so?"

"I was working for so long. Numbers, and loopholes, and tax codes, and it just didn't make sense to me."

"So what you're saying is you were a lousy accountant."

"Shut up, no." He thought. "I guess. Okay. One night, I was called into work. 3:30 in the morning, because the servers were down, and users were unable to trade for about an hour and a half, I'd say. Which honestly - big picture - you would think, well that isn't that big a deal. But, it was. In that world, in my business, it was a huge deal. Like, enormous. I didn't even go back to bed, or back to the condo because I had to go into a meeting the following morning and listen to this guy just scream and yell and berate my IT guys because a server went down for an hour and a half. An hour and a half."

"Can suck."

"Yes. Well, it wasn't a new situation. I'd been yelled at before, I mean, that's work, right? But it was just this thought, you know. Popping into my head. One thought."

"What was your one thought?"

"I'm there in the meeting. Laura's dad is there, and we're all standing around the conference table like it's a fucking war room. And as I am apologizing for the error and making amends to the clients and assuring him that something like this will never happen again, because as the account manager that is what I am supposed to do - this thought came into my head. Just 'Who the fuck cares?'" David gestured up to the sky. "I mean, honestly, 'Who is this helping?' The availability of server data for people to trade at 6 AM in the morning in Australia. Is anyone's life really going to be seriously - I mean, seriously - going to be affected by the loss of an hour and a half of trading time? My companies are not feeding the hungry, or housing the elderly, or curing the sick. 'Who is this helping?' No one. It wasn't fucking helping me, I'll tell you that much."

"So you had an epiphany."

"Yes. Yes, I did."

"So? The boat is your epiphany?"

"No. Yes, but no. It is easier out here, Jules. Easier because it's simple. I don't work, or I don't fish, I don't eat. I am responsible for me. I am not the cause for anyone to stress or worry because no one needs to take care of me and I don't have to take care of anyone else. I have whatever I need right here. And no one needs to worry."

"So, how is this helping?"

"I don't know. I haven't gotten to that part of the epiphany yet. But you know what? I sure as hell am not hurting anything."

"So that's why you got the boat?"

"Well, not really."

She lay there, her hands folded on her chest, "This is a rip."

"What?"

"This is not The Story, Dave. I feel like I am being ripped off." She tried to sound serious. "Yeah, work epiphany, but that's not The Story."

"Give me a second," he shook his head. "Impatient." And then, he paused for a good long while. She thought the pot may have caused him to lose his train of thought, but he began, "Let's see. I... got... the boat," he started, dragging out his words, more like he was trying to figure out how to phrase it, or if in fact he wanted to tell her or not, "for Laura."

"But, you have it..."

"If I am going to be perfectly honest," he hesitated, "it was a gift, for her, she grew up spending her summers on the Cape, as I think you may remember, and I bought it, to, ahhh..." He took a very deep breath, deeper than the ones he had down in the cabin, and he breathed out, "...to celebrate the upcoming birth of our first kid."

Lull, gone. *Wait, what?*

"Didn't happen though."

Julia didn't move, but she heard him breathing deeply again, maintaining some type of control over his message.

"She, uh, had complications and a miscarriage. She was a coupla months along and it was you know, rough."

"Oh, David," was all Julia could breathe out. She felt the sheer unexplainable brutality of his statement and she didn't know what to do. Her first instinct was motherly - a hug, or something, to acknowledge the depth of his loss. She felt at least she needed to offer some comfort, especially after, after that, *oh my God, what did I say last night? 'No collateral damage?' What the hell is wrong with me?*

But the window lay between them.

He kept looking up at the sky. "We were in therapy, for a solid year, even before that. Before the baby. Things weren't... great. It's funny because therapy is good for a lot of things, don't get me wrong, but I think it makes you start to believe that you can badger someone into perfection - 'I'm sorry Laura, you're not reflecting back what I am saying and so I am not hearing you understand me,' or 'Dave, you know how leaving the toilet seat open makes me feel like you're invalidating my presence in our home.'

"And if we fuck up, you know, just once, we can easily convince ourselves that the other had deeper and more nefarious reasons as to why they forgot to pick up the goddamned romaine lettuce instead of the iceberg so clearly, we can't be right for each other. I mean, why can't we just promise to be nice to one another? What would be wrong with that? Or maybe, just maybe cut each other a little fucking slack from time to time and have some laughs over what total idiots the two of us really are?"

"I don't know, Dave. Hard to laugh sometimes?"

"Yeah, well, what else is there, Juju? If you can't laugh, your ship's fucking sunk" he said, bitterly. "When we were pregnant, it was good, we laughed again, it was like sharing some secret, something deep and real, I guess, meaningful. That being together was important. But, you know, just after, things just sorta fell apart all over again.

"So she got her little condo and I got the boat. Back."

"Dee never told me…"

"Dee doesn't know. We weren't going to tell anyone, not until it was obvious, you know. And then, we found out that the due date was, well, this coming Saturday…."

"The day of the wedding."

"Yeah."

"Oh, David." She couldn't think of anything else to say.

He puffed out his breath, and cleared his throat, "So, yeah, when it came to that, and then, we, uh, were at the hospital and it was over. And Laura couldn't look at me. She was just so disappointed. In us. Mostly, in me, I guess." He shook his head, "But you know, even before that, with the job and all of my bullshit, I guess, she was always just so disappointed in me."

Julia breathed out too.

"So the story goes… what I told everyone else was that I just fucked it all up. Got a boat, a midlife crisis, and I left. I don't know. I didn't want to expose her, maybe just expose that disappointment, I guess? And she just let me, a couple of weeks after. Maybe it's easier that way."

"Easier." *There was that word again.*

"Yup."

"Is easier better?"

"I guess. I don't know."

"Neither do I."

He turned to his body slightly toward her, but didn't look at her face. He spoke to the stars, "I know you're having a hard time, I know that this hasn't been easy on you, but I would like you to stay, Jules. Because right now, the only thing that is keeping me - I don't know - here, I guess - physically, mentally - is well, going through this, with you."

He finally looked over at her, his brows drawn low, his eyes unable to erect their protective defenses fast enough, she could see the earnest plea deep in his irises. She answered his eyes, saying simply, quietly, "Okay."

He grinned just slightly, gratefully, his cheekbones lifting the crinkled corners of his reddened eyes up, his brows lifting slightly, and she watched him as he turned on his back again, she reached across the window with her left hand, her palm up.

He didn't look at it, but he reached across and took her hand with his right, and held on for a good long time. One set of hands warming the other, and at one point, it was hard to tell just by feeling whose fingers were whose.

David liked the soft stillness of her palm under his, the quiet beat of her pulse against the thin skin of his wrist. He wanted to move, to somehow coax her warmth closer, to hold her against him, just hold her so he could feel that soft quiet beating against his chest instead, but they were kept separate, chaperoned by the thick plastic molding that sealed the window above his bed shut.

And it was hard for him, but he did his best to not fiddle with the ring he could still feel was on her finger, as they stared up at the ever-whitening sky.

CHAPTER 13
From This Day Forward

Tonight was the rehearsal and then what Dee had dubbed "The After Party." Julia had slept gratefully for most of the early morning after she and David had rolled back in with the tide. The bridal party and Julia would spend about an hour or so in the ballroom late this afternoon and then David had said he'd meet her at the bar where the "After Party" was supposed to take place. Dee had arranged for the usual rehearsal dinner to be more festive. "No speeches, no fancy clothes, just fun!" she had enthused. She had even gone so far as to hire a local band for a bar and arranged for pizzas, burgers, and beer to be served until the wee hours of the morning.

Julia had gone to change after the rehearsal and leave the dog with Gary, the hotel manager, who had agreed to kennel the Golden Retriever for her until after the wedding. She kissed her pup on the head and told him she would miss sleeping with him as she handed the leash to Gary. Gary's eyes widened as he gave her the once over; she stood there decked out in skinny jeans, a t-shirt, and sandals, with dark gray eyeliner and her hair in a ponytail, ready for a night of fun and loud music.

"You look uh, different," he stammered.

"Yeah?" She had looked down at herself briefly. She hadn't gone casual to work since she had slogged in the kitchen. "I suppose I do."

"Good-different."

"Well, uh, thanks Gary." She went to hand him the leash,

But he stood there, still looking.

"Um… the dog?" she pointed.

"Oh yeah, the dog." He took the lead from her hand, backing up, "Bye."

"Bye," she replied, shaking her head, perplexed.

She headed to her car, and drove to the address Dee had given her. How long had it been since she had been out dancing? It felt like forever. The shuttle from the hotel hadn't arrived yet, and as she walked through the front door, she noticed there were a few locals at the bar. She grabbed a tall beer out of the ice and looked around at what had to be *the* dive college bar in town. It looked like any of the dozens that her buddies had inhabited for those few brief years in and just out of college, back before they had money, lives, responsibilities. It smelled typically like beer, and although Julia tried to make herself feel at home, her forty year old mom instincts told her that this was the kind of place that in a few years she'd have to pull her son out of.

The band was setting up on stage, and she saw the lead singer look over in her direction. He nodded his head at her and smiled tentatively.

Julia looked from side to side, *is he smiling at me?*

She looked back at the stage.

The lead singer, had stopped what he was doing, now gave her a small wave, then pointed at her, nodded and waved again.

She raised her eyebrows. He was. He was waving at her. She didn't really know what to do. She just smirked, and gave a small wave with the hand holding her beer. Her only thought: *I am easily fifteen years older than that kid.*

The rangy singer grinned happily and went back to strapping on his axe. She smirked to herself, *Jesus, is he even old enough to be in a bar?*

She glanced around the room. Her eyes trying to find a place to rest. But unfortunately, they stopped again in the general area of the stage.

And he looked over at her again.

She shifted her weight, uncomfortably. *Could he want me to score him some alcohol or something?*

She sipped her beer; she found that his eyes were on her again. He kept on watching, and then smiling, looking away, and smiling again. Julia honestly wasn't sure how to react. She couldn't scowl at the kid. Or ask him if his mom knew he was there. Or scream at him in an elevator because he happened to look at her and find a resemblance to his aunt. *Oh God...* So she tentatively smiled back, again.

His grin deepened.

There is a boy here. And he is looking at me. A boy. Well, a young man. A man-boy. Looking. At. Me.

She didn't know where to look, what to do with herself, her hands, her beer, the way she was standing *Oh my God, what is wrong with me?* She was fidgeting around so much, the kid probably thought she was having a seizure.

An age-induced seizure.

Her phone buzzed. *Oh thank goodness.* "Hello?" She put her head down.

A breathy, deep bass voice came over the airwaves, "What are you wearing?"

"Hi, Dave."

The overly deep voice continued, "It's not Dave."

"I have your number on my phone," she explained.

His voice went back to its normal baritone, "I'm on your phone? That's a new kind of sexy." He continued, "So what are you wearing?"

"Dave..."

"I don't want to wear the same thing?"

"When will you be here?"

"We're wrapping up now, what's up?"

"Oh nothing. Just be glad..." she glanced over at the stage, the singer saw her look up and smiled again, "...when you get here."

"Wow," he expressed. "Good. Okay, I will be there as soon as I can."

She hung up.

Dave flirting with her was... well Dave, and that Richard Brighton flirting thing was, yes, vaguely disconcerting, but at least it was age-appropriate. This kid, this kid who couldn't be more than *Oh My God,* ten - maybe twelve *at best* - years older than her son? *He must have very bad eyesight,* she assured herself as she sat at the available seat on the opposite side of the bar, out of sight of the stage. *Blindness is going around - legal blindness or debilitating cataracts.*

Mary Ann's wedding had been different than Hannah's graduation. Julia had been seated on the sidelines, her hand resting gently on the enormous belly in front of her, William had gone for the both of them to congratulate the bride and groom, and she spotted David with his fiancée, Laura.

He looked great, smiling and happy in the receiving line. She smiled involuntarily at his happy profile, and Chris Billings, her ex-boyfriend from college, came over to greet her, thinking the smile was for him, "Hey!" he leaned in to kiss her cheek.

She kissed him back, "Hey Chris! How are you?"

"Good, great," he had said, hesitatingly. He looked down at her, "A lot of Good Juju going on there," using David's nickname for her.

"Yes," she had laughed, looking down at her belly. "A lot of Good Juju."

"You, uh, heard about me and Kristen?" he looked at her.

"Yeah, Chris, I was sorry to hear about it." At the time, she couldn't imagine how he was dealing with an impending divorce with his wife who was pregnant with their first, and soon to be only, child. "You here alone?"

"Yep."

"You sitting with Will and me?"

"I think it's you and me and Will and Dave and maybe a couple others from school are sitting together?"

Oh boy, she had thought. "Well, that will be okay. You know," she thought, "I think Deidre is here alone too."

"Dave's little sister?"

"Yes," she had encouraged.

Julia had watched his thought process as it happened, she looked up at him, "Hey, I actually need to know if Dee had bought a gift off the registry or if she was just giving cash, and I just need to sit for awhile, could you go ask her and then let me know? I'd call her over, but I don't want her to lose her place in line."

"Um," he looked down at her, "yeah. Yeah I will."

"Thank you, Chris." She watched him walk away and go up to a pleasantly surprised Deidre, and when she saw he was ready, she got up to meet William, who was engaged in a discussion with - *oh Christ* - David.

"Hey Julia," he had said affably, leaning in to kiss her cheek, quickly.

She was taken aback, "Ah, hi."

"Hello, I'm Laura," the pretty blonde at his side introduced herself and held out her hand.

Jules shook it, "Nice to meet you."

David continued, "I was just telling Will that he may have met some douchebag who looked a lot like me a few years ago, but not to worry, I killed him."

"Oh," Julia had smiled at Will, who just clapped David on the shoulder, "Okay. So Laura, where are you from?"

At the reception, it felt as though nothing had ever happened to ruin that perfect friendship Julia and David had built over that summer when she was twenty-two and he was twenty-four. And witnessing their odd, fast-paced conversations soon had the entire table doubled over with laughter, entertaining the wait staff and the tables surrounding them. "I feel like I'm on a sitcom!" Laura had hooted out, wiping away tears of laughter.

Julia found that her face had begun to get sore from her ever-widening smile and pressed one hand to her cheek, and one hand to her belly. She let out a big breath.

Dave, coming down from a large laugh as well, his eyes crinkled in the corners, noticed from across the table. "You good, Juju?"

"Yes, David, I'm fine." She nodded. "Thanks." Will had placed his hand on her shoulder and then went back to his conversation with Jacob.

Dave had looked over at her, and caught her eyes in his. She saw him wink, just once, quickly, at her, and then look away, grinning to himself, and then glance furtively back. She found herself chuckling at his silent communique, and his grin broadened at the sound. Chris had then come up and asked him a question and that invisible thread across the table between Julia and David was snipped.

And she remembered, in those few brief seconds, as they had looked at each other from across the centerpiece, how long and how hard she had worked to make herself forget completely how much she had missed him.

But, *oh, stop it*, she was just being overemotional, overly sentimental - *the pregnancy and all.*

Still, it would take her a little while to work those little thoughts back out of her mind.

But she would.

He had been the first one off the shuttle bus his sister hired for the night. He tried to be casual, but he ended up inside the bar easily a minute and a half before anyone else even approached the door. Julia said she would be glad to see him. Julia had apparently needed him. Julia would be there waiting for him. He found her sitting at the bar, drinking a beer, talking with some guy with a guitar across his back. He sprang into action.

Dave strode over, put his arm over her shoulder possessively, and said, to the two of them, "Hi honey, I'm home," He stared over at the punk, then grabbed her left hand and interlocked his fingers in hers, waving them slightly for emphasis so that the kid could see that she was wearing a ring.

"Um, hi Dave." She said, lowering her eyebrows, pulling her hand from his. "This is Christian, he's the singer in the band."

"Hello, Christian." The greeting was almost like a challenge.

Julia looked up at him, and then back to the kid, she gestured toward him, "We were just talking about the fact that he is going back to college in the fall."

"Yeah," the punk affirmed.

"Oh, good for you Christian. Tough making it out there in the world?"

"Not so much. Band's doing fine. Just never thought I'd be twenty-seven and still in a band, you know."

"I get it, I do." David replied.

The kid nodded, "Plus, I promised my mom."

"Aww, he promised his mom." David mocked.

"And she died last summer, so…" Christian admitted.

Julia put one hand to her heart, the other to the kid's forearm, "I'm so sorry."

Dave took his arm off of her shoulders, *what the fuck?* "Sorry to hear that, man," he conceded. *A dead mom, really?*

"Yeah well, it was nice to meet you, Julia. Dave. Let me know if there's anything we can play for you." The singer moved off to do sound check.

"What a great kid."

"Yeah, a 'kid.'" Dave mumbled, suddenly grumpy, but neither he nor she was exactly sure why.

"Well, he said twenty-seven," she considered.

Hey... "Looking for a sympathetic ear." David growled. "A hot sympathetic ear."

She looked at him, fully. "Really?"

"What?"

She just rolled her eyes, got off the barstool and started to walk away towards the group that had made it in.

"I have a dead mom too, you know," he yelled at her back.

She frowned over her shoulder, and kept on walking.

Argh, why had he done that? Why had he been in such a rush to get to her? She had had a funny little note in her voice when she had told him that she would be glad to see him - her voice had made him stir, actually. Why did he feel the urgent need to save her from that kid? *Because that kid was so clearly hitting on her.* And she was just released out into the wild and it was too soon. And what was she going to do now, suddenly single and unaware of men's intentions like that. *Christ,* she still had her fucking wedding ring on and the kid sharked in. She was sitting there, blind, BLIND to that boy's intentions.

To the boy's intentions? But not to mine?

Mine are different. I am different. I am not a kid, and I am not looking to just score with a random hot chick in a bar.

A specific hot chick in this particular bar.

He grabbed a beer off of the table. *Okay, so last night.* They were together all night last night. He shook his head. *History repeating.* She held his hand for so long under the stars and he had felt close.

Closer to her than anyone else in a really long time. Just from holding her goddamned hand.

But what did he expect? He had been foolish to think that there would be any possible way for him to escape being near her for so many days, completely unaffected. Anytime the two of them spent any portion of time together, he had always felt like there was something there - still - between them. There was a closeness, a connection, an actual physical chemistry only the two of them could create - *the air fucking changed when she came around* - something.

And not just because of those last three weeks.

Although, in his personal history, no one had ever come anywhere near to those three epically hot weeks - *like Sahara* desert hot, like Death Valley hot, like center of the Earth magnetic core hot.

Never had there been hotter weeks. Not for anyone, any time, any place, *ever*. There was no denying that.

She couldn't have even denied that.

Nope, not that gorgeous woman standing there in a t-shirt and ponytail, looking just as incredible today as she had on the day she had walked into that party on the Cape when he was twenty-four and she was twenty-two.

CHAPTER 14
We Are Gathered Here Together

"Oh shit, it's Julia fucking Santos."

"Who?"

"Julia Santos, my best friend's ex-girlfriend. She hates my guts."

"Whoa."

"Yeah," David had been trying to duck down, but he wanted to peek, and it was 85 degrees on the Cape that night and the tall girl was wearing a short tan skirt that showed off her long, brown legs and a thin t-shirt that just hugged those lovely tits of hers. Her hair was off her face in a ponytail and her eyes were made dark, like a rock star. She stood out in a sea of well-scrubbed five foot six Yankee blondes with their shoulder-length highlights just brushing the collars of their oversized pastel Oxford shirts that was for damned sure.

"Why does she hate you?"

"I took a TV from her room."

"What?"

"She had my buddy's TV after they broke up. I showed up one day and took it."

"You stole her TV?"

"No, I took my buddy's TV back," he explained slowly.

"And she knows it was you?"

"I didn't take it when she wasn't there. I told you, I didn't steal it. I just went to her room, unplugged it, and walked out."

"Why?"

"He told me she had his TV."

"Was it big?"

"The TV? No, just some little piece of shit. I think it was black and white."

"You're a fucking idiot."

"He was my friend!"

"He's not here now."

"So?"

"I want to meet her."

"I told you she hates my guts, no."

"But I'm your friend."

"Shut up."

He watched as her dark-lined eyes scanned the crowd, flicker over him, hesitate, return, widen and then narrow ever so slightly in his direction.

Julia had spotted him, *Oh, crap.*

Julia had walked in, scanned the room of blonde heads and her heart sunk right back to where it originally had been when her roommate Molly had invited her to a Townie party of rich kids where she would know no one. Molly had convinced her, but it was just as Julia had imagined - just her in a grubby concert tee lost in a sea of pressed Polos.

But wait, hold on. She knew that face, that guy's face right there.

Oh shit, it's David fucking Diemand.

The last time she had seen him, his broad swimmers' shoulders had swung off with the TV that Chris Billings had given her the summer before in his paddle-like paws.

Okay, so maybe she had played a teeny tiny bit naïve when it came to Chris' broadcast entertainment generosity, and maybe it had been just a way of Chris trying to maintain an open line to a still available ex-girlfriend, but *hey,* Julia hadn't been stupid - *a free TV was a free TV.*

And Chris didn't even have the decency to come and get it himself - sending his best friend David as some kind of repo man proxy. Dave, who just sauntered in, unplugged the little set, gave her a "Hey Jude" like he was so fucking funny and then gone.

That was the last she had seen of her once "friend."

Until just now.

She had known that when she finally broke up with Chris it would be the end of an era - the end of late nights hanging in the dorm room with Deidre and her brother and Chris, just shooting the shit and making fun of one another.

Out of all of them, Dave and she had actually gotten along famously. Over the two years she had dated Chris, the peripheral friends had been dubbed "the Smokers." They had shared insults, scores, fake fights, headlocking hugs, playful punches, and big slapping high fives. David had always taken on the role of the Big Bad Brother of the group - coming up with ideas, making plans, calling friends, driving them around, making the plans to let's-all-go-get-into-trouble. And street-wise Julia had the know-how to get the craziness done.

Dave was good to have around. He'd even keep an eye out for her as well as his sister at parties, making sure that they all got home okay, even sometimes just her when his sister or his buddy wasn't around, or maybe one of them was just too drunk to deal. Chris was just passed out somewhere, he'd say, waving his big hand dismissively. I've got it Dave, she would grin sideways at him, I'm good. But he would insist he couldn't just leave her, despite her insistence that she could take care of herself. He had to, *for you know, my boy Chris*.

Ah, Chris. So classically handsome, nice family, well off, good muscle at a party, well, when he didn't end up face down in someone's toilet. Chris was almost the total package.

Almost.

Just one thing.

He was boring.

Chris was good in bed, but only because he had all of the best equipment - not a lot of thought in the technique but he had a lot to work with. With the gorgeous physique of a running back - those lovely large muscle groups and incredible stamina - Chris really just had to show up and you could have yourself a pretty good time. The problem was there just wasn't a whole lot to talk about before, during, or after. And so, after a while, it had gotten to the point where Julia knew that she had to end it with him. There was no point in keeping on a long term relationship just to keep the sex going, especially with Chris' complete lack of real imagination. And so the deep and wonderful friendships that had blossomed on the periphery of Chris' and her involvement would have to suffer. And the only thing Julia knew that she would regret is that she would lose Dee and David as collateral damage.

She wouldn't have admitted it, but she had cried over the loss of the four of them being together more than she had wept for just Chris.

A thin little shock of thrill ran up her spine and she took a deep breath, glancing over to where she had seen his face again. She watched him practically dive behind his friend.

Really? You fucking coward. A smile cracked at the corners of her mouth. She made a beeline for him, leaving Molly in the dust.

"Hi, Dave," she had said coolly.

"Hey there, Julia."

She turned to David's right, and spoke directly to his leering friend, "You know this motherfucker right here?" she pointed at David, "He stole my fucking television set. Right in the middle of a Saturday Night Live when Paul McCartney was singing. Paul Effing McCartney. He walks into my dorm room, says 'Hey Jude, you owe Chris his TV,' unplugs the damned thing and leaves with it. I wouldn't have been so mad, but seriously, in the middle of what has to be one of the best Beatles' songs ever!" Watching Dave putting his hands up in front of his face, cowering down in front of her, she had a lot of trouble holding in the laughter.

"I'm sorry?" he chuckled out, still half-afraid.

"Pathetic, David Diemand." She shook her head at him.

"You should have seen him all badass just a second ago. 'I took it for my friend!'"

Julia laughed, "I think you owe me."

"I do?"

"Yeah," she blustered out, right in her old friend's grinning face, "Hey Jude, you owe me some alcohol."

She had darted off back to her friend. "I am in love with her," Tim had said.

"Yeah, you and every other guy she's ever met," Dave had warned.

Tim had shot back, uncharacteristically quickly, "That would mean you too, idiot."

David had furrowed his large brow, "That's not what I..." but he had stopped and just had gone with, "Shut up."

A few seconds later, she came back to Molly, grabbed her hands and pulled her, encouraging breathlessly, "Come on, there's someone I know here!"

"She dumped me by association," Dave handed her a second beer. He, his friend, and Julia and her friend were talking.

Well, more like the two new friends were watching the two old friends talk.

"Oh, that's rich!" Julia had shaken her head.

"I was mad. You dumped my friend, and so you dumped me too."

"Whatever, David, I just can't believe you cowered behind Tim when you saw me."

"You're scary."

"I knew seeing you was inevitable. Dee told me you were here somewhere. Are you teaching this year?"

The other two had moved over slightly to begin their own conversation, but neither David nor Julia particularly noticed.

"Yeah, this will be my second year, high school English." He asked, "What are you doing down here?"

"Molly and I are working at one of the hotels on the shore, waiting tables. The manager has an in at the Plaza in Boston, promised to get me a spot in the catering department by the end of August."

"Very cool."

"Yep," she looked around, finally, "it was nice to see you, Dave."

"Yeah, definitely, you too." He leaned over, "Watch out for my buddy, he wants your phone number and et al."

"Oh, uh, him?" She hooked her thumb over her shoulder, and glanced back.

"Yeah, he's kind of a wannabe dog."

"Thanks for the heads up."

"Anything for an old friend."

She had smiled and walked off.

And he had watched her walk away, and watched the heads turn as she walked away. And then they watched the guy who had been yelled at by this new girl – hey, he knew that chick, she looked dangerous, and he had talked to her alone. Dave had flicked his eyebrows and chucked his chin up, smiling at them generously, nodding, enjoying the stark admiration in their eyes.

The two of them kept tabs on one another for the remainder of the night. He would see her chatting with a couple of girls outside, she would see him and turn and smile. She would catch him, pulling a beer out of the ice and he'd wave the bottle at her. It was nice, friendly, familiar.

"I am so hitting that tonight." Tim had slurred in his ear. Tim had been a sloppy drunk.

"You think." David had raised his eyebrows.

"Oh my God, look at that ass! I have to, what's she like?"

David had looked at her ass, but not so blatantly as his buddy. He then swigged his beer, "She will eat you for breakfast."

"That's what I'm hoping for." They watched as Julia turned her head, looked one way and then made her way to where they were standing. "Oh, yeah, she's coming for it. Come to breakfast, lunch, and dinner, baby."

"Dude," Dave warned.

"So, you thinking a midnight snack?" Even to her untrained ear, Tim made that sound obscene.

"Um, not really." She looked askance at Tim, and then grabbed Dave's shirtsleeve in her hand, pulling him slightly towards her and away from his only slightly discouraged buddy. She looked at the leering friend and pulled David further away, and asking furtively, "I'm sorry to bother you Dave, but I have to ask you something, and as I see it, after you stole my TV, you kind of owe me."

Despite her insistent teasing, he was enjoying this - her familiarity, their conversational ease, coupled with a few beers, had made him feel loose, comfortable, warm. He liked joking with her, wanted it to keep going, so he pulled his head back on his neck, "Okay first," he explained, mock-exasperatedly, his gestures exaggerated, but not too wide, he didn't want to drive her close presence any further away, "I didn't steal your TV. My friend wanted his TV back."

She tucked her pretty little chin in and tilted her head at him, "You mean the one he said I could have, months after I broke up with him, because he said he had no use for it and was going to just throw it in the trash?"

"What?"

"Yeah."

"See I didn't know that." David shrugged slightly.

"No you didn't." She pointed at his chest, pushing him back a bit. "And you didn't bother to ask."

"Dumped, By Association. What is it about that you don't understand?" He grinned at her.

She shook her head. "Shut up, Diemand," pulling him further aside. She had stood up on her tiptoes and steadied herself with a hand on his chest. He felt her warm breath on his ear, "You know, this place is pretty straight and you are the only guy I know who'd have some."

He pulled back and looked directly in her honey brown eyes, reading her hesitantly hopeful face, and making the quickest calculations in his head that he had possibly ever made, he replied "I don't on me, but," he said, grinning widely, "I know where we can get it."

She grabbed her bag and they had gone out the back door.

The rest of the night was kind of a blur. Julia remembered smoking with him, and a lot of walking. They had talked themselves hoarse about school and then once all of that ground was covered compared notes on television, movies, books they had read, people they had met, bars they had gone to, random items they stumbled across on the road and *where the hell were they walking to?*

"I have no idea," David laughed, as they stopped and looked around.

"I can hear the water," she said, "Can't be far from the shore."

They started towards the sound, but as they neared the shoreline, Julia noticed that they were about to cross the main road to downtown. His place was to the left, her place was to the right.

"Starting to get light out," she looked up. "Glad I don't have to work until 3." She yawned.

"I don't have to wake up 'til September."

"Lucky."

"Nah, I'm running out of money all ready."

"You didn't plan well."

"Guess not."

"Yeah, well, you can just call your dad."

"Oh, you think that's how it goes?" He cocked his head at her teasing, nodding, like he was thinking it over.

"I know so." She grinned, "I lived with your sister, remember?"

He chuckled. "Poor little rich girl."

They glanced at one another.

"I'll have you know that my rent checks go to my *uncle*." He informed specifically.

"Oh well, then." She nodded at the difference.

They laughed.

"Well, it was nice to see you, David."

"Yeah, you too."

They both lingered for about a half a second, and then turned, heading down their respective directions on the same road.

He turned and walked backwards for a second, "Hey!"

"What?" She turned to walk backwards as well.

"I'll probably see you around!"

"Yeah, probably!" she yelled back, turning around and heading down the road.

He kept walking backwards for a few steps more, and then turned and jogged home.

He showed up at her work.

Just showed up. Walked in, said hello, shook some hands like he was the mayor of Osterville and came over to where she was standing at the desk with Molly. "Hey," he said to her.

Molly said hello first.

"Hey, um, whatcha doing here?" Julia said warily.

"I just wanted to let you guys know that," indicating Molly as well, "we're playing darts at the Regatta in town."

"Um, okay." She replied slowly, "Thanks for coming all the way out here to let us know that."

"I didn't have a number."

"True." Julia admitted.

"I can give it to you," Molly brightened.

"I just figured I'd drive out and ask if you guys wanted to come and…"

"Yes!" Molly answered.

"Oh, well, thanks Dave. I'm working," Julia shrugged, "but you know, Molly, if you want to."

"Yes!" Molly enthused. "I will see you there," to him, breathlessly.

Dave smiled and nodded, "Yeah, okay. Well, Jules, we'll see you another time."

"Yeah, sure."

He left, and Molly took her arm, "You cool if I go?"

"Um, yeah, of course."

"I just thought, the other night… you left with him…"

"Oh that was nothing, we're just you know, old friends. Buddies from college." She shook her head, "Please," waving her hand.

"Oh, I didn't really care anyway." Molly smiled at her, with her mouth, but not with her eyes, "He's hot."

Julia was kind of taken aback, by both the unabashed female treachery, as well as the sentiment, "Okay."

Hot? I guess, Julia mused, *if you're into the Howdy Doody type.* She had never really given it a lot of thought. David's face was not much more than a loose collection of freckled features - regular mouth, big nose, strong chin, wide forehead.

Sure, he was good-looking, she had to admit. *But he would never have been considered pretty,* that was for damned sure, not like Chris was. Next to Chris, David was - well, just different - maybe his attractiveness not as noticeable. Where Chris was finely made, David was rough hewn. Chris was lace curtain Irish - porcelain skin, fine aquiline nose, bright blue eyes, slender dark brows, smooth muscular frame. David was freckled, tall, rangy and strong, big shoulders and skinny hips, like he had just come off of the fields stricken by some potato famine. Chris' features could have translated into beauty, David looked, if nothing else, like a - well, a guy.

So yeah, David wasn't unattractive, and I guess, he could be considered a hot guy. Plus, Chris wasn't here on the Cape to be a comparison. There wasn't a whole lot here to compare him to, really.

David did have nice eyes too, Julia had remembered sophomore year in college being caught up in them once when he had come to drive her home because she and his sister had been drunk at some frat house. Dave hadn't liked the frat parties, and Dee had called him to come get them and he, despite all of his bitching, showed up to save his sister.

Julia was faring better than Dee and had gotten as far as getting her friend into David's back seat before she had slurred out to him from the passenger seat. He leaned in closer to hear what she had to say and she had put her hand on his cheek and pulled his eyes to hers. It was just a moment - their eyes had met and Julia had drunkenly noticed that rather than the usual let's-all-get-into-trouble gleam, there was a stillness, a cool calmness, like the ocean on a sunless, gray day. She ran her thumb up his cheek to his heavy eyebrow, murmuring softly, "What color are they, David?"

"Hazel," he had answered quietly, looking into her focusing and refocusing eyes. She had smiled openly at his reply and he had smiled back for a half a second, still looking at her.

And then he just stopped. He shook his face out of her grasp, and looked away. He pushed her gently back into the passenger seat and buckled her in.

"Hazel," she had cooed, "that sounds…"

She vaguely remembered that she had never finished the sentence, having laid her head on the cool glass of his side window and promptly fallen asleep before he had opened his car door and started the engine.

"Too bad for you," her roommate snarked, turning her uniformed back toward the kitchen, and throwing back to Julia at the desk, "I do have to admit I am SOOO glad I am not getting your sloppy seconds."

Julia was tired when she got home from work, but more than that, she was disappointed. Her roommate, the only girl - the only other Not Rich Girl - she knew in this whole damned town was willing to step over her to get to a guy. Granted, Julia had only known Molly a couple of weeks, but really? *What happened to Working Class Solidarity, or even just Girl Power?*

It's not like Julia had a thing for David - *I mean, yeah, it was nice to see an old friend* - but that wasn't the point. Because, hey, what if she did have a thing for him? *Way to give a real shit about my feelings there, Molls.*

What feelings?
Friend feelings.
Julia sighed.

It had been a decent night and she had even made about $100 in tips, but she smelled like meat and cigarettes. She jumped in the shower, put on pjs, went to bed and fell asleep.

She didn't hear when Molly came in. With company.

She was up early, was picking up the kitchen, putting dishes in the sink. Julia was going to head out for a walk before work, when she heard Molly's door opened, which was unusual, Molly was a sleeper. She said coolly, without turning around, "What are you doing up so early?"

But it wasn't Molly who had come out of the door. "Juju, shush."

She turned quickly, her eyes popped open, "Oh, you slutty, slutty man." She laughed.

"Julia, please." David put his finger to his lips.

"Oh, my God, is this David Diemand and the Walk of Shame right here in my living room?" She whispered out, pointing. "This is the best morning ever!"

He was trying to be mad at her, but it was hard to be mad at her. She was so goddamned pretty - the other night, last thing in the goddamned night, and now, first thing in the goddamned morning. Plus, she did catch him trying to sneak out before the pushy girl woke up, "If you wake her up, I swear to God..."

She was practically jumping up and down, "What happened? What happened? What happened? Tell me."

"No!"

"Come on, please! I have to know."

"I am gentleman, I don't kiss and tell."

"I'll buy you breakfast."

The offer stopped him. "Seriously?"

"I am totally serious."

"Let's go."

She grabbed her keys and they went out the door.

They sat at the town's only diner, an actual converted railroad car that served breakfast and lunch whenever and however you wanted it. "You could get steak and eggs, or steak and French fries at pretty much any hour of the day," David informed.

"That sounds good."

"Which one?"

"Both."

They ordered both.

"So," she took a large bite of her steak, "when did you become such a whore, David?"

"Shut up, Santos," he tried hard not to blush. He reached over and grabbed a handful of her French fries.

"You're so cute." She grabbed his forearm across the table, then reached up and pulled back her fries, "You've never done that before."

"Yeah, I have." He fought her off.

She only managed to save two and shoved them in her mouth. "Okay," she chewed, "but not before this summer…"

"Whatever." He ate most of the handful in one bite.

She pointed her fork, "I'm glad you're having fun, but I'm not sure if you want to keep it up with Molly…"

"Whoo, I kinda got that impression…" He slit open his egg and dipped French fry into the yellow goo that oozed out.

"Gross, David."

"What? It's like hash browns."

"Well, she was willing to step over me to get to you."

"Step over you?"

"Yeah, you know, like I'm dead, she wouldn't care. Just step over me to get to you." She flipped her hand in a gesture to show Molly's imaginary motion over her imaginary dead body.

"Huh?"

"The other night, she thought, you and I had hooked up and when I told her we hadn't, that we were just friends, she told me she didn't care if I had or not, she was gonna get you."

"Yikes." He sat back.

"So how'd it happen?" She took a piece of his toast off of his plate and held it up.

"You can have it." He added, "I don't know, you know, we had some drinks, she put her arm around me…"

"You talked…" She ran his toast in the juices of his steak.

"Not really," he looked around trying to recall.

She tilted her head, "You just started macking on her?"
"I think she started it."
"And hey, free pu…"
"Be quiet!"
"What?"
"I am a teacher in this community, behave yourself," he whispered vehemently, but there was a tone of amusement in his voice.

She said louder, "I'm not the one kissing on a girl I've never talked to in a bar."

He was up to her challenge, "No, but please tell me when you do. I would like to bear witness."

She ended up saying, "Shut up, David." She looked down at her plate, now just fries, there was a long, crispy one on the side of the white plate, she held up the French fry, "This one's sharp, I bet I could poke your eye out with this."

"Yeah, you could. Let me see that sucker."

She handed him the fry, "Don't eat it."

"Why not?"

"I don't know, too crispy."

"I like 'em crispy."

"Put ketchup on it." She splooshed some of the red thick condiment on the side of his plate.

He dipped in the pointy end, then held it up. "Is this a dagger I see before me?"

She found herself giggling.

He took a regular fry off of her plate and laid it in the middle of his plate, then he plunged the red end of the pointy fry into the center of the regular fry, so that it stuck out, standing straight up out of the red ooze. He said in a crazy British accent, "Someone call the police! There's been… a murder!"

"Dun dun duuuuh!" she added.

He laughed up at her.

She looked at his plate and decided, "Everyone, clear the area." She pushed back the other pieces of toast, glanced around the table, grabbed the salt and started shaking over the murder scene.

She then removed the two French fries, ate the murdered one and stuck the pointy one in his mouth and pointed down at the salt lines and ketchup stain they had left behind, saying simply:

As he nodded and chewed and said simultaneously:

"Chalk outline."

"Chalk outline."

He put his chin in his hand, and gazed down at the scene they had created in front of them, and unknowingly, around them, "Genius."

"I've got to get going to work…"

"Again?" he looked up, surprised, maybe disappointed.

"Some people work more than 180 days a year, David."

"Dumb people."

"People who like money."

"Like I said."

"People who can buy breakfast." She laid down some of her tip money to cover the breakfast.

"You said story in fair trade."

"What story? You couldn't remember what happened!"

"The Great French Fry Murder of Osterville, Massachusetts?"

"Come on," She rolled her eyes, "Want me to drop you back off at my house?"

"No!"

It was at that point when they became, much to Molly's, and ever other male within the general vicinity's chagrin, inseparable. Their relationship was completely different than it had been in school. There was no Dee or Chris to act as a buffer between them, and they just found that they had some connection that had gone unexplored too long. Many girls tried to get his attention away from his friend Juju, but as soon as he was done with them, David would be on the phone with her, or on his way over to her house to just "you know, hang out."

Molly had given her that evil eye for about two weeks after the incident with David but announced she was leaving for Boston early and Julia would be stuck with the rent for the remainder of the summer. Julia didn't see that as much of a problem, she was making good money, she had plenty of cash from tips and hey, she'd have her own place until she headed out to Boston at the end of August.

Dave was always there now anyway, on her couch, watching her TV, or eating her food. She should have minded - she certainly pretended to - but he kept her from getting too lonely, and they would talk late into the night about her day, about his ideas for the coming school year, about the intrinsic differences of swimming in the pool versus swimming in the ocean, about pretty much anything that came to mind.

At varying times, they each had one or two brief love affairs with others in the Town, but their bond had quickly become too strong to be broken by some easy lay they had come across.

They'd gotten into a habit of heading out and having a couple of drinks, playing darts or whatever. And then he'd walk her home. They'd watch some form of Star Trek or a late night Sci-Fi movie, or play cards or get high and just wander around the neighborhood. He'd leave around 1 or 2 in the morning on the nights she had to work and occasionally they would talk when he called her to tell her something he had thought of on the way home. People at her work knew him. The regulars at the bar wondered where the other one was when one showed up alone.

He was dating someone when it happened, actually - that first time, when there was nothing left but a few weeks left for the summer.

Timing had never been - nor would ever be - their strong suit.

Being friends with a very beautiful girl was not without its benefits, and deficits. He had definitely risen in the social ranks of the guys he knew around town, but he had stopped trying to explain the nature of their friendship - "Yeah, okay, like you wouldn't hit that."

"You know," he had joked back. Yep, *joking*. But Julia was different, he had never known a friend he could be with like that - guy or girl - never running out of stuff to talk about, commenting on every thing around them, finding something they both liked, or just noticed. Juju, she was *you know,* just a great friend - a best friend - she just happened to be a girl.

An incredibly beautiful, ridiculously sexy, girl.

And a few of the preppy summer girls who a month or two ago wouldn't give him the time of day, now seemed to show him some interest. He had been on several dates, some of them more than once. Julia called them "his Flavors."

"This the Flavor of the Week, Diemand?" She would ask when the girl would shyly walk into the Regatta Bar and wave over at him. "She's pretty!"

The girl he was seeing now, Laura, was, in fact, pretty - a petite blonde, really nice, very sweet. They had gone on a couple of dates and it seemed to be going okay.

He had never really talked to Julia about Laura - he wanted to, but just didn't. The girl didn't hang out at the bar with them, and it seemed that as soon as Juju came into view, the sweet blonde and pretty much every other girl just went right out of his head. *Well you know, Julia'd show up in these summer dresses, or these short skirts, or Jesus, those days when they were nursing their hangovers on her blanket on the beach and she'd be just lying there next to him in nothing but sunglasses and a bikini - holy Christ.*

He once had this really fast, fleeting fantasy that one sunny, sweaty day at the beach, he would just lean over to that particular hot spot on her hipbones where the strings tied together the bottom parts of her suit and he would just pull the knots apart with his teeth.

That particular sequence would, in fact, help him get through a couple of lonely nights.

Still, he knew that in real life, had he attempted such a stunt, he was pretty sure Julia would have bare-foot kicked out his teeth, so that untying thing would never have been a problem again. But even that thought of her kicking his ass - in her bikini - gave him a little electric shock of pleasure way down in his nether regions.

She is a friend, *but I'm not fucking blind.*

A lot of times, over that summer, he would just completely flake out on a girl. He was supposed to meet a Flavor later, he ended up wandering around the town with Julia until all hours or sitting on her futon couch. Not doing anything special or anything in particular, they just got caught up in another one of their weird conversations.

"Jealous" would not be a word she would have used.

Did she feel out of sorts, imbalanced, uneven when she went to the Regatta without him?

Did she feel lonely when he went out with those other girls?

Did she wonder what he shared with them that he didn't share with her?

The answer to any and all of those types of questions would be, in her mind, nothing more than the simple, but maddeningly provocative word:

"Perhaps."

She was very well aware at how he looked at her, acutely attuned to the twitch in his cheeks when she would come in the room, as though he were trying to suppress a fully automatic smile, beating the expression back into his usual devilish smirk. She had begun to enjoy the fact that she could have his constant attention, could torture him to her heart's content with endless questions, literal pokes and figurative prods, and that he would still hang around and keep her company.

So much to the fact, that she hadn't realized it, but she herself had stopped looking for *other* company altogether.

That real Perhaps feeling really kicked in however when one night, after a particularly trying night at the hotel, he had come over to have a couple of drinks, share a smoke, and watch some TV, when he found her already on the futon, under a blanket, dazing out to an episode of STNG, "You okay?"

"Yeah," she answered sleepily.

"You want me to go?"

"No, s'okay. Sit." She patted the futon beside her, absently.

He sat down next to her, he had seen this one a thousand times, and said robotically, "He is Locutus of Borg."

"Second part's on next."

They didn't get through the whole episode before the two of them were fast asleep on the futon.

She woke briefly to hear him softly snoring next to her, Patrick Stewart was somehow back in his Starfleet uniform on the TV, so she put her head next to Dave's shoulder and then pulled the blanket up over his lap so he wouldn't be bothered by the cool night air off the ocean coming through the open window across the room. She pulled her eyes wide open so that she could at least finish the second episode, but the weight of her lids proved too much and she was soon sound asleep again.

He had fidgeted a bit and moved his half asleep arm up and over her head and shifted his legs off to the side of the futon, stretching them out and over and was soon snoring again.

Her body craved the recently lost warmth and she slid her feet down to his. Their combined weight slid them down the back of the futon and they adjusted sleepily until they were both comfortable under the blanket.

First, his arm went under her head.

Then, his other arm was thrown around her waist.

She fussed until her back tucked into the space against his chest.

She couldn't get it right until she put her hands around the bicep just under her cheek.

Their feet found themselves tangled together and he adjusted his stubbly chin until he got it to rest softly in her hair as they finally fell in to a deep, satisfying slumber, the greedy instincts of sleep drawing the warmth of their bodies ever closer together.

They slept soundly for hours.

She was the first to awake in the early morning light still locked in a soft embrace. Her body became more conscious of their entanglement gently, and as she became slowly more aware, she took a physical inventory of arms, feet, torsos, hips, legs, and most importantly, hands.

Everything seemed to be where it should be.

But, oddly enough, she didn't move. She didn't pull away from the length of his large, warm body, she kept her breathing soft and her body mostly still. She may have in fact curved herself further into the space between his arms, and may have closed her eyes and feigned sleep until she felt him stir awake under the blanket that they had shared.

"Hey, hi, sorry," were the first words out of his mouth, as he pulled his arm up and out from under her head. The morning news was predicting heavy rains all that day.

"What?" she opened her eyes and spoke raspily. She then laughed out a little, at the pressure she could feel against her butt, "Wow, what's happening there, Diemand?"

"Pay no attention to the man behind the curtain," he grabbed the blanket and shoved a good portion of it between the two of them in the space where their hips had aligned. "Morning," he offered for explanation. "Sorry."

She sat up on the edge of the futon, and then stood, heading for the fridge, she opened it, "You want coffee? I've got work in about an hour, but I think I have time to make some"

He tried not to watch her, he said to the room, "Um, no thanks. I think I'll just head home."

"Oh, okay. Do you need a ride?"

"No, I'm good. I'll just, uh, I'll just walk." He added, "You know when I can stand up."

"It's supposed to rain, I think."

He stood and stretched his long body 'til he could practically touch the ceiling, letting out a huge, "Ahhhhhyaaaaahhhhh! You know what? I'm good, now, I think," and went out just as casually as he had come in, "I'll see you later, Juju."

"Oh, yeah, okay, see you later, Dave," as she watched him walk out, the coffee pot filled with water still in her hand.

And she was, for all intents and purposes, extraordinarily pissed.

Holy fuck, he had to get out of that house. She was walking around in a goddamned tank top with no goddamned bra on, in these tiny little boxer shorts after they had been sleeping together under that blanket all night, like he was some goddamned sexless eunuch. *What the hell was wrong with her?*

He heard thunder rumble overhead.

What the hell was wrong with me? He had given up on plans with Laura because Jules had called and she just wanted to hang out and she was his best friend, and because Jules was fun and Jules was crazy and Jules was just up to relax and he wouldn't have to worry about what to do on dates he couldn't afford or what he was going to say next or if she'd be upset or offended by one of his stupid jokes.

And then a sprinkle on his freckled nose. And then his arm. And then steady drops down his shoulders.

But he had given up the possibility of getting LAID for friendship. AND he ended up SNUGGLING on the couch all night with Julia.

Lightning crackled. He started to jog, and then a boom, and the heavens opened up on him.

Snuggling.

I should give up my goddamned Man Card, right now.

But they had just fallen asleep watching TV. And it had gotten cold in the night. And he hadn't wanted to get up, and he hadn't wanted to leave when her warm little body had been pressed up against his, and he had liked having the scent of her hair in his nose, *it smelled like apples,* and he had liked feeling that he was there to protect her as he had looked down onto her gorgeous face late in the night and seen the light of the moon just touching her eyelashes, her cheekbone, her neck, her shoulder, so softly alive and sweetly vulnerable.

He ran his hand over his face, clearing his vision, he seriously needed help.

No guy, not a single one, had ever EVER done that to her before. Not a single man had ever walked out on her after a night together. EV-ER. They wanted to stay, they wanted another round, they at least wanted breakfast for the love of God.

But Jules and Dave hadn't been together.

They had just fallen asleep on the couch.

And they weren't together - together; they were just friends.

Right?

Right?!

The thunder startled her. The storm was right over them. She ran to close the window.

But would a friend do that? Just jump up with an "I'll see ya later, Jules" and howdoyado out the door? What the fuck was that?

An asshole, that's what it was. An asshole friend.

Should she go out to her car and look for him?

But what was she expecting? What did she think was going to happen after that? After a night of just lying in one another's arms, surrounding each other with the entangling

warmth of their bodies, sweetly intimate, incredibly close, as the gentle rise and fall of their breath came together as one?
What do you follow that up with?
I don't know, but it isn't "I'll see ya later, Jules."
He can get hit by lightning for all I care.
Douchebag.

Tim was just getting up when David walked in. "Ah-ha, niiiiiiice," Tim insinuated.
"Shut the fuck up, Tim." He shook himself, like a dog. "You don't know shit about shit."
"Whoa, dude." He held up his hands, "Bad night?"
"Yes! No." He sat down like his knees had given out beneath him, "Yes. I need to get my fucking priorities straight is what I need to do."
"What's up?"
"I don't know, Tim. I don't flipping know. I have Laura who wants to be my girlfriend, wants to be, she's perfectly nice and perfectly sweet and she's pretty, what's wrong with that? Right? That's pretty good, right?"
"Yeah?"
"Yeah. Then what the fuck do I need? What am I looking for?"
"I dunno. Sounds like that is a good set up."
He stood up, pointed at Tim, nodding, getting it, "You are absolutely right. That is a good set up."
"So?"
"Nothing. I don't need anything else." He looked over at Tim, grateful. "Thanks, man, I appreciate it. Good talk." He went to his room and closed the door.
"Anytime dude." Tim nodded to himself. "Good talk."

She decidedly did not call him that afternoon to tell him that she was home from work.
She came in, turned on the TV and went through her bills. Bills, calculations, money, plans. She could concentrate on those.
She estimated that if she made enough tips this week, she would have enough to buy that red suit - the Jones of New York one that she had been saving up for from the Nordstrom's

catalogue. If she waited until next week she could pay to have it tailored, unless she picked up a couple of extra shifts this weekend, then she could order it on Monday. She probably should offer to pick up some of Sally's hours, the other waitress would like the Saturday night event off. And Julia had been such a bitch this morning, she'd offer her her night off to make up.

She would do it, it made her feel a little bit better, working toward something for the end of the summer, which as of this morning, she could hardly wait for. Five more weeks. That's all she would have to endure in this stupid, tiny little one-horse, wannabe resort town and the stupid, tiny little people who lived here. Soon, she would be in Boston, working toward a future, a career, an actual real important life. Like she had figured all along.

She tried not to notice that her phone remained silent all afternoon and there were no messages when she came back home that night and that there were no knocks on her door after midnight for nights on end.

Every night, she glared at her futon couch on her way to her bedroom, flipping off the living room light with a slap of absolute disdain.

He wasn't going to call Jules either. Who the hell needs a girl best friend? Not him. He had Tim, right? Ah-HA! *Tim. Busted, dude.*

And Laura, he had Laura.

He was set about, determined that he was going to focus his energies on his Actual Girlfriend.

Laura seemed very pleased that he wanted to stay out with her longer than his usual, that he called her a couple of times just to see what she was up to, that he invited her out for drinks with the guys.

He had always been so, well, distracted, before, off with that girl - Jules? He'd said she was his best friend, and as far as Laura had seen from afar, that's all she had been. But it was hard to believe. Still, she was sad to say that she was petty enough to enjoy that he had been choosing her over his best "pal" for the last week or so. Katherine Huffington could just shut up about him now.

But Laura could see that despite this new energy and intended enthusiasm of the first few days, now he seemed, well, even more distracted than before.

They were walking along the shore together, he had been quiet for about five full minutes when she finally asked, "David, are you okay?"

"Uh, what?" he came out of his head, "Yeah, yes, I'm good. It's a nice night, huh?"

"Yes, it is." Laura added, "Thanks for inviting me out tonight. The uh, darts, that was fun."

"You'll get better at it with some practice."

"Maybe." She had shrugged.

"Oh no. You didn't have fun. Don't tell me that throwing sharp objects when you're drinking alcohol isn't exciting enough for you?"

"What?"

"You know, throwing darts while drunk can lend itself to all sorts of injury possibilities."

"Oh." She nodded. "I suppose so. Yes."

"Yeah, like a dart to the hand, or to the eye...Argh!" He slapped his hand to his face, covering his eye, "Argh!" and then he saw her slightly horrified expression, "Just joking" he said, slightly deflated.

"Oh," she giggled, but it was a little late to be convincing. "So, you want to come over?"

"Um, yeah," he said, turning himself fully toward her, "I do."

This was going to work out. The sex was really nice and he lay there next to Laura, knowing that this should be enough to satisfy him - that this could be everything he needed, everything he could ever want. A really sweet girl who enjoyed his company, who was nice to him, and who liked him enough to not just sleep with him, but to have actual sex.

It should be enough.
It could be enough.
It was enough.
Wasn't it?

"You want to go out for breakfast?"

"Yeah, sure." He added, "What are you doing today? Do you want to hang out?"

"Um, actually, I am supposed to go shopping with Katherine." Laura added, "You could come along with us if you wanted?"

"I guess."

"You don't have to David, it's okay."

"Oh, thanks." He smiled up at her, *See? Concerned for his thoughts and feelings. Not just there for her amusement.*

"But I'd really love for you to come."

Dammit. But okay, she was his girlfriend(!) and girlfriends want you to do that stuff because they're your girlfriend(!). "Oh, well, I guess that would be okay."

She beamed at him. "Good."

He got home at around 3 pm, inexplicably exhausted. He didn't understand how it was possible but the relative time he had spent watching Laura and her best friend forever Katherine - not Kathy - look at Ralph Lauren Polo shirts in pink and green and khaki shorts made his Massachusetts Teacher Certs seem like the intercoital timing of a 19 year old virgin who had somehow hooked up with Cindy Crawford.

Laura had asked him if he wanted to meet for dinner, but all he really wanted to do was to go back to his apartment and watch something incredibly stupid on his television, and numb his goddamned brain from figuring out how much those goddamned Bass penny loafers would cost as opposed to the boat shoes.

"Need a night off?" Laura had said coyly.

"Yeah, maybe." He had just smiled and kissed her forehead before finally being able to make his way to his place.

He lay there on his bed. *Laura wasn't awful. She was a girl. A regular girl. He shouldn't expect that she would be any different.*

Maybe it was him. He just didn't feel, I don't know, right. Like somehow things weren't in their places, like that some part of his body was physically missing and his balance was off in trying to compensate for its absence.

He was the one being weird and awkward with Laura. It wasn't her at all. She was nice.

Nice. The word rolled around in his head for a bit.

Until it bumped up into a thought that had been sleeping in there for bit, waking it up.

You know, it would be *nice* of him to just find out where Juju was.

It was kinda weird that he had just not called or anything. That wasn't nice. And that she had not called him.

Why wouldn't she have called him?

Wait a minute.

What if something happened to her?

She lived there all by herself, a pretty girl. A very pretty girl. Alone.

Who would know if something did happen?

Work? Who would they call? Did she have an emergency contact? Would she just be dead and disappear and he would never know what had happened to her?

I could just call. He should just call. His sister Dee would never forgive him if her college roommate disappeared on his watch.

He had to call. You know, to be *nice.*

"Hey," he said into the receiver.

"Oh, hey."

"You're not dead," he stated matter-of-factly.

"Not yet," she replied, without hesitating.

"Where you been?"

"Had to go up to Boston, pick up a suit, went to the hotel, stuff like that."

"Cool for you." He added, casually, "You playing darts tonight? I mean, you haven't, so I just asked…"

"Um, yeah I think so."

"I'll probably see you around." Repeating the words from their first night together, *would she get it?*

And he could hear her smile into the receiver, "Yeah, probably."

Her meeting in town went well. Mr. Joseph Cavanaugh had complimented her suit when she had arrived at their morning appointment. He had given her a tour of the kitchens and their function rooms and she had impressed the head chef as well as the sommelier when she had been able to suggest an appropriate

Beaujolais Morgan for the upcoming Thanksgiving menu. "You will have a bright future at the Plaza, Miss Santos. We look forward to your arrival in a few weeks."

"Thank you, Mr. Cavanaugh," she had replied, shaking his hand firmly. And her first thought was - of course after thinking about how proud her mother would be as Julia turned to walk out of the bright lobby, lit by the afternoon sun reflecting off of the gilded mirrors, the polished marble floors, the glinting metal and crystal of the giant chandelier, that her mother had once cleaned - *I can't wait to tell David!*

Oh, crap. She remembered as she got behind the wheel of her car, pulled out of the parking garage and headed down 93.

Why had she been so mad at him? He was her best friend, and they had shared a blanket on her futon couch. What the hell had she been so worked up about? That he hadn't done something - what? - special to acknowledge the closeness of that night?

Why would she have wanted him to?

They were in fact, best friends. Close pals who expected nothing from one another but good company and a few laughs, right? And what was wrong with that? And after a couple of weeks, she would move off to Boston and he'd be teaching on the Cape and they would look back when they were old at some school reunion and remember all the good times they had had together.

Onward and upward in just a few weeks. Might as well have fun while she could.

They were together for approximately six minutes before they were crying tears of laughter, gasping for breath, as Jules had pretended to toss a casual dart at Tim's left foot, causing him to actually jump without the sharp metal object even leaving her hand. Tim had shouted at her, and then stalked off, "Oh my God, Tim, I am so sorry!" She apologized at his back.

"She didn't actually throw it!" Dave had laughed out.

Tim had given them both the finger over his left shoulder, which sent them howling further.

"Did you see him move?"

"He was like a cat! The reflexes!"

"I didn't think he had it in him!"

They whoo'ed out, together, inciting laughter again. It took them a solid two minutes to finally get it under control.

"You wanna go?" she suggested.

"Yeah, let's walk or something."

They walked out of the bar, and turned a dark corner, she pulled out a joint from her wallet, lit it, and passed it over. "I impressed them today, Diemand."

"I never had a doubt you would," he croaked out, holding in the smoke.

"I can't wait. I can't wait to go to Boston. I really can't. I feel like my life will begin, you know?" She said, "I think I might just miss you, though."

"Yeah? You think?"

"Maybe." She punched his shoulder. "If these past few days are any indication…" she admitted.

"It was weird…" was as far as he'd go.

They just stood and looked at one another for minute.

Julia looked away, "See you tomorrow?"

"Yeah, call me when you get home from work."

"Okay."

"Night."

"Night." She walked off, down the street toward her little house.

And he headed back to his apartment.

And much to his girlfriend Laura's dismay, their private little best friend world has suddenly righted itself and started spinning again.

Just this time, a little faster, toward the sun.

"Oh my God, you used to have an earring!" She reached over and grabbed the lobe of his left ear once when they were watching Empire for the one thousandth time.

He pulled his head out of her grasp. "I did. I was hot."

"Were you? Didja get all the middle school girls to think you were dangerous?" She slid close to inspect the now faint pinhole in his ear.

He kept watching TV, trying not to think about the fact that she was practically in his lap. "A highly dangerous, freckle-faced kid. Tried to punk up my look a bit."

"Was it a stud?" she said, "Or a hoop?"

"Does it make a difference?"

"Stud said stud, hoop said, I don't know…"

"Pirate?"

"No!" she said, "The code was left was right, right was wrong."

"Not wrong, just gay."

"Ah, yes." She looked at it some more. "Let's re-pierce it," she said.

"No."

"Come on, David, I'll do it."

"Definitely no!"

"I'll be gentle!" she prodded. "Come on, it'll be funny."

"Funny?"

"Sorry. It will be hot."

"Yes it will."

"Alright, come here." She pulled him into the tiny bathroom between her kitchen and her bedroom.

She placed him on her bathmat, where he stood, feigning impatience as she gathered up supplies. She told him, "Haven't done this since I slept over my friend Maria - that girl had no boobs, like at all - at her house in ninth grade."

"You are not making me feel any better about this procedure."

"Don't worry, ya big baby." She lay out her instruments on the back of the toilet, pulled him toward her to face the sink, while she balanced herself, sitting over the edge of the sink. She pulled him close, he put his hands on her knees to help her keep steady on the edge of the sink as he stood between them.

His head turned away from her to the right, but he could smell the salt watery warmth coming off of the skin of her arms as they moved around his head. He cringed at the ice cube being placed on his earlobe, "Why do I let you do these things to me?"

"Because," she had said offhandedly, "you love me, that's why," holding the ice to his ear, while she grabbed the pin out of its rubbing alcohol bath. "Just like Maria."

"Love, true love," he crooned. "Wait, was Maria a lesbeeeeeeeee-oooooooooooowwwwwww-ccccccccchhhhhhhhhhhhhhh." as she slid the pin into his flesh.

She pulled the pin back out, her eyes widening, "Um, it was totally closed."

"Yeah, I figured that out." He grimaced, reaching up.

"Don't touch it!" She hopped off of the sink and pushed by him to run to the kitchen.

He watched her leave, and called after her, "Why?"

"You'll freak out at the blood."

He looked in the mirror in front of him, "Jesus Christ, Jules!"

"We've got a bleeder!" She ran back in from the kitchen with a wad of paper towels, and turned him to face her, as she dabbed his neck and the side of his head. They stood close together in front of the mirror.

He looked down at her, finding her eyes.

She smiled sheepishly, "I'm sorry, David."

"Should be." He smiled back. His eyes held hers and he watched them change right there in front of him. Fascinated, he kept looking, *where was she?* Her pupils grew large, and then he couldn't stop, even as he became completely aware of her lovely body in a smooth line against his, as the hard edge of the porcelain sink dug into his hipbone. He asked, softly, "I'll live, won't I?"

She took her hands away from the side of his head, and placed her hands on his forearms at his side, not breaking the stare between them. She just kept looking too, into those hazel eyes, that changed with whatever shirt he was wearing, that changed when he came out of the sea water or out of the pool, that changed when they had laughed so hard the two of them had to lay there exhausted from the whole body effort. She had looked into those eyes before right now and seen them both stormy and calm. But now, they were affecting her, deeply. She found her pulse pounding in her neck, her heart leaping up into her throat, her hands suddenly warm, and every instinct in her body screaming at her to, *please just...DO IT.*

She looked down at his mouth, her lashes lowering over her cheeks, and then, he leaned in and she found his mouth with hers, just softly meeting, electric shocks conducting through the hypersensitive nerve endings and the warm, wet sweetness.

She heard him inhale sharply and a small sound came from her throat. Her eyes flew open at her own body's reaction, "Oh, wow," she expressed, looking down, stepping back, taking her hands from his arms. "I'm sorry, Dave. I just..."

"Just what?" he stood there, slightly dazed, his eyes half open, his arms still trying to hold on to elbows that were no longer there. He couldn't think, he could only feel what had just happened, his mouth still warm from hers.

"I just wanted to see what it was like," she whispered.

"Well, what..." he tried to clear his throat, his eyes refocused, his face earnest, he stepped even closer, whispering hoarsely, "What did you think?"

"I liked it," she said slowly, thoughtfully, backing herself against the wall behind her in this small space.

"Enough to do it again?" he looked down at her, right there in front of him, so beautiful, *so unbearably beautiful,* a lump had risen in his throat. *Please.*

He leaned in. He was achingly close, his voice was rasping, his surprisingly delicious mouth just inches from hers. She should duck out, run, go! She could hear the blood pounding in her ears. But she looked up into his eyes again and just said, "Yes."

His hands came around her back as she pushed herself into him as hard as she could. Their lips, their arms, their tongues softly intertwining, picking up speed. They wanted to feel, to smell, to touch, to taste as much and as quickly as they possibly could.

They broke contact, long enough for her to pant out, "Bedroom."

His hands came under her lovely, lovely ass and he lifted her against him, her legs came around his waist and he carried her out of the tiny bathroom, careful not to bang her back or legs on the doorframe.

His mouth, not wanting to leave hers, but he needed her to know, "You don't understand..." he managed to get out, between deep, astonishing kisses, "how long I've wanted...this is crazy..." He gently deposited her on the end of the bed and stood in front of her. "You're so beautiful... and you're like my best..."

She got up on her knees and once again, came level to his face. She looked right in his eyes and directed, "Stop talking."

She pulled back and lifted the hem of his shirt up over his head and twisted it around her hand at the back of his head, just keeping the collar around his eyes. He couldn't see a thing, he could only feel her, and all of the marvelous things she was doing to him. She leaned in and grazed over his softly freckled chest, down his belly, his thighs, over him, biting, kissing, her lips, fast and then slow, "Holy shit, Julia," he breathed out. She smiled a little triumph between her kisses.

He couldn't bear it much longer. He pulled away, taking his shirt off of his head. Now it was his turn, he pulled the straps of her sundress away from her shoulders, exposing her tanned skin, his mouth just skimmed over her collarbone, her neck, the intense combination of his rough stubble, his persistent lips, and his hot breath causing ripple after ripple of goosebumps to appear all over her.

He pulled the straps down her arms further, slipping them gently over her hands, peeling the dress away from her incredible breasts, he slid the fabric down over her stomach, hooking his fingers into her underwear, sliding them gently down her legs, he trailed the path of his hands with his mouth, sweet, salty goodness. She sighed softly, stepping out of the ring of her clothes, now rumpled at her feet. And grabbed his shoulders, pulling him up to her.

But he stood back, breathing heavily, just to look at her.

Julia slid herself back on her white cotton sheets, just skin, with her funny tan lines marking all of those delicious borders, and her hair loose and spilling down her back and his heart was in his throat.

A girl, a girl who he thought about so much she invaded his sleep, a girl who could tell a joke and swear like a fucking sailor, who worked harder than anyone else he had even known before, who made him feel as though he was the only one in the room with her who knew what she was saying, how she was feeling, and knew exactly what he would think too.

This girl that he had spent so many nights with, just talking, was now before him, her cheeks flushed by his kisses, her nipples rosy from his hands, her thighs damp from his mouth, she was there in her bed, ready for him to come to her, waiting for him now to make love to her.

He had been carried away by the depth of words before, been awed by the beauty of priceless works of art in museums, stood before the stately majesty of the mountains, even been struck by fear of the raw power of the ocean, but he had never been witness to anything like this before in his entire life.

She was just...*wonderful.*

Julia saw him looking at her, and she said his name, just once, softly. The sound of it in her mouth shot right through him, and she lifted her hand.

And he took it.

And if it had been possible, he would not have let it go.

They worked hard to impress one another, using up an entire lifetime of sexual education within the first few days, and so they tried new things they had heard of and even made some things up as they went along. On her days off, they would get up in the morning, have coffee and bacon and then head back to bed. On the days she had to work, they wouldn't bother with the coffee and bacon.

They made plans to go out for dinner, or to head out to the Regatta for a drink or two, but he would come by and pick her up at work, and they would smile when they saw one another, and then work very hard at keeping their hands off of one another on the drive home.

They weren't always successful.

In those moments when he had been alone, he came down enough off this Juju-induced high to feel bad about Laura. He tried to call her a couple of times, to say something, or maybe apologize, but he couldn't help this incredible thing that was happening with Julia, and he couldn't seem to get a hold of Laura. He supposed he should go to her place, or call her friend Katherine, but truth be told, he just didn't.

Just the thought of Jules, his funny, beautiful Jules - her laugh, her body under his hands, or her face when he was inside of her and she would bite her lip, or even if she just happened to smile at him during the course of the day, or the rare warmth in her eyes when she would look at him when they lay together in her bed after, just tangled up, not wanting to move, not wanting to separate in the cooling dampness - it made him feel... well, he wasn't sure at first how to describe it.

The closest thing he could think of was when he had once seen a guy on TV who had won the Mass State Lottery for something like thirty-three million dollars. The guy had been handed the lump sum check by the state lottery commissioner and he had been photographed with the biggest, dumbest grin on his grateful face.

Dave felt that if someone had taken his picture during these days with Julia, the look in his own photograph would have been more stupidly happy than that lottery-winning-never-have-to-work-another-day-in-his-life-sonofabitch's.

"I'm getting sore, David," she had limped out into the kitchen one sunny morning to grab them some water.

"You need some time off?" he had followed her out, concerned.

"I didn't say that."

He came up behind her at the sink, putting his hands on her shoulders, and she leaned into his touch. He offered, "Perhaps, just not the main event, and we use other ways to entertain ourselves?"

"You mean, like TV? Or a movie?"

"No, you brat." Dave smacked her butt.

"Ooh, that's new," she laughed out.

"Excellent," he cackled evilly. He had tried to grab her tight but she wiggled away from his grasp, he chased her out of the kitchen to the bedroom hallway, and she leaped around him and jumped for the futon, he caught her in mid-air, and pulled her down on top of him, she was screaming laughing.

He flipped her over and pinned her down and she wrapped her legs around his, moving against him. She glanced down, "Thought the main event was off the table?"

"If you don't want..." he started.

Now with him, circling her hips, "I never said that."

"Well, how about spanking? Is that off the table?" He whispered in her ear, moving against her, one hand holding her wrists firmly between his fingers, one hand pulling her clothes aside, gently stroking her.

"No," she breathed out.

"Interesting." He kissed her neck and she moved beneath him, breathing harder, and then steadily harder. He kept himself steady, cool, alternating his free hand to the changing wonders of her body, letting her go where she wanted to go, but keeping her hands down against the rough cotton of the futon. He watched her eyes shut tight, her body getting distinctively tense, and then she called out his name, and her whole body softened against his, she sighed gently, her muscles rippling in rapid, then slower, succession.

Her eyes sprung open, "Now you need to be punished," and fast as anything, she had freed her hands, flipped him onto his back and slid herself fully astride him, pinning his muscular thighs with her ankles, pushing her hips down over his, first slowly, then harder, faster, again and again, her beautiful breasts absorbing the incredibly deep shock of her thrusts.

All composure he had tried to maintain was completely lost in a fury of her skin, intense sensation, and moisture, he gripped her hips and was lost in her momentum.

"That was punishment? What else," he panted, "what else can I do wrong?"

She smiled, and lay herself on top of him, catching her own breath, brushing his hair back. "Speaking of, were you ever spanked as a kid?"

"Wha...?" he had been enjoying the feel of her fingers on his head, shook his head, gaining focus, "Um, no. We were smacked around a bit, but oddly, not spanked. Were you?"

"My mom's dirty looks were scary enough. That woman could turn your insides to jelly with one little glance."

"Apple doesn't fall far from the tree," he bemused. "Okay," he considered, "that's good."

"Whaddya mean?"

"Well, besides the weird psychological issues that could come up when and if we explore those sexual options later, I don't want to hit or spank our kids."

He didn't think anything of her moving off of him, "Our kids?"

"Yeah, I don't really believe in spanking." He got up and went to the sink for some of the water he had never gotten, then laughed, "Well, unless you ask for it. So for you - yay! For the kids - boo."

"You keep saying 'kids,' David." She stood up in the kitchen, her arms crossed in front of her.

He nodded, turning to her, "Yeah, well. Just for future reference." He added matter-of-factly, "You'd make a pretty cool wife."

"Wife? For you?"

"Yeah," he shrugged. "You know, somewhere down the line."

"I think this is a really inappropriate conversation."

If he could have made the sound effect of a wall suddenly coming up in front of him, it would have sounded a lot like the swooshing silence that filled the room. "Inappropriate how?"

"Well, Jesus, we're having incredibly hot sex and then you're talking about our children, and marriage. I'm not looking to get my claws into you David - not all women dream about having kids and being someone's wife."

"I know that. I was just... talking."

"David, you do realize that I'm leaving here real soon. I'm moving to Boston and starting a job, I mean, I just got out of college last May..." she was starting to hyperventilate.

"Whoa, okay, Julia, it's okay. It's not a big deal. I swear to God, I didn't mean to, make you panic."

"I'm not panicking!"

"You kinda are." He laughed gently at her, but then saw her expression, "Okay, is that your mom's thing - the jelly glance - right there?" He needed to pacify her, "It's really okay. C'mere." He moved in to hug her.

She jumped back. And put one finger up for him to stop his approach. It did. "I think I just need to get some air, okay?"

She was out the door before he could say, "Okay" back.

She came back two hours later, looking vaguely sheepish. "Hey."

"Hey," He got up, but wasn't sure if he should go to her. He stepped slightly forward but then thought the better of it, and spoke from where he stood. "I didn't mean to freak you out, it's just that I thought..."

"No, it's not you, it's fine. What you said was nice, it just, surprised me a little. I just don't think of myself that way, you know..."

"I didn't mean..."

"Hold on, please. Just give me a second, I've been thinking about how to say this for like an hour." She breathed in deep, "I just, I just want to keep this light, Dave."

"Okay," he said.

She nodded.

He waited, but nothing more came. "That's it?"

"Yes."

"That took you an hour?"

"Yes."

"You need to stop smoking pot, Juju."

She laughed, in spite of herself, "Shut up, Dave."

He moved in to hug her, and she put her arms around his waist, "We good?"

"Yep."

"Why don't we get out of here? Let's go out for a bit, see where the day takes us?"

She nodded into his chest.

They spent the day walking around town. They ate lunch, they saw friends who wondered if they had fallen off the face of the earth and if they could point out where, they picked out books for his class this coming school year, ate out for dinner, stopped in at the Regatta for a drink before walking back to her house, where they made simple love and fell asleep spooned together under her white cotton sheets.

He had never had a happier day in his life.

He was starting to spend afternoons cleaning and setting up his new classroom. He came back to the house after a particularly productive afternoon to a small gift wrapped on the kitchen table. "For David - Julia" he read on the card.

He ripped off the carefully tied purple bow around a yellow daylily, decimated the brown paper packaging and dug inside the yellow tissue-filled box, and pulled out a small metal school bell. He dinged it, laughing out involuntarily at the little sound, "God, I love you," he said, smiling, and then clapped his hand over his own mouth, looking around the house, checking to be sure she wasn't home to hear him.

"Who is that guy?" The blonde waitress who had recently been hired to take Molly's place had asked, looking over at David, who had bumped into one of his Dad's yacht club buddies at the hotel.

Julia looked over at his tall, lanky frame next to the short, stodgy man, and she smiled, "Which one?"

"The not ancient one, duh. The one talking to my uncle."

"That's, David Diemand. He's…"

"Oh, David, yes, I know the Diemands, from waaay back." She flicked her eyebrows, "Huh, he's all grown up. I am going to go ask my uncle to properly introduce me."

"Oh, okay. Go do that." Julia grinned to herself.

The blonde noticed and turned to fully face her, "Oh, he's here for… you?"

"Yes," Julia found herself almost blushing, "We're, well…"

"Together? You and him…" She looked, cocking her highlighted head at Julia. "He's gotta taste for the…exotic, I guess."

Julia's eyes darted around, confused at what she thought the blonde was implying, "I guess."

She pursed her lips and looked Julia up and down. "You are super hot and all. Spicy." The blonde nodded approvingly, "Well, good for you, girl."

"Good for me?"

"Well, you know. Cha-ching. He must be taking you out all over town."

Julia laughed, "He's not. It's not like that."

The blonde frowned at her, "Ooh, he's keeping you on the DL. Don't put up with that, honey."

"No, I mean, he's, you know, just a teacher. He's not working right now, and…"

"He may be just a teacher, but his family is most definitely not."

"I know his family. I went to school with him, and his sister."

"Mhm, upwardly mobile. Well, then you know. And if you are college-educated, you should get him to own up. That family is your first-class ticket out of Waitress-ville, you know what I'm sayin'."

The little blonde snapped her fingers in what she thought was sassy solidarity and sauntered off toward the kitchen; Julia couldn't speak. She just watched her go, her mouth open in fraught indignation.

It was on the Wednesday night before the Saturday morning that she would leave for Boston that it all went to shit. He watched her folding her laundry. She was so hot, folding goddamned laundry, and all he wanted to do with his stupid life was sit here and watch her fold her fucking laundry.

He forced himself to look away from her, he frowned, "We haven't talked about it."

"What?" she asked offhandedly.

He had been thinking about this all day. Maybe all week. Maybe all summer, and he was ready to go, "What do you mean 'What?' You're leaving on Saturday."

"Yup." She stopped, with a pair of her lacy panties in her hand.

Goddammit. He had to look away again, "Yeah, and we haven't talked about it."

She put them in her basket, and went on unthinkingly to her bras, tucking and folding the straps neatly into the aligned cups, "I told you when I saw you at the party. I'm getting the job in Boston. I reminded you a few weeks ago, I was leaving this Saturday morning. What is there to talk about?"

"Okay, then." He opened his hands, "Where do we stand?"

"What do you mean, where do we stand?" she said to her laundry.

"Julia..."

"David." She finally looked back, putting down that black lace number she had worn last Thursday.

You could almost see her nipples through that lace, he recalled automatically, *oh, last Thursday...*

She enunciated her point, "We stand here. And on Saturday, I will be standing in Boston and you will be standing in Osterville. And that's it."

He repeated, "That's it."

"Yes."

"End of discussion."

"What is there to discuss?"

"Oh I don't know - feelings, ideas, plans."

"What kind of plans?"

"Let's put it to a scale - where are we on the scale?"

"What kind of scale?"

"A scale of one to ten. Ten - we're together, not seeing anyone else, we figure out how to see each other, I come to you, you come to me, we make plans. A One - well, I guess, the opposite of that."

"You already know my answer."

"You don't know mine."

"So?"

"Can't we add them together and average it out?"

"Oh Christ."

"Doesn't it matter how I feel?" he sputtered out.

"No."

"What? Why?"

"Because this wasn't supposed to be anything, David."

"Yeah?"

"This summer was a stopover until my life began."

"But then there was you and me."

"What about you and me?"

"You slept with me, that changes things." He stood up.

"It does? Really, because I slept with Justin and that guy Bob, too, and it doesn't seem to have changed a damned thing."

"This is different, Jules. You and I are different." He pushed his hand toward her and back to him.

"How are we different?"

"We're friends, for chrissakes, we're more than that, we've been together pretty much every second of every day since that first time - I'm waking up to you in the morning, and going to bed with you at night."

"David, it's been a couple of weeks, what we have is... fun."

Oh no, she wasn't dismissing it that easy. "Fun?"

"Yes, but the reality is, I am moving away, and I work weekends, my business happens on Friday, Saturday and Sunday. You'll be in school during the week and honestly, I know that there are women here who would stab me in the neck to get to you..."

"Julia..." he tucked the corner of his lip in.

"No, I'm not kidding. And I can't worry about what you're doing and who you're doing it with while I am trying to build a career for myself. I have a whole life to worry about a husband and kids, I'm twenty-two years old for chrissakes. I can't even believe that you're trying to pressure me into this, now." She slapped her open hand onto her thigh in frustration and whirled away from him toward the kitchen.

He followed her, "I'm not trying to pressure you into anything…"

She spun back toward him, "Yes you are, a scale of one to ten, make a decision. Well, you need an answer so desperately, it's a negative ten."

"Funny."

"It's been two weeks - a summer fling, ya know? Good while it lasted. It's not like we're in love or anything."

Dave hung his head.

"Oh come on! Two weeks, we're not in love, David."

He looked away.

"David, cut it out. We are NOT in love."

He said to the floor, bitterly, "Yeah, we're not. You call the shots." He looked up at her suddenly, yelling, "I'm not asking you to fucking marry me!"

"Good!" she yelled back.

He threw up his hands, "I get it!"

"You apparently don't!"

"Julia, just please listen! Okay, so it's not love, but I'll tell you it's something."

"What is it, David?"

"It's just…"

"What?"

He shouted, "I want you!"

She frowned and shook her head, disbelieving, "Really? You think now we're going to have sex?"

"No." He registered her slight expression of shock, and almost disappointment, and he stopped her, but more calmly, "No, that's not what I mean, I want… you."

"Yeah," she rolled her eyes. "I heard you. You want me. Big surprise."

"Julia, stop." He grabbed her arms and turned her to him, He looked right at her, her dark lashes narrowing over her eyes, he needed for her to understand, if she wouldn't hear what he really wanted to say, she would have to at least understand this, "I just... want...*you.*"

She pulled out of his grip, "What the hell are you talking about?"

"I just want to have you. Just... with me. All the time. I go places without you - while you're at work, or when I have to leave, and all I can think of - the entire time I'm gone, or you're gone, with every thought in my head - is, I wish you were with me. That's it." He shook his head at her, "That's all. You know, so I could talk about what was happening, or who was there, or where we were. To you. To make jokes to you. Whisper in your ear while we're together in a crowd and make you laugh. And no one else would get it or know why the hell we were smiling and I wouldn't care. Or if we couldn't talk, you know, I could even just stand there. Next to you. It would be fine. That would be just fine." He shrugged, her arms still in his big hands,

"David..." she caught her lip between her teeth.

"Do you know that I can't ever wait to just get back to wherever you are? Like, I'm jumpy. And weird, and impatient. Like I've forgotten something - you know, that feeling you get?" He shrugged a shoulder, and looked around, "That something's missing and you just have to get it back to feel right again? Like my keys are lost, or I don't know where I parked, or I've lost an arm for chrissakes and I can't figure things out. It doesn't make sense."

"No, it doesn't." She frowned at him, her eyes darting about uncomfortably.

"Julia," he looked at her, again, pulling her a little closer, forcing her eyes to meet his, and he continued, his voice softer now, "I just want to get back to wherever you are. I just want you to be with me. Or, me be with you. Whatever. Wherever. It's been that way the whole summer. That's how I've felt. And I mean, yeah sure, I want to have sex with you. Duh. Like every time I look at you. Here's me, ready to go! But, it's more than that. I just want you. Here - or there - with me." He practically laughed out the last words, as though saying them out loud actually had surprised him. "All the time."

He half-expected her to laugh too, at this emotional outburst, so odd coming from his lips, so unlike any words they had ever said to one another before, in a long friendship built mostly on shared sarcasm and cynical observation. It was crazy really. But she looked serious. Very serious. Her lip was sucked tight between her teeth, and her brow was furrowed deep.

She was silent for a solid minute, just looking up into his earnest face, so close to hers and he watched as her eyes changed in front of him once again. They began to swim in the deepening tide that rose in her lids. They sparkled and shone softly in the light and he knew that she had to understand exactly what he meant.

She did. She knew.

She had been pulled into the soft swell and fall of his voice, and she felt her body sinking, deeper, and deeper, almost drowning in his sweet and soft sentiments.

And the depth and scope of her own reaction to his words, his look, his touch scared the shit out of her.

He could see there was a sea change. He watched as she gathered herself like darkening storm clouds. He saw her expression harden and firm as she steeled herself with hearty defenses. The sparkle vanished and a hard flashing light came into the honey brown of her irises.

She pulled away. "That's just stupid," was all she said. And she had to look away. She busied herself with her laundry again.

"What?" he couldn't get it, couldn't understand.

"I mean, it sounds real nice for you, David. You've had me at your beck and call all summer. But it's going to stop, David. Saturday morning, when I leave for Boston."

He looked around, flustered, but then stepped to her, "What if…" he hesitated.

"'What if' what?"

"What if I said I wanted to go too?"

She blustered out, "That's not fair…"

"Why not? I could figure something out, after the start of the year. A sub position somewhere."

She couldn't take it anymore, he was trying to divert her, *he would not change her path,* all of these feelings, these wants, he just wanted more.

More would stop her from achieving her goals, from making money, from making a life.

That would not happen. He couldn't have more. She pushed him back from her with the sheer power of her voice, her intention. "Leave the job you actually have? Come and sponge off of me for another three months? Because, you know, what's the big deal? That's what *you* do."

"What? Who the hell are you talking about?"

"You guys, you people, from around here, or from college. You pretend that you could care less about cash and where it all comes from and then when things look desperate, just call Daddy." He had never suffered, never knew what it was to want anything in his goddamned life and now he wanted to trap her with him so that she would never get ahead, never break free of the world she grew up in, never make good for her family.

"You think that's what I've done? You think I rely on my parents to support me? Do you know me? I mean, have you seen me?"

"I see you. I know you. And I know me. And I am not that girl. I cannot rely on other people. I have to do these things myself and that's the way it has to be."

"It doesn't have to be just you."

"Oh yeah , I can see that, with no job and me buying us food, booze and pot all goddamned summer."

"I'm getting ready to go back to work now..."

"So how did you make it this far, David? Are you trying to tell me that you didn't have a little help from the Diemands - because that's how you people work. I know, I see it every day at the hotel."

"'You people.' There it is again. Who are you talking about?"

"Rich people!"

"I'm not rich, Julia! My parents - yeah, but I'm not."

"Oh come on. That's such bullshit, David. You pretend you've got nothing, and you sponge off of me, thinking like it's some kind of joke. And if all else fails, just call the Diamond Diemands. But that's not me, I can't do that."

"I don't do that either."

"Maybe you don't, but you can."

"So?"

"You don't understand. That is not, nor has it ever been, nor will it ever be an option for me. You have that option."

"Julia, how can you not get me? All of the things that I have always stood…"

"I get you. You want me," she threw back his words. "You just expect me to support you, feed you, and fuck you on the regular."

"That is not what I said!" He had backed near her door.

"But that's what you've gotten, so why not keep it going right? That's just the type of girl I am, right?"

"I've known you for years, Julia. Years." He pointed at her, "And I never thought much about what 'type of girl' you were…" She could see in his pained face, his brows pulled low, his mouth twisted, "…but what it seems right now is, you're just a pretty cold bitch."

"I never pretended to be anything else," she replied.

"When the fuck did this come up?" he shook his head.

"It was going to eventually. You know it, I know it."

"No, I don't. I think you are blaming me for something I have no control over, because it gives you an excuse."

"I don't need an excuse for anything."

"Yes, you do."

"No, I don't."

"Please."

"I am leaving here. I am going to have a life. I am going to make it, on my own. I am not going to be trapped here by some guy, who thinks that we have something we don't."

"We've got something, Julia." He snapped, "But because you feel something and you can't control it, it scares the fuck out of you. The tough girl from the city."

"There! There it is."

"Don't get it twisted…"

"I'm sorry – 'don't get it twisted' is that some sort of slang you're trying to use to speak to the city girl?"

"Julia!" he shouted.

"No, David, no!"

"What is it, Julia? You don't love me. Fine. I don't have money. But I could have money because my family has money. What is your excuse?"

"I don't need any excuse to leave you behind, trust me." Her little chin out, she glared at him, her eyes glittering and hard.

"I think you need one to leave me behind without feeling bad about it, Julia. And that's just fine. That's just fucking fine. I'll make it easy on you, actually, and take my rich, lazy, over-privileged ass back to my crappy, roach-infested, fucking hole in the wall apartment."

"That your uncle owns," she added.

And for the first time in several weeks, he again, voluntarily, walked out her door. "Fuck you."

"No, fuck you," she called at the door as he slammed it shut.

He didn't come back. *He didn't come back.*

It's been hours and he didn't come back. She was surprised at both the time on the clock and the feeling of overwhelming panic that spread down over her shoulders, made her stomach clench, her knees buckle underneath her.

He'd left before. It's not a big thing. But not after they had been together.

But that didn't mean anything, did it?

She put her hand to her head. Was she coming down with something? *Jesus, she felt like she was going to throw up.* She laid down on the futon, shivering, pulling a blanket up and over her shoulders, willing herself to sleep, to dull this *whatever it was*, among the unpacked boxes that dotted the house around her.

She woke up, discomfited, it was dark in the apartment. She flipped on a light. She had an incredible headache and she got up and got a drink of water. He still wasn't here.

Why had he done this? Why? Most guys would be thrilled with a quick and painless summer fling. Just a thanks for the sex and I'll be seeing you. Why had he made something of it?

But it wasn't that simple. Dave wasn't just some random guy she met, they *were* friends, they *had* history.

But it could be that simple, if he just let it. What was wrong with just a summer of sex and fun? What the fuck was wrong with it?

The sad thing is, she could see their future, both of them together in this little Podunk not-even-tourist town, stupidly happy, two kids years before they were thirty, him pleased as punch with his goddamned tiny little teacher's salary and she hustling her ass off as some glorified waitress to make ends meet.

I don't want that. I don't want that. I never said I wanted that.

Her mother didn't scrape and struggle and fight every single day to send her daughter to college to end up like that.

He wants me.

But no, Julia had a plan. Nothing was going to make her veer from the plan.

Not a goddamned headache, not a goddamned fever, and not a goddamned *guy*.

A sweet guy.

Who may, actually, love her very much.

But just *a guy*.

If he had just let it go, if he could just let her be, let her think about it, then maybe, just maybe she could have worked this out on her own. But he was right. And she had to feel it, had to just know it, deep, deep down in her bones that nothing would feel more natural, more right than the two of them being together. If he had just let her think it through, given her time, space, let her go, do what she needed.

But he couldn't.

He could barely contain himself - he was angry, fidgety, pissed, sorry. He wanted to punch the fucking wall, he wanted to kiss her, he wanted to run away, he wanted to hold her in his arms and sleep with his face in her hair, he wanted to fuck her silly, he wanted to just talk to her, to be next to her, knowing that if he even just went and sat inside her house and resigned himself to whatever punishment she would dole out, if she was there, somehow he would feel better, quieter inside, at peace.

And she had to know, deep down inside, that he was right.

He couldn't handle it for much longer, he dialed the phone. The other end picked up.

"Hi Dad, it's me, David. Listen, I gotta talk to you. Yes, sir."

David and his dad had never been exactly close. He had grown up, saying, "Yes, sir," and "No, sir," and "May I refill your drink, sir?" Once, when he was sixteen, his father had made the mistake of trying to hit him for not being respectful enough to his mother when she had demanded a fifth gin and tonic. Although David had caught his dad's right hand as it swung toward his face, he didn't see the left one follow it.

David never thought of himself as abused, or even that his parents' drinking was out of control. He just knew the rest of the family before him had all just laid down and taken it, or fled the house as soon as legally able. He figured on the former rather than the latter, he'd just leave a little earlier than the rest of them.

At twenty-four, he had been out of the house for almost seven years and in that time, he'd forgiven them a lot, and forced some of the more unpleasant memories to the back of his brain, not to be aired out or dusted. *What would be the point?* He liked to remember what was good about them, like the fact that even after thirty-five years of marriage, they still sat together in their den, night after night, talking and laughing together, as though no one else in the world existed. Although he never understood and had made a promise in his heart that this would never extend to his life, sometimes, even their own children were part of that plane of unimportant nonexistence.

His dad met him at the diner. "This is serious, Dave."

"I don't know, sir."

His father's large hand shook around his coffee cup, "You know something."

"I really like this girl, Dad."

"And?"

"She's leaving on Saturday for a job in Boston."

"So?"

"She doesn't want to keep seeing me."

"Then, that's it."

"Why? Why is that it?"

"Have you stated your case?"

"What do you mean?"

"Have you told her how you feel?"

"Kinda."

"Kinda? What sort of bullshit is that? 'Kinda.' Listen, how long have you known this girl?"

"A while. But we weren't ...together... up until two weeks ago."

"Two weeks, huh?"

"It's too soon to feel like this."

"I knew with your mother within the first two hours. I didn't tell her that then, but I did." He went on, "All I can tell you is, time is not on your side, it's forcing your hand. Your only option is to tell her the truth. Tell her how you feel and then let her decide, knowing the whole story."

"I just don't think that's going to work."

His dad laughed, a hoarse, coughing laugh, "Of course it's not going to work. But at least you know that when she leaves, she knows."

David put his head in his hands.

His dad stood up, sweating, "Listen, son, I've got to go. Wish I had had a chance to meet this girl."

He looked up at his unsteady father, "You have, Dad, she's Deidre's friend."

"Which one?"

"Julia. Santos. Julia Santos."

"Ah, interesting."

"Dad..."

"Does your sister know?"

"No."

"You might be wise to keep it that way."

"Yes, sir."

His dad got up, threw five hundred dollar bills on the table, and patted Dave's shoulder. "I'm sorry, son."

"Don't Dad." He pushed the cash away.

"David, for chrissakes."

"No, I don't want it."

His father began a slow burn, "Take it."

"Dad, no, I'm good."

"David, this," he held up the bills, "is what got you that pansy ass liberal arts, social work degree you've got..."

"Education, Dad." David looked at him, narrowing his eyes, giving him the same look he had when he home for Christmas his freshman year and announced that he would not be moving back home for the summer. Or ever again. Chris had helped him pack.

"Education, social work, same thing. This did, so don't turn up your nose at what my hard work and opportunity gave to you, 'so you can go out there and help the world.'" His dad growled at him, "And you and your 'I'll do it without you' bullshit has gotten you down in this shitty little Cape town…"

"I have a job, I got it on my own credentials, not on who I'm related to back in Manchester."

"Yes, and here you are, high and mighty, with the girl you love about to leave you in the dust."

"Jesus Christ, what does that have to do with anything?"

"Shut your disrespectful mouth, son. because I'm about to give you the best advice I can right here and now." His father raged at him, quietly, fiercely, "Right here, for free. No, in fact, I will pay you to listen to it - no woman worth anything in this world - no smart woman anyway - I don't care how much she loves you, is going to go anywhere with you, without a little bit of this in your goddamned pocket. And I am very well aware that right now, you've got nothing." His father threw the bills down on the table and stalked, as well as he could, out of the diner.

It would be the first and the last real adult conversation he had ever had with his father. His dad died of liver disease in his home hospital bed, as his wife sat next to him, talking and laughing about something she had seen on the evening news. She would follow him not more than a year later, the dutiful widow.

He showed up late Friday night. In homage to his dad, he was stinking, falling down drunk.

"I'm sorry, Juju," he slurred at her doorframe. "I just, just can't take it anymore."

"You're a frigging mess." She grabbed him under his arms and eased him into the house, sitting him down on the futon couch. The only thing in the place that wasn't packed up.

"I know. I'm sorry."

She sat down next to him, "I think you picked the fight because you didn't want to help me pack."

He smiled loosely, she wasn't mad. "I hate packing," he breathed out, his eyes closed.

She laughed softly down at him, "This is not how I pictured our last night together, David."

"Me either." He spoke softly, his voice husky from the repeated sting of alcohol, slowly opening his eyes, "I thought there would be outfits involved."

"Props. Lighting, maybe?"

"Cameras. Action."

"Too bad."

He swallowed hard, his eyes glistening up at her, "You can't stay."

"No."

His voice caught, "I can't go."

"No."

"Thought so." Dave's eyes closed again, "You can tell me as much as you want that it's not true, as much as you tell me I'm not right, I know that I am. And I don't care about anything else. I am in love with you. Sick and stupid, and pathetic and sad, in love with you. Head over heels type shit."

She rolled her eyes, "Very romantic."

"You know what I mean," he whispered out. She looked down at him, his breathing became softer, more even, his face relaxed, but he managed to get out finally, before he fell completely asleep, "I love you, Julia. I love you so much."

She pulled a blanket up over his shoulders.

She wished she had it in her to just tell him, just let him know that, hell, she might, against all possibilities of reality, that despite the fact that it didn't work, it didn't make sense, that it was just plain old dopey, that she thought she could, possibly, maybe be in love with him, too.

But she couldn't. She just couldn't bring herself say something so impossible and *improbable* and *dumb*.

And he was asleep now, anyway.

He wouldn't even have heard her if she did.

He awoke to the smell of coffee, the pattering sound of her feet, and a slicing pain in his frontal lobe. "Four food groups," she handed him down Advil, a Solo cup of water, a paper cup of coffee, and a paper towel filled with bacon.

"Thank you," he rasped.

"Welcome."

She left the house with what looked like the last two boxes and came back in the door.

"Futon staying or going?"
"Can't fit it in my car."
"Ah."
"Just about ready."
"Okay."
She stood there, hooked a thumb over her shoulder, "I've got to get driving."
"You want me to drop off your keys?"
"Yeah, David thanks." She looked over at him and the depth of what she was feeling took her by surprise, seeing him just sitting there, and realizing that this was going to be it.
She could barely breathe.
He shifted on the couch.
Please don't get up and come over here and kiss me and put your hands on me and hold me against you. Please just stay there.
He just sat, cup in his hand. "Welcome" he said back to her.
"Good luck," she ventured.
"Yeah," he cleared his throat, "you too."
I can keep it together as long as you stay there. Right there. She breathed in deep, her throat burning. "Goodbye, David."
"Goodbye, Julia." He remained cemented to where he was seated, his knees open, one hand awkwardly deep in his pants pocket, and she was able to turn back to the open door, "Hey!" he called out.
"What?" She had stopped, turning to him, half-terrified, half-expectant. *Oh God, please...*
"I'll probably see you around." He repeated the words he had said to her that night out on the road and he mustered up a smile for her.
She smiled back, grateful to him, "Yeah, probably." she said back, turning herself and heading out to the car, and down the road.
He whispered softly as the door had shut behind her, so he could be sure she didn't hear him, again, "Don't go," as he held hard onto the fold of hundreds in his front pants pocket.
And she, despite every smart, savvy, survival instinct in her body, cried a trail of hot, aching tears all the way to Boston.

Thankfully for David, love, like smoking or any other addictive substance, could be quit.

Once he got the smell of her out of his clothes, and school was starting up, he would keep his hands busy, carefully replacing old routines with new ones, concentrating long and hard about not thinking of her at every moment, every second of every hour, forcing himself to sleep, focus, work. He tutored in the afternoons after school, and then, bartending nights and weekends at the Regatta. Anything, anything to keep his brain occupied.

Oddly enough, he was now making more money than he knew how to spend. He was keeping his tips and tutoring money in a big jar on top of his dresser, and as the rumpled bills stacked higher and higher in the large plastic Poland Spring container, a brilliant idea had popped into his head, something he could do with all that cash.

He fell right off the wagon, if only for a while.

The fantasy started out simply - he had a week off from school at the end of April; he would take his money and go to Boston, and give Julia a call - but by the time February vacation had come and gone the fantasy had built itself up into an epic love story, a monomyth, a mythological quest: Ulysses to Penelope, Yuri to Lara, Orlando to Rosalind, without the cross-dressing part.

He would see Julia at her hotel in Boston, where he would happen to be staying, for some nameless educational conference. He would ask her out to an expensive dinner which, at first, she would think it wasn't a good idea, but he would smile and she would smile and she'd shyly say that she was out of work at six, and they would go to a beautiful restaurant and they would laugh and talk and buy expensive wine and he could take her back to his room, and she would protest unconvincingly how she was not allowed to fraternize with the guests, making it somehow forbidden and infinitely sexier and he would kiss her and she would say how she didn't care about the rules and they would fall into the sumptuous sheets of the expensive hotel room he had paid for the entire week and they would have hot, sweet, crazy make up sex for like hours, days, and she would whisper to him late in the night that she didn't want him to leave. Ever. And then he would go out and get a job and they would move in together and get married and have sex and babies and a minivan and a dog. Maybe a cat, too.

But *you know, whatever.*

He even got as far as making the reservation.

The real fucking wake up call was when he heard, from his sister, on a dark, dreary Wednesday night in March, the longest month of the year, that Julia Santos was engaged to be married, to some guy, William Rosa, some high level CPA or real estate guy, or something like that she had met in the City while she was working.

"Can you believe Julia's going to be the first out of all of us to get married?" his sister had gossiped.

Deidre didn't understand when the line between she and her brother suddenly cut off, but the phone lines on the Cape could be funny like that.

He went back on the wagon with a vengeance, he wasn't sure what he was going to do over the long, impossible summer that would be coming up. He had to work, he had to do something, he had to find something that would keep him busy, he needed another job, or a new one altogether, so that he could never allow himself another moment to just daydream and remember how good she felt against his lips, slowly inhaling, taking her in.

Over a few months' time, he was able to sublimate the intense cravings, push back the need, replacing it with new feelings, until even just the whiff of that sweet, salty scent could make him hate himself for ever being under its spell.

CHAPTER 15

Pon Farr

Julia looked over at him, standing there at the bar, as she chatted with Dee. Her friend was going on about how annoying Chris' ex had been about her mother-in-law's rings, and on the outside, Julia was nodding and frowning and sighing with sympathetic exasperation with Dee. On the inside, she was mentally chuckling at how badly David had handled her talking to that kid from the band - *God, he could be a moron,* she smiled at the thought. She hoped Dee didn't think she was smiling at this distressing story, so she quickly pressed her lips together. She tried to refocus on the whole problem with Chris having that pavé diamond set sized appropriately and "Julia, have you talked to Chris at all about…?" but Julia's mind rebelled against the Wedding Machine.

David wore his big idiotic heart on his sleeve.

He didn't think he did. But Julia could always tell what he was thinking or how he was feeling.

So unlike Prince Charming.

Will? Never would he make himself a fool for her. Never would he be too affectionate. Never would he yell in anger. Never would he show too much emotion. He was like a fricking Vulcan.

Just like she was.

Cool, calm, and always in control.

God, he could be so irritating.

Am I like that?

Overscheduled. Overcontrolled. Overplanned.

Afraid to show real emotions?

Not being fully human?

How had this happened?

Her husband left her last Tuesday and all she could think about was that his timing was *inconvenient.*

What have I become?

She used to be fiery, fierce, spontaneous, loving.

Back when she had to protect herself, feed herself, find a place to rest at night. Back when she was hungry. Back when she needed to fight to be alive.

The closest she had come to that fierceness had been her feelings for her children. She had been a Mother Lion again, providing and protecting. But not in her work, not in her love, not in her life, not in her marriage. Things just moved along as she had instructed them to, as she had made them run efficiently, flawlessly, automatically, as they had gone on for years.

David had never lost that emotional edge - he had been called immature because of it. But was it really immaturity? Or was it that he couldn't dull his senses to everything around him? He felt everything. He had never lost that strange ability to be this incredibly masculine man who would holler with the boys and tell them what to do, and then on a dime, turn and put his hand to her cheek and be incredibly tender and caring and sweet. Or tell her flat out that she was wrong, but then defend her wrongness to anyone who had ever challenged her way of thinking. He had that deadly, devilish combination of rough and gentle, dangerous and docile that had drawn her in so long ago, when they had been alone together down at the Cape in the first place.

Julia suddenly felt that she had to get back to him, as quickly as she could end her talk with Deidre. And she liked the feeling. "Hey Diemand," she demanded as she sauntered over to where he was standing, "you've been flirting with me."

"What?"

"You heard me. I know how you work, and you've been legitimately flirting with me."

He said, defiant, "Who's going to stop me?"

"Maybe me."

"Or your friend over there?" He smiled at her.

"Cute."

"I've been flirting with you," he paused, and looked around, his gaze stopping at her, "because you're letting me."

She looked long and hard at him, trying to figure out a smart retort, a quick rebuttal, but she couldn't. "This is dangerous territory."

"Why? You don't like it?"

Or maybe I do? "Hey, do you think Dee's acting weird?"

"Why do you care, Jules?"

"She's my friend and I don't know, I should be able to tell her." She looked down at the bar, then back up at him, "And you, she'd be on your side you know."

"Bullshit, Julia."

"It is not."

"I fed people a story in which I am the asshole, the irresponsible jerk and not a single one of my family has ever thought for a second, 'Wow, that doesn't sound like Dave.' I worked at that accounting firm for years, Jules. I made great money, but no, I didn't get married, and no, I didn't buy a house. So, of course, David would just up and leave and believe he's fucking Peter Pan. My family equates things, possessions, with success."

"Yes, most people do."

"Yeah, well then, I've got a boat." He swigged. "None of them have a boat."

"I think it's hard for them to see you as anything but the baby boy of the family."

"She's the baby girl, Julia. I wish people had more faith in me. But they keep falling for the story I give them."

"Maybe I have faith in you."

"Maybe that is bullshit, too. Who is flirting with whom now?" he grinned into the top of his bottle.

She shook her head, "Why don't you just give them the truth?"

"Because Julia, as you know, the truth hurts. A lot."

"I'm in the same boat you are."

"That's not true, Juju. You're lying to avoid the pity. I'm lying to direct it right at me."

The music started up, all but ending any shot for this kind of conversation to become a little more real. A little more truthful. Julia was sort of sad about that.

"Dave," she shouted "you up for pretending?"

"Why not?"

They ordered shots. "Shots should hurt going down – these taste like Kool-Aid!"

"Makes you think you're not even drinking!"

"It's wrong!"

He looked around, "I don't want to talk to anyone else here, do you?"

She grinned, "Not really."

"Do you think we should?"

"Probably." She suggested, "We can go back to talking to that hottie up there."

He frowned at her.

She grinned. "I don't know, David. This plan seems risky."

"We can do it, if we stick together," he grabbed her around the waist and pulled her along, shouting, "Chris!"

Chris met them halfway with a Woohoo! And a High Five!

"You're getting married in the morning!" Julia shouted.

"I am!"

"Ding dong. The bells are gonna chime."

She smirked. *What other guy could quote "My Fair Lady" and get away with it?*

He winked at her.

She turned to the groom, "It's wonderful Chris, I'm so happy for you both!" Jules said into his ear.

Dee made her way over, eyeing Julia and David, "You guys having fun?"

"Great idea, Deidre!"

"What?"

"This was a great idea!"

"Thanks! Wedding planner approval?"

"Stealing it!"

"I wanna hear a song from back in the day!" Chris yelled out.

"Juju can hook that up for you!" Dave teased.

"Yes I can!" She hoisted one boob and then the other, higher up in her scoop neck t-shirt and made to march off towards the stage, Dave grabbed her shoulders and turned her around and placed her firmly under the crook of the arm of his beer-holding hand. "Not a chance, cradle-robber." He had her captive, but she didn't move out from under his arm.

He pulled her close to face him every time he swigged. It felt nice to stand there with him, to put her hand on his chest and look up at his tanned neck and stubbly chin as he swallowed down a gulp of beer. She felt like a kid, with the music playing loud and a guy - whose entire face smiled when he looked at her - trying to hold her close by all night.

They jumped in place more than danced. Jules found herself caught between laughing, smiling, screaming-along-with-the-music friends she hadn't spent time with in years. They always had reasons not to see one another - sick kids, or parents, or birthday parties or work. But here they were, and having a great time.
What was particularly interesting is mixing the college memories up with the memories she had of that summer on the Cape. Never had she spent the night in the company of these people with David's arm around her, but oddly enough, right now, it seemed to fit just fine.

He was just coming back from the head when she had come to find him. A song had came on, and she leapt on him, impulsively flinging her arms around his neck, putting her cheek to his cheek, "I love this song!" she shouted and slid down his chest, not taking her arms from his shoulders. She looked right into his eyes and her gaze went right through him, up and down his spine, capturing him, holding him fast.
She was laughing, and he watched her face as it transformed from a happy grin to a slow smile and then quietly serious as they continued to stare right at one another. He had to shake himself, break that invisible thread and push her slightly from him, "Okay."
She stepped back, sheepish, unsure, embarrassed again. "Sorry."
He touched her elbow, "No, not you. I'm sorry."
"For what?"
"Muscle memory, I guess."
"Huh?"
He stepped closer to her, turning her body to his, putting one hand lightly on the side of her neck, his large calloused thumb resting on her chin turning her head slightly to the right and up and he could whisper directly into her ear.
He wanted to be sure she could hear him.
He confessed, over the noise of the bar around them. "Weird flashback, drummed up from somewhere in the deep

recesses of my brain." She could feel the heat of his skin coming off of his hand, his chest, his neck as he moved in closer, the scrape of his rough cheek against her smooth one.

"What..." she cleared her throat, "what was it?"

He moved in to say into her ear, "I just had this... feeling," he paused, she could feel his mouth just hovering over the fine bones, the soft lobe, "that it would be perfectly normal" stopping again, moving his mouth millimeters closer so that the hairs on her neck started to raise in a ripple of goosebumps, as he said gruffly, "to kiss you right here and now."

Those last words, whispered warm and husky into her ear, made her breath catch in her throat.

"But," he pulled back, grinning down at her, letting her go, as her chest heaved in some kind of unseen effort, "I wouldn't kiss a married woman." He stepped back.

Christ, was this the beer? This gentle push, this subtle pull was making her dizzy as hell.

He looked out into the crowd. "Not in front of all of these people anyway," then he turned to her and smiled, just for her.

That smile, the familiar magnetic pull of those eyes of his were somehow directly affecting her center of gravity. She found that she had to lean up against the wooden paneling behind her.

And then nonchalantly, as though he had had no intention at all, he said simply, "I'll go grab us another." He walked in the direction of the bar, she watched him get swallowed up by the crowd and then reappear at the side of the bar.

Her whole body felt elastic, taut, then soft, warm, pulsing, alive.

He caught her eye across the bar, where she stood where he left her, and grinned. That sweet, sweet grin that extended up to the crinkly corners of his eyes. And she felt her pulse jump.

Oh dear lord, she put her hand to her forehead, steadying herself, taking deep long breaths in an attempt to slow down her heart rate. *What the hell am I doing?*

She had this thought - the briefest flash of a thought of her walking up to him at the bar, taking the beers out of his hands, and looking into his eyes. And she would see that he knew, and he would take her out to her car, and they would, *um, re-pierce that left ear of his all over again.*

She had to shake that thought right out of her head. *Nope. Nuh-uh.*

But it would be okay, wouldn't it? They weren't kids, anymore. And who would know? Only David. And they were grown ups. And this was not new territory for either of them. A quick period of oh, okay, and yes I remember that, and that's new and then, it would all be just easy and familiar and hot and sweet, like it was - like he was - so long ago.

But what was she thinking? She had a husband.

Yes, she did. Despite all of these dramatics, things were not over yet, the fat lady had not sung, Julia was not free and clear to do whatever she liked, she was still legally, contractually obligated.

Rendered null and void by her husband? Say, around, last Tuesday?

Just days ago. Last Tuesday could only qualify as a few days.

Her husband left her days ago.

And, he was already sleeping with someone else.

True.

But.

No buts. When really had he left her? When had he checked out emotionally on her? Months? Years? Maybe, of going through the motions of married life? Just waiting for an excuse like Ellen to come along?

Or maybe he really just did not know better. Maybe William just hadn't known that their love wasn't quite that mythological thing, that deep connection that could span time and space called IT? Not until he

Met.

That.

One.

Could she even hear herself thinking? God, what a cliché.

One that Julia knew might be true. A summer fling, right Juju?

Stop. Stop it. I can't justify this. No way can I justify this.

Really?
No! I am thinking with my...
Yes, please.
No. Not now. Now was just not the fricking time, not the time to start anything up. No, this wedding was certainly not the time, and she had gotten into waaay too much trouble at weddings.
No, she would not go through that again.
With David...

The last wedding she had seen David and Laura at was approximately four years ago.
Tim Laughton was getting married. Yes, David's former roommate from the Cape. He had found her on Facebook and decided that he would love to have her come to the wedding.
She had lied to herself as to why she almost immediately accepted.
"You hardly know this guy."
"That's not true. And we'll know David and Laura."
"Ah, yes, your friends."
"Think of it this way, Will, a weekend night in the City, drinks, food, away from the kids, just time with you... and me."
She didn't have to connect the dots too much more for him. Annie and Billy had been so little, and the two of them had been perennially crossing paths with each other on the way to daycare, on the way to work, on the way to soccer. It hadn't affected their relationship too much, but they were adults, and they did have needs to be met. And so he had agreed, she booked a suite for one night at the Plaza. Being a hotel employee had its definite perks.
The wedding was nice enough. Julia had tried not to spend too much time scanning the church for the back of a familiar head, but there was noticeably none to be found. She did however, feel the warmth of David's thigh against hers as he slid easily into the pew next to her, a grin on his face and pretty Laura right on the other side. "Hey, Juju."
"Hey!" she had whispered enthusiastically to the both of them. "I was almost afraid you guys weren't coming!"

Will shushed them; Julia rolled her eyes, "You'd think this one had been the schoolteacher, wouldn't you?" and Laura laughed.

They all sat up straighter though, "I know I wouldn't have put up with your behavior in my classroom I'll tell you that much." David had said out of the corner of his mouth, enacting their bad habit of private conversation in a room full of people.

"You could have and you would have."

"Whatevs." He made a W with his fingers and thumbs and held it up to her face. Julia snorted, which made him cackle, which made Laura start in her pew, which made people turn, which made Will glare.

The night was the most fun Julia had had in ages. She and Will and Laura and David had talked and laughed and danced and drank until late after the band had packed up and the wedding party was cleaning up. Tim and his new wife were about to leave, and so the four of them decided to head out to a local bar in an old converted railroad station.

They sat and drank martinis in the puffy seats of a large circular booth, "We need to go out, the four of us, this has been so great!" Laura had enthused across the table to her when Dave had reluctantly taken up Will's offer to have a good cigar. "Dave's had so much fun getting to talk to you guys, I haven't seen him laugh so hard in a long time."

"It's so good to see the two of you." Julia confessed, "We'd love to get together, but truth be told, we don't get out together much. We'll have to make plans."

"We can work around whatever you've got, we're just two single people, you guys have the kids."

"Yeah, it's so hard for Will and me to get out. He works five, sometimes six days, I work weekends. Then there are the kids and their schedules and it's like we're constantly running. Unless we have a scheduled event, we don't really see even each other."

"That's too bad."

"I'm not complaining, we want to finish up the backyard and redo the kitchen, finally."

Laura frowned for her. "You're busy."

Julia nodded, frowning along with her.

"Why the faces?" David had returned and looked from one to the other.

"Just talking."

"'Bout what?"

"Not you," Laura reproved. "And on that note, I will take the opportunity to use the ladies room."

Laura slipped out of the booth and he slipped in.

"Not a cigar fella?"

"Not my kind of smoke."

She laughed up at him, "Mine either," she agreed. "It didn't make you puke, did it?"

"No," he admonished, then, "Wait, is there still some on my shirt?" he looked down. "Thought I cleaned it up."

Julia laughed again.

He watched her for a second, his fist at his temple, "I'm lucky, you know."

"Laura? Yes, she's so great."

"Well, yes of course." He sighed, "Laura - the lovely Laura. But I mean," he said, "with you."

"Me?"

"Yeah, how many guys can say that they can still stay pals after all these years with their first love?"

She tilted her head at him, frowning slightly, "Um, I don't know, David." She could see his smile was made as easy as this confession by the amount of vodka flowing through his veins. She grinned, "You're soo drunk."

"Might be."

"And you may have a little cigar-induced vomit right there," she pointed at the side of his face.

He caught her hand and held it in his, clasped together, elbows on the table, mock-exasperated, "I didn't actually throw up, you know."

He kept looking over at her face.

She smiled.

And he smiled.

He dropped her hand and she dropped his warming gaze at the same time.

It was all very innocent.

Laura had come back to the table a moment later, and Will came in to gather Julia up and take her back to the hotel.

They all embraced good night and walked off to their separate accommodations across the city.

Julia snuggled herself into the space between her husband's arm and his chest as he walked briskly back to the hotel. Her heart had been beating fast and she had the sudden feeling of wanting to get back to the room as quickly as possible. She smiled up at his handsome face, her husband, so finely gorgeous, so classically handsome, *she was lucky too, wasn't she?*

They slipped into their beautiful room and Julia turned to Will, right there at the door and kissed him deeply. She felt his slight shock but pressed on and he responded. She pulled off his coat, grabbed at his tie, his shirt, as his hands made their way to the hem of her dress, lifting it up, pulling down her underwear. Their mouths open against the other, panting out breaths. They had never gone after one another like this, never had sex this raw, but it had been so long. She ripped at her husband's zipper and reached deep inside, made him ready, and lifted her left leg around his back, pulling him to her. He slid himself inside her with one hand and reached under her ass and lifted her up, her back against the door, his other hand now on her breast still under the bodice of her dress, she bit at his neck, stifling her cries in his shoulder, the sounds of their movement only muffled by the pile of clothes at their feet.

After, they sunk down to the floor, Will had stumbled back a bit, and landed on the soft carpet, his shoes still on his feet, he quickly stuffed himself back in his pants and zipped up. He looked over at Julia propped up against the door, her breath still heavy in her throat and she grinned between gasps.

But Will's face was odd.

"Good?" she laughed.

"Different," he answered. His voice sounded a million miles away.

"Not necessarily a bad thing."

"I guess not." He had caught his breath and stood up, he walked into the main part of the room.

There was a solid minute of silence between them.

"Will," she broke it, saying warily, "is something wrong?"

"I don't know," he shrugged, "You're just, I don't know, different. You act different when you're with your friends."

"Different?" she furrowed her brow, and stood up, drawing herself to her full height, straightening her dress. "Different how?"

"I don't know, you're louder, you swear, you're like that," he pointed at the door. "That's not the kind of sex you have with your wife, Julia, that's like…"

"Like what, William?" she warned.

"I don't know," he was buttoning up his shirt, "Prostitute sex."

Did she just hear him right? "I'm sorry, what?" She put her hands on her hips, "What did you just call me?"

"I didn't call you a 'prostitute' I just don't think that's the kind of sex you have with the mother of your children."

"But you're saying that's the kind of sex you would have with a prostitute?"

"No," he shook his head, "That's not what I mean."

"So we only have certain 'kinds' of sex?"

"It's just, I don't know, disconcerting?"

"'Disconcerting?' Most men would be happy to have lots of different kinds of sex. I'd be happy with different kinds of sex. I'd be happy with sex, William!"

He ignored her last comments, "Most men?" He asked quietly. "You mean, like David."

"No."

"I've seen the way he looks at you."

"Why don't you try looking at me like that once in awhile? And then maybe we could have a little more wife-appropriate sex on the regular."

"'On the regular?" he repeated, "See? What does that even mean? You're talking like a teenager."

"I'm talking like a normal fucking human!"

"You're just proving my point."

"Your point that I am not acting wife-appropriate, that, only in retrospect, you didn't like the very hot sex we just had, that you get prissy when I swear, that you think I 'act different' when I'm with my friends. Well, ever think of this, Mr. Rosa? Maybe I am actually just acting with you?"

"Maybe you are." He straightened up, put on his coat.

"Where are you going?"

"I don't know." He turned at the door, "I just know I can't stay here with someone I don't really know."

Dave, had he known, would have been jealous of Will and Julia's evening together because, although he, across town, was receiving a somewhat similar reaming out, at least Will had gotten laid first.

Julia and Will had driven home together in silence, but the routine of life kicked in after a couple of days. Their fight was soon buried by the needs of new estate development, the spring wedding season, Billy's baseball practices, and Annie's rehearsals. They soon found themselves sleeping closer together at night, pecking one another goodbye in the morning, wishing the other a good day.

Whereas Laura pulled herself and David completely off of the radar, closed down their Facebook pages, canceled any thoughts of plans with friends, and invited a therapist to what had once been their appointed Date Night. David and Laura hadn't the Rosas' luxury of such a busy existence to sublimate the complete upheaval brought about by the leftover insecurities of a girl who had been left *by him, for her* once before, so long ago.

Thankfully, Chris came by to use the bathroom, saving her from her Smeagol/Gollum argument with herself.

Or, maybe not so thankfully.

"JUJU!!! My GIRL!" He hugged her, or more exactly, over-hugged her, "W'ZUP?"

"Not much, Chris, you excited?" She tried to extract herself from his overenthusiastic grip.

"I'm pumped!" He looked around, dropping his arms, "Werz yer boy?"

"Dave?" She pointed, "At the bar."

"Gemme a drink!" he bellowed.

She was taken aback at his sheer volume. "Um, no."

"Iwanotherone," he slurred in her face.

"I'm pretty sure you don't, Chris."

"Idon?"

"I think you've had a little too much."

"Nah, nah, jesskiddin, I just, juuuusssss... I valways liked you, evenaffer college. Yerrrran ice persn."

"We've been friends for a long time."

"It's weird rightu know, we'rrrall married but-cherboy."

"As of tomorrow."

"As of tomorrow. YEAH!" he overhugged her, again.

Julia caught Dee's eye looking at them and waved her over from behind his back. Dee hustled over and Julia advised, "If you want your groom to make it through tomorrow morning, it's time for him to go. Now." Julia heaved his arms onto his wife-to-be's shoulders.

Dee buckled under her guy's weight, "I can't... can't..."

"Hold on," Julia grabbed an arm. "Dee, I have some emergency supplies in my bag at the hotel just for this kind of thing," Jules called over to 'her boy,' "Dave!"

He saw her attempting to distribute the weight of a very drunk Chris between her and his sister's slim shoulders and stagger towards the entrance. David leapt to her rescue.

There was some brief scuffle over who would sit in back with Chris and who would drive, but David conceded that he was probably best sitting next to his moaning best friend. They tried their best to ease Chris' obvious discomfort as Julia drove down the long road that wound through the sea grass.

"Uhhhohhhnoooo."

"David, you tell me if he's going to blow, okay."

"Yep."

"The lease is under Will's name."

"Gotcha."

Julia, to Dee, "We'll get'im back to my room and I'll fix him up."

They sat in silence, well, relative silence from the three sober ones, for about two minutes.

Dee, in the passenger side, turned herself in her seat and faced the driving profile of her college roommate. "Julia?"

"Yes?"

"What are you doing here?"

"Uh, driving your drunk fiancé back to the hotel."

"No. I mean, what are you doing here at this wedding? What are your intentions here?"

"What do you mean? You called me, you asked me…"

"I mean, besides the hotel, besides the business, you are here. Without Will."

"Yes, he's in Boston, couldn't make it," she glanced at David in the rearview mirror, and kept on talking, "something with there being another buyer and the deal not being solid and there was some sort of counter…"

"Julia, stop, you're so full of shit."

"What are you talking about, Dee?"

"Just tell me straight…"

"What straight?"

"Are you here for your ex-boyfriend?"

"What?!"

David tapped his sister on the shoulder, "Um, which one?"

She turned to her brother, "What are you talking about, 'which one?' Chris!" She turned back to Julia, "Are you here to stop my marriage to your ex-boyfriend?"

A moan emanated from Chris' barrel chest.

"Oh my God, no!" Julia glanced at her friend. "Dee! Of course not. Why would you think that?"

"I don't know," Dee started, "It's just, it's just been so long and Chris just told me you asked him down to the dock the night you were here and then, the tuxedo and you were with his son Jackson all day the other day and then tonight, he was all over you and I don't know, I just thought Will's not here for seven days and maybe you're looking to, you know, I don't even know…"

"Oh my God, honey, no!" Julia reached over and rubbed her friend's arm. "You know, I love you two together! I've always thought it'd be perfect!"

The moaning was longer and deeper, "Arrrrrrrrrrrrrrrrrrrrrr-ghhhhhhhhhhohhhhhhhhhhhhh."

"Just, why isn't Will here?" Dee sat up, her voice an octave higher with emotion.

Julia sat up again, "Business, I'm serious."

"Noooooooooo, sheeeeeeeeezzzzzzzzzzz."

"Are you sure?"

"SHEEEEEZZZZZZ"

"Yes, I'm sure."

"You just seem like you're keeping something from me, Julia, we've barely talked…"

"We've talked all week, I don't know what you mea…"

"You've been avoiding talking about Will all week…"

"Well, I don't know what to say, I do know that your wedding has brought you and I back together," She avoided again, "and I've been so grateful to be able to see you all again."

"So many years, Julia, I did close you off and I can't believe I've been so…"

"I know, and I understand! You've been busy and I've been busy…"

"SHEEEEEEEEEEEEZ NATHE ONE!"

"Wait," Dee turned back to her brother, "Dave, why did you say 'which one?'"

"Huh?"

"Earlier, when I asked about the ex-boyfriend, you asked, 'which one'?

"SHHHHEEEZNATHE ONE TO CHEEEEE."

Julia, to Dave, interrupting his sister's train of thought, "Dave, is he okay?"

"I'd pull over, Jules."

Jules screeched over to the gravel and Dave pushed the door handle on Chris' side, Chris did lean out toward the side of the road, but didn't vomit instead he merely breathed out, "Sheez nah the one to cheat!"

"What?" Dee asked.

"Juleziznt the cheater, Deidre. We are - we're the cheaterz. This is no way to start a marriage, Dee, with lies. In fronna ourfrenz."

"Chris, this isn't the time." David started.

"Thizizth'time. Itiz. So many yearz," He slurred at Dee, "I thought Dave tolder, you know, when the two ovem were boffing down on the Cape, but she didn't know, she never knew." He pointed at Jules.

Dee looked at Jules, slightly struck, "What?"

Jules looked at Chris from behind her head rest, "What?"

"When wewer togethern college, I cheated onyu witDee," he flung his head forward, "like, a LOT. I thoyou know, knew. But you didn't knew, know." He pointed at Julia and looked over at his fiancée. "David ne'er toldher."

"When my brother was - did you say - boffing her?"

Chris, to Dee, "You dinno that?"

Julia, to David, "You told him that?"

Dee, to Chris, "No! I didn't know that!"

David, to Julia, "I didn't think it was supposed to be a big secret."

Julia, to David, "Not a big secret, huh? Nice, real, nice. Did you happen to use the word, 'boffing'?"

David, to Julia, "Of course I didn't. Listen, I was in a lot of pain when we broke up…"

Dee to Julia, "Broke up? Hold on. So it wasn't just sex, you had a relationship with my brother and never happened to mention it to me?" She turned to her brother, "That is why you asked 'which one?' Oh my God, you were with Julia and you never told me?"

"Dee, it wasn't that like that. It was a summer fl…" Julia tried to soothe, but then realized something, "And wait a second, you had sex with my boyfriend in college and never told me."

"I'm sorry, Julia, it just happened."

"That's a load of crap, Dee, it never just happens. We girls try to pretend that 'Whoops! It just happened,' but you know as well as I do, that shit is planned in advance. You're shaving for a reason."

"I knew it!" Dave slapped the back of the seat.

Julia said, "What?"

Dave, "I knew that girls planned the sex."

Julia, "Of course."

Dee, "You're fucking forty-two, Dave." She shook her head, "I just can't believe you never told me, my own brother…"

David, confused, "That…girls…plan…"

"No! About you and…" she tilted her head quickly to the side.

David, to Deidre, "I told Dad. That summer."

"You told DAD? But not ME?"

Julia, horrified, to David, "You told your father we were sleeping together? Oh my God, I went to his funeral!"

Dee needed clarification, "So that summer on the Cape, you two were just sleeping together?"

"Yes," Julia answered.

"No," David answered.

They glared at each other.

"After all this time, you can't even admit it, not even once. Can you?"

"And after all this time, you are still making something out of nothing?"

"Oh ho, that was not nothing, love."

"Stop it, David!"

"Even now, all of this... electricity between us,"

"Electricity..."

"Yes. I know it, you know it. Just then in the bar. I felt it. I could feel it. Just then."

"David, I can't think about..."

"No, see. There has always been a connection, Julia, beyond husbands, girlfriends, we have always had it, we've always been able to keep it - that's not nothing!"

"Because we're friends, David. Friends have a connection to one another, that's why they're friends!"

"Friends don't have this, Julia! Not this!" He pushed his hand back and forth between them. "Dear God, do you know how many therapy sessions I have had to endure over the years trying to explain away why I 'laugh like I do when we're together,' why I 'can't seem to talk with anyone the way I talk with you,' why I 'happened to hold your hand for twelve seconds at a fucking bar four years ago?'" He sat back, his hands on his legs, palms up, "That one, oh yeah, that one just kept coming up!"

Julia yelled at him, "Shut the door!"

"What?" He yelled back.

"Shut the goddamned door!"

Dave hauled Chris out of the way and slammed the door. Julia turned back around in the driver's seat and shoved the car into gear, spraying gravel on the road. She stared ahead at the road, "That's not my fault, David."

"Wait, that was what that was all about? Julia?" Dee asked. "Julia was the girl he was hitting on in a bar after Tim Laughton's wedding?"

"I wasn't hitting on her."

"He wasn't hitting on me."

"Yes, he was - Laura told me all about it!"

"Laura told you? For chrissakes!" David threw up his hands.

"She didn't say it was her!"

Chris moaning, "Oh Chrisss, hewuz always hittinon her."

"What? Chris was?" Dee asked.

"NO! I said CHRIS-T. Davidwuz, Davidwuzhittinonher. Hewuz so ma't'me for cheatinon you Juju, he kept telling me how perfeck youwer an'howbuful anhowcoudIdotha? NIwuzlike, dude, shut up."

"So you knew about them, David?" She looked at him in the rearview and then set her gaze back to the road. "You knew and didn't tell me?" She looked at him in the mirror again.

He met her mirrored gaze, "Yeah, I knew."

"I thought we were friends."

He looked out the window, "Just friends though, right?"

She pulled the car over again, throwing them all against the left side of the vehicle. Chris' moan turned to a grunt. She slammed it into park and turned on him. "David, you haven't been the only one to suffer consequences from what I thought was our private little affair, you know."

"How could I have possibly known that, Julia? You didn't consult me when you got engaged like a week later!"

"It was seven months."

"I'm sorry - not a week, seven months! Months that I went through agony! Physical withdrawals - from you! Like you were heroin or something. And I had to go cold turkey because I didn't fit into your plan, while you're up in the City being wined and dined. I have never felt like that in my life ever and then I hear you're up and marrying some rich asshole from Boston? What the fuck was that?"

"It just happened, David."

"No, see, nothing just happens, Jules, you just told me. 'The girl makes the plan.' I could have been that rich asshole, Julia, I wanted to be that rich asshole. I was fucking ready to be that rich asshole!"

"It was not the money, David."

"Bullshit, Julia."

"It was effort, ambition, taking the initiative on something - you couldn't even kiss me first, David!"

"What? Ho, ho, you…oh, okay… There's a lot, a lot you don't realize here…" she had taken his assault back a step with that one. He regrouped, "Wait a minute! I tried, I tried to take the initiative and remember, I was putting too much pressure on you. You couldn't deal with that, Juju. Because everything had to happen according to your plan. Will fit in with the plan, everything in perfect fucking order, not a hair out of place, not a wrong word, and good lord, not some wild run away emotion!"

"Yeah, here we are, in perfect order," she laughed bitterly.

"And then you come back and you tell me about the fairytale, how he's got the fairytale, and you're sad because you don't," he mocked. "And I should be bullshit at you, and I should be mad, but I'm not, I feel bad. Me. I feel bad. How stupid can I be? I feel bad that you are upset and I'm a - a sap! - when it comes to you. I shouldn't feel bad for you because honestly, it's your fault, Julia. You could have had the magic. You could have had the fairytale, but no, and you know what? It's your flipping fault."

"It was three weeks, David!"

"Three fairytale weeks, Julia!"

"What are you talking about, guys?" Dee looked from one in the backseat to the other in the front.

She started back on the road, hitting the gas, not so worried about the passenger in the backseat as she had been earlier. "So what do you want me to say? That you were right? That if I were to say that yes, back then, I did love you, David, it was messy and stupid and completely improbable, but yeah, what if I did? And that if I were to say that, yes, I remember now that I used to think about you even when I was marrying that rich asshole, and that if I were to say to you that I had to make myself forget about what it was like when I was with you, and that sometimes, I may have let myself wonder about what would have happened if we hadn't stopped whatever it was we were doing and that we were together for all these years, what would that do for you now, David?"

"I don't know!" he said to the back of her head.

"What do you mean you don't know?"

"I don't know! I'd feel… vindicated, I guess, maybe, for that time, back then…"

"Vindicated, knowing that you were right?'
"I guess."
"And you could go about your life, feeling pretty good about yourself. That almost twenty years ago, you were right, because that was what was important."
"That's not what I meant Juju, I didn't think…"
"But that's what matters right now, in this car, that I admit it?"
"That's not what I said…"

She pulled into the driveway of the hotel, just making it into a parking space, her tires spun on the crushed shells in the lot as she once again, slammed it into park, pulled her keys out of the ignition, opened her door and walked away. Deidre and a woozy Chris opened up as well to see as Dave flew out of the side door of the car, trying to catch up to her.

Julia spun on him, stopping him in his tracks.

"You know, you'll leave this place, sail off into that easy sunset, knowing that all along - yes! you were right! And then I get to go home and have a fucking nervous breakdown, because my asshole husband, whom you - again! Rightly! have never approved of - is fucking my neighbor and I have to figure out how to deconstruct seventeen, SEVEN-TEEN years of my what you would note as MY VERY WRONG LIFE. Does that make you finally happy?"

"Oooh, I knew something was up." Dee whispered to no one in particular.

"That doesn't make me happy, Julia. None of this does, I never wanted for you to be unhappy."

"Well, now I believe that is bullshit, David." She started and then stopped again, whirling on him, "So you know what? Own up. Take it, enjoy it! Take my misery, take my cheating husband, and my cheating ex-boyfriend and even my cheating best friend and have them all and tell every single one of them you were right. You and I, David and Julia, yeah, we…you were right! And then you can even blame me for you fucking things up with Laura, and the baby, and you can blame me for quitting your job and having nothing in your life except your goddamned beautiful boat. And you know that you really have it all, because you can say you were right all along. Okay? We had it!"

"What it, Julia?" He squinted at her, leaning forward, he wanted to hear it, he needed to hear it.

"IT." She leaned toward him, her hands on her hips.

Dee yelled over, "WHAT 'IT'?!" Then clamped her hand over her mouth as the two shot her equally scathing looks.

She yelled over to Dee, "We were actually in love with one another. Deeply, stupidly, sickly, pathetically, sadly in love. After three weeks together. Nothing, no time." And then turned herself back to David, "And I didn't have a clue, I didn't know what it was, I figured we were just kids, who had been friends, and we were lucky, you know?" She straightened herself up a bit, slapping her hand on her thigh in frustration, "Lucky enough to carry that feeling, that connection - yes, our connection - to sex and it was wonderful. And being with you was wonderful, David, in every sense of that stupid fucking word." Her voice broke, "I remember. I do. But I was naïve, I guess, I thought that was just, the way it would be, for everyone. I thought I could figure out how to love Will the way I loved you." She had to stop, just for a second, but she gathered strength, "What did I know, right? So, there. I gave it up. Motherfucking true love. You and me. Three weeks. Almost twenty goddamned years ago." She spat out, "How's that?!"

"Didn't you tell me you thought true love didn't exist?" he jabbed quietly.

"OH MY GOD! I AM IN THE MIDDLE OF A GODDAMNED LIFE CRISIS, DAVID! WHAT MORE DO YOU WANT ME TO SAY TO YOU?"

"I DON'T REALLY KNOW!"

The swerving vehicle, the vodka chased by beers, and finally the verbal back and forth between the two of them proved too much for poor Chris to handle any further. And so, without much more ceremony than a loud, "Bluuuuuuuurrrrrrrrrrrrrghhhhhhhhhhhhhh," the groom to be vomited in the parking lot of the Nantucket Plaza by the Sea.

Dee wanted to help, so she absentmindedly patted his back, but she needed to listen and see how this was going to end between her brother and her friend. "Did she say something about a baby?"

"I dun-NOOOOOOOOAUURRRRRRRGHHHH."

"Then there's only one more thing to say to you - fuck off, David." Julia spun on her heel, walking away, "And to think, I was going to have sex with you tonight."

"Wait, what?" He yelled at her back. "What? Why would you say that?!"

"Because there was electricity, asshole!" She yelled over her shoulder and disappeared into the brightly lit lobby.

"Goddammit." He kicked at the crushed limestone, "Goddammit! I didn't even know that sex was on the goddamned table tonight!" he flung his arms into the air, shouting. "I mean I had hoped - but Jesus! Julia!"

He saw that she was gone, so he spun on his sister and the kneeling mess of his best friend, whispering fast, triumphantly, "See? I knew there was still something there! I knew there was electricity! I knew it! I WAS RIIII ..." and then, he realized, he realized what he had just pushed away, the little thing he had been working for all week long - his perfect shot, "...ight. Oh my God. I'm Such.

A Fucking.

Moron!"

His yell echoed across the water, answered by the soft dinging bell of a boat gently bobbing with the tide in the harbor.

"Captain Moron, David," his youngest sister corrected as she helped her fiancé stand. "And of course you didn't know it was on the table. We just told you - the girl makes the plan."

Chris, now seemingly able to walk, since he emptied a good deal of his stomach of half-processed alcohol, stumbled toward the door with just the help of his lovely bride-to-be, and said in passing his extremely frustrated best friend, "The girl makes the plan, David."

Her phone buzzed: 'Talk to me.'

BUZZ: 'Please, I mean. Please talk to me.'

BUZZ: 'Shouldn't have pushed the issue. Not important right now. I get it.'

BUZZ: 'Still care about you. Want you to be happy, no matter what.'

BUZZ: 'Sorry.'

Her phone went silent.

But then, there was a knock on the door, Julia started up, angry, *he shouldn't have come up...* but when the voice that said "Julia?" was that of the youngest sister Diemand, she felt the briefest flash of... *I don't know.*

She opened the door. Dee came in, Julia said, "Hey, how is he?"

"Chris? Sleeping it off."

"Get him a huge water and make him drink it when he wakes up in the night. And then tomorrow morning, just give him toast and eggs and bacon and some Advil, he'll be okay."

"Will you be?"

"I don't know. I don't have any idea. I don't know what my next move is supposed to be or what it's going to be like when I go home. I've just been here, hiding out from the world, pretending that everything is just fine." She play-acted, "'I'm good, Will's good.'"

"It's not though."

"Oh crap, I know." Julia sighed and went and sat down on the bed. "I'm sorry, Dee, the last thing I wanted at your wedding was this awfulness."

"Timing is everything," she said sarcastically. "I'm just surprised you were able to keep it together this long, Julia. I don't know if I could control myself. I would have just been so angry..."

"I was angry, Dee. I am angry. But is it at him? Yes. I guess. Maybe I'm not mad at him, maybe I'm mad at this situation he put me in."

Dee sat next to her, "You can still be mad at him, you have a long relationship and you want to fight for that."

"Do I?" Her eyebrows shot up. "Will said he's gone. He made it pretty clear in fact. So, I guess that's just the end of the story."

"That's the end of the story?"

"The End."

"Just like that."

"Happily ever after," she resigned.

Dee squinted at her, just like her brother did, *really? Come on.* "So what will you fight about?"

"What do you mean?"

"Seemed pretty worked up in the car."

Julia flopped herself down, "Okay, I'm sorry I never told you about David and me."

Dee flopped next to her, "Let's start with, why didn't you tell me?"

"It was so long ago. I just couldn't say anything to anyone."

"Why?"

Julia lay flat on her back, "I don't know. It was just weird, the whole thing, those three weeks, it was like time out of the world. We weren't in any type of reality, just some fantasy romance novel bullshit set on Cape Cod." She laughed out a little, ruefully. But she felt her throat get tight. She looked over at her prone friend, looking up at the ceiling and she turned her face away, her eyelids were starting to burn, "It was amazing, really, I guess. But I didn't understand it, or even if I did, maybe I didn't want other people to understand it and tell me I was making a mistake. You know, one way or the other." She felt some water from the corner of her eye pooling in the hollow between her cheek and her lower lid, she tried to casually wipe it away without Dee seeing. She was unsuccessful. Julia croaked out, "So…" she couldn't finish her sentence.

Dee propped herself up on an elbow. "So you just tried to pretend it didn't happen?"

Julia, "I don't know. I just wrote it off in my mind - over and over again - as a summer thing."

"Can I ask you something?"

"Why not?"

"Did you even know why David was down the Cape, Julia?"

"I don't know, he wandered into a classroom somewhere and they figured he was too old to be a student?"

"Good one!" Dee laughed, "But no."

"Okay."

"Did you know that David could have gotten a job in Manchester, a city job, or even at a school - Dad could have arranged it - right out of college, no questions asked?"

Julia wrinkled her forehead, "That would have been so much easier on him."

"Yes, but he was a stubborn son of a bitch. He didn't want a handout, he didn't want to take our parent's money, he wanted to make his own way. He heard about a possibility of a job down the Cape, with his Mass license, and he took a substitute job for an entire year teaching Townie kids about Shakespeare for a crappy per diem in a dinky little system with no real funding until they gave him a position. He worked for it, on his own, as shitty as it was."

"Please don't tell me this," she groaned, and put her hand over her eyes. "This does me no good."

Dee said, "It's just that he was ambitious, he did have a plan, but it wasn't about money. He always told me that we had been given so much in life - so many gifts - that we were somehow in debt to the Universe. And to pay back all that generosity, it was our responsibility to help people who didn't grow up with the White Picket Fence."

Julia thought, "Like me."

"No, I mean, yeah. But, we were all in awe of you. You know, you were always working, working toward something. God, you were always so determined, so ambitious and driven."

"Yeah, well, I think you've mistaken 'determination,' 'ambition,' and 'drive' with a case of semi-crippling obsessive compulsion and the overwhelming need to control outcomes. Jesus, that's practically my job description."

Dee chuckled, "That is how you got here, from there."

"You know, when I met you guys I didn't know Tommy Hilfiger from Ralph Lauren."

"Who cares about that?"

"I did. I did because I didn't have it. It's funny, because you don't understand what it's like not to have it, but to be constantly surrounded by it. Always feeling like an outsider, no matter how smart, now matter how savvy."

"Really, because I didn't feel that around all you beautiful people?"

"What are you talking about?"

"Come on, Julia. When it was the four of us, 'one of these things is not like the other...'" Dee sang.

"What do you mean?"

"Pretty. Juju. Standing next to you. Standing next to Chris. God, my own idiot brother even is prettier than me!"

"That is not true!"

"Julia, you talk about people not understanding what it is like to have…advantages. Yeah, I get it, I didn't have all the advantages you had either."

"Dee, I always thought you were lovely."

"That's nice of you to say, Juju. But," Dee sighed, "I didn't always feel it. I feel it now. I feel it today. Chris makes me feel it. Those shoes you gave me made me feel it. But I was an outsider sometimes, too."

"I didn't think of it that way, I guess."

"I guess then I could say the same."

"Look at us now. We got all the stuff we've ever wanted."

"Will you have it for much longer?"

"I'm not sure."

"Is it worth holding on to?"

"I'm not sure of that either."

They lay there quietly.

"Do you even know how happy you and David would have made me? God, when we were in college, he used to help me try to figure out how to break you and Chris up." She thought, "Makes more sense now."

Julia huffed out another laugh, "All you had to do was tell me what you and Chris had been doing." She added, "Sluts."

Dee laughed. "It was college. And it was weird, and the four of us were friends."

"Why do you think it took me so long to break up with Chris? God, I missed you." Julia smiled. "And then the boys graduated and now you and Chris are getting married."

"Funny how it can turn out that way. Twenty years later."

"So betrayal, lying to ourselves and to each other? All's fair in love and war? Will and I will be fine? In twenty years."

"No. Will sucks."

"Not you, too."

"He was always too perfect. Beautiful, generous, polite. The hair, the teeth, the chisel-i-ness. Too perfect. I bet he even cheated perfectly."

"How would one do that?"

"Damned if I know, I just got caught for some thing I did twenty years ago."

"Yeah, so did I." She turned to Dee. "Am I that easy to fool?"

"What?"

"Well, Chris cheated on me with you. Will cheated on me with Ellen. Is that it for me?"

"What do you mean?"

"I'm a woman men cheat on."

"Not all men."

Julia frowned, "You're talking about Whatshisface."

"Yes."

"He didn't get the chance."

"You didn't give him the chance."

"Because I wasn't with him long enough you mean?"

"No. Because I think he wouldn't have given up any chance to be with you, for anyone, or anything."

"Oh boy."

"So, how do you fix it with Whatshisface out there?"

"Why? Why should I fix it, Dee? He lied. I lied. We all lie and all it does is hurt - hurt, not just you but everyone in the periphery, everyone who is either dumb enough, or unlucky enough to get involved."

"So?"

"What do you mean, 'So?' Whether it is friends or kids, or family, you and he are not the only ones who get hurt. It isn't just you and them anymore, everyone feels that hurt."

"Of course they do!"

"So what? What could be the good of that? What is the point of all of this, Dee?"

"Oh grow the fuck up Julia," Dee snapped. "We get scratches, we get dents, we get vomit in our shoes for the love of Pete. And people lie and they don't always do what we hope they will. And as a matter of fact, I can almost guarantee you that in every successful adult relationship there is some unhappiness, some betrayal, some kind of denial, some level of unreached expectations. I'll tell you that if anyone who's been with someone for any good amount of time tries to tell you that it's not true, they're lying. Lying through their teeth."

"Why is that okay? Why do we just accept that?"

"Because we're human beings for goodness sakes! We're emotional, and stupid, and we fuck up, we do and say dumb things and no one is ever perfect for any significant period of time. But you know, time goes by, and we get older, we get knocked down. Emotional involvement is never elegant, or even pretty. God, do you know what I have to deal with with Jackson's mom? She's nuts. And an ex-wife was never on my list of life dreams, I'll tell you that much, but I get to have Jackson and I get to have Chris - you remember that guy just vomiting in the parking lot?"

"Yes, I do."

"I'm marrying that man. And so after all the nuts, and the dents, and scratches, he and I figure out that we can still be friends. And that, in and of itself, is pretty much worth fighting for, isn't it?"

"I guess."

"You guess? You just had a screaming match in a parking lot with someone who has done nothing but protect you and your big ole secret all week."

"I know," Julia conceded, and then, burst, "I know!"

"So there is still hope. Maybe. For you two morons. Captain and Mrs. Moron."

"Why does he get to be Captain?"

Dee laughed at her indignation. "What?"

"Can't I be a Captain? Why can't I be Captain too?"

"He owns the boat and you are ridiculous."

"I know." Julia put her hand to her forehead, "So what should I say?"

Dee shrugged, "To start, sorry is always good. For example, just throwing it out there, I'm just giving you a place to start - you could say that you're sorry that you didn't tell your old college roommate that you were in love with her brother."

Julia's shoulders dropped, "I'm sorry I didn't tell you that I was in love with your brother."

"And I'm sorry I slept with your boyfriend in college."

"Ah, you can have him." Julia added, "Tomorrow."

"Thanks."

"You're welcome. I think."

Dee got up, "So any advice for the bride-to-be?"

Julia sat up, "You mean, as a wedding planner, right? And not as someone dangling on the precipice of a failed marriage? Not as someone who fucked up true love?"

"Right."

She ticked off on her fingers as Dee walked to the door, "Okay, no simple carbohydrates at breakfast or you'll bloat. Drink a lot of water until about an hour before the ceremony. Do not let your groom drink like he did tonight, and don't let anything else bother you. Like, say, the unnecessary dramatics of an old friend. If you enjoy yourself, your guests will enjoy themselves."

"Huh."

"Huh, what?"

Dee opened Julia's door and took one step out, turning back to say, "Yes, well, it's just that, on your wedding day - if you had asked me, and I had been there and I had known about you and David - I would have probably told you something a little different."

"What would that have been?"

She spoke slowly, "Not denying your seventeen years of marriage or your beautiful children, Julia, but I think I would have told you that - at the time, mind you - it might not have been such a great idea for you to marry, what appeared to be, your Rebound Guy."

Dee closed the door behind her and Julia just lay back down on the bed and closed her eyes.

Chapter 16
Let Them Speak Now

She had been a mess.

She had gone to work, had come home to her tiny one room city apartment and had cried.

She had met up with Hannah and Mary Ann in the city, cried on the car ride there, and then, cried on the car ride home.

What the hell had been wrong with her? Funny commercials had made her cry; a golden Labrador puppy playing in the Public Gardens made her cry; a baby passing her in a stroller on Mass Avenue had made her cry.

She had figured then she had to be homesick. Homesick for your mom's apartment five miles away?

Except that I wasn't homesick down in Osterville.

You know what? She was bored during her hours outside of work. She was feeling maybe a little lonely in the city, by herself. That was perfectly normal. She needed a hobby - like knitting, or drinking, maybe - some type of distraction.

She was homesick, dammit. She had made a choice and she couldn't, wouldn't turn back on it now. Her work at the Plaza was amazing. Mr. Cavanaugh had actually given her the management for the catering department for an entire corporate event for a group of real estate agents to be completed on her own - she had worked late into many nights in the kitchen, emailing the sponsors, taking ideas, making suggestions, and coordinating with staff and kitchen to make sure her menu went off flawlessly. This was her proving ground, this was her break.

And she wasn't going to fuck it up, for anything. Everything had to be perfect.

Her mom had shown up at her apartment a week before the event, "My baby, what's wrong? You look terrible."

"Yeah, hi Mom, glad to see you too."

"Why do you look like this?"

"I've just been working a lot, for this big meeting for these bigwig Boston real estate people."

"Ah, this is important."

"Very."

"Well, you want to impress, you want this big fancy job, you need to look the part."

"I work in a kitchen right now, Mom. I've got a suit for when I'm at meetings and stuff."

"One suit? Look at your nails, your hair! You're like this every day, you'll never leave the kitchen. Trust me, I know. You want to be the part, you need to look the part first. You know this." He mother advised, "You want a beautiful life, you want to be happy, you need to look like you deserve it."

"Mom, I've just been working so much, I haven't had time…"

"No more, baby. We'll go out. You will be ready for this big event. I promise you. You do this and life will open up for you." Her mother had held her by the arms and made the decision for her.

It wasn't a bad plan. Julia had been up until two AM, covering the last details of the linens and the bar for the two hundred and fifty guest event. But that morning, she had little to do but to be on hand to make sure that the servers and the chefs were able to keep to the schedule. She wasn't due in to the Plaza offices until eleven AM, but she left her apartment for all of the appointments her mother had made for her on Newbury Street.

Julia arrived at the Plaza Event Offices in a cream colored suit to set off her freshly coiffed hair, her eye make up toned down, and her feet, although completely covered up in the expensive shoes her mama had bought her - "Just let me get these for you!" - were as soft as a baby's ass. Julia had smiled to herself knowing that her toenails were painted a shiny black, if only to remind herself of who she really was. She had shaved, plucked, groomed, lotioned, powdered and perfumed.

And she felt… good. Better than she had since… well, she wasn't going to think about that.

"Julia," Mr. Cavanaugh had called her in, "I'd like you to meet the young man who is to host this event."

"Oh yes, sir," she had stepped into the office and looked up to see a tall, slim man in a navy blue blazer with a light blue shirt and khaki pants - more casual work attire for Boston, but appropriate for an out of office event. Julia noted the high quality of the materials and the same shoes she had appreciated just days before in a store on Newbury Street when she had gone shopping with her mother.

He turned in her direction and she saw that his eyes were as blue as his shirt and his dark curls pushed up and off of his high forehead. His dark brows looked surprised as he saw her come in the door, but pleasantly so. He held out his hand, and she shook it, his skin soft, his nails short, even, his hand firm, but not overly so.

She knew he was undeniably attractive; she knew that most women would be stuttering, possibly drooling, at this point. But she was able to remain pretty cool. She was dressed just as well as he was. Her hands were as manicured as his.

"Julia Santos, William Rosa."

"A pleasure to meet you, Miss Santos," his deep baritone was clipped and precise. *Surely it had sent many shivers down many a spine.*

But she replied equally as coolly, "You, as well, Mr. Rosa."

"Call me, Will." His smile was full of straight white teeth, clearly the work of a master orthodontist. This guy was no joke, this guy was the actual - almost mythical - Tall, Dark, and Handsome.

And Julia was able to take all of this in, without an ounce of nerves, without a moment of worry about if her hand may have been sweaty or if her breath still had coffee on it. She enjoyed the feeling of power of looking this good and still not giving a shit. That coolness, that detachment. She was invulnerable. She was in control. *She was powerful.* Her work was all that mattered.

But still, he *was* good-looking.

Huh.

If she could get through today, this guy might just be the distraction she needed.

Distraction from what, Juju?

She knew today would be a success, felt it in her bones, knew it through her preparations. Julia had planned for success. And after her success, she might just convince this man right here to buy her a drink.

Yes, a guy like this? He could be... perfect.

CHAPTER 17
Or Forever Hold Their Peace

David was amidships at the wheel of his boat. What the hell had he done?

I mean, actually, *what the hell just happened?* The last hour was a blur of emotion, information, kicking things, and monitoring a potential vomiter from violating a lease agreement.

But he was aware of one big thing. A long-awaited victory.

Okay, so not the best time to bring it up, but he had been right, motherfuckers. RIGHT.

Julia had loved him. And she had said something about wanting to have sex with him, and not then, but actually now. Tonight!

Two victories!

Kind of, as the sex part wasn't actually happening right now, so one victory. And, she had said she couldn't admit that she had loved him and she fucked it all up for the both of them and he had been right all along and she was the one to ruin what the two of them had had.

But why? Why? Why had she ruined it?

That was the question wasn't it?

Because he had a teaching job, and no money, and all of that didn't fit into her plan.

Well, fuck her and her plan! Didn't do her any good in the long run, did it?

Well, the really long run.

I mean, she was married for a while. A long while. A really long while. Enough to have two beautiful children, and a home and, well, a life.

Not like him.

Jesus Christ, he was worse off now than he was then. Years experience at a job he couldn't go back to. His cash was running low. No kids, no home, just a bed on a boat.

A really, really nice boat.

But here they were again. The playing field completely in her favor, even with a cheating husband. Her life and his life still didn't sync up. The only advantage he had was that he finally knew he was right about them.

For three weeks.
Almost.
Twenty.
Years.
Ago.

Why didn't it feel like it was so much of an advantage?

Although… she did say she had planned on having sex with him.

Crap, he pushed it. He had pushed it too far, pushed her too far, too fast, he had glimpsed something - something real within his grasp out there and he had grabbed for it and held it and then choked the life out it.

Just like he had done on the Cape.

What?

Had he been just as guilty as she had been?

Christ, and right now, she is dealing with the death of her *seventeen year marriage* and he was so, just, selfish? Stupid? This wasn't amateur hour, he should have known better, but, God, he had always been just a sucker for her.

He took a deep breath and started up his engines. He just needed some time, some time to think. She hadn't answered his texts. He could go out, out there on the water, and maybe, it would just be easier if he didn't come back to this harbor.

CHAPTER 18
As Husband and Wife

And then there had been Valentine's Day.

Valentine's Day, that had stretched out into St. Patrick's Day when she had finally thought it all through and said, yes.

A Yes that would determine the course of her life for the next seventeen years.

Three weeks.

Seventeen years.

Julia hadn't a clue as to what Will had planned but he had told her he wanted to do something special for Valentine's Day. The last few months had been very exciting. Mr. Cavanaugh had given her the opportunity to manage the menu for the Plaza's Annual New Year's Extravaganza to the high praise of the Society page in the Boston papers as well as the head chef and the Human Resources department. Cavanaugh had given her a bonus and was promising a raise at the end of the next quarter.

Will had proven to be as perfect in all other environments as he had been on that first day they had met in Cavanaugh's office - at the bars, out dancing, out to dinner, in the bedroom. He was handsome, well-mannered, polite, ambitious, particularly attentive to her needs - everything a man should be.

He could be occasionally critical of her dress, her apartment, her car, but he wanted her to have the best of things, so that the Boston people would see her as the bright, beautiful professional woman she wanted to be, just like her mother wanted.

He was a real companion, a partner, an ally.

So why, when he pulled out the blue box out of his jacket pocket, and she found him kneeling in front of her in the restaurant and saw his mouth moving, and his eyes looking up at her and she saw people clapping and found herself in his arms and crying, could she not stop once the ring was on her manicured finger?

The evening did not go as Will had planned. Although pleased with her answer, he found himself with a suddenly inconsolable bride-to-be, in which he had to call over the waiter, and ask for the check and his car to be pulled around front, *quickly*. He had ushered her out of the door to the furtive stares of the crowd that moments before had been congratulating him, as she sobbed, apologetically, "I'm just so happy, I don't understand it," she hiccupped. "I'm sorry... to ruin... such a perfect... surprise."

It was a disaster. She couldn't catch her breath in the car and the tears just kept pouring out of her. Will brought her to her apartment and had put her down on her bed, pulled up her covers, and went to grab her a glass of water. She had put her head down on her pillow, laying her left hand on the sheets in front of her. There was a gorgeous square cut two carat diamond, set in platinum, in front of her eyes - the promise of a life with a handsome man who respected her plans and wanted to stand beside her as she forged ahead in life.

Will kissed her forehead, when he came into the room. "Will," she said to him, "I don't think I can do it." She held the ring out for him to take back.

"Of course you can, Julia," he admonished gently.

"I just don't know, if this is right, you know? It's only been a few months and I'm not sure..."

"I know it's soon, Julia, but I have to say I think you are perfect for me. We have the same ideas, the same goals for our future. But," he said, sitting himself down on the side of her bed, "if you aren't sure, you don't have to give me answer now. If you want, you can keep the ring, and keep the box, and just think about it."

He was so wonderfully understanding about something she didn't even understand herself. "I really, I really appreciate it, Will, but it doesn't seem right, you planned this big surprise and the nice dinner, and Valentine's Day, and I'm just... I don't even know."

"There's no rush, Julia. I will be ready when you are."

"Thank you, Will."

"I mean, how many announcements will be coming out in the papers this week anyway. Ours would be lost in the crowd." He smiled gently.

"I don't want a big wedding. Just too many people to think about, you know?"

"There you go, planning already."

"Will…"

"I'm telling you, Julia, take all the time you need. We'll let everyone know when you decide, okay?"

"Okay."

"Goodnight, Julia."

"Goodnight, Will."

He had let himself out. And she had lain there, staring at the ring on the sheet in front of her. It would be another month, before she decided to slip it back on her finger for good.

Or at least, what she thought was for good.

CHAPTER 19

Please Repeat After Me

David cut his engines. *Christ,* he couldn't just leave.

Well, he could. Chris would get it, but his sister would be pissed. He could go down to Key West again, the hurricane season wasn't for another few weeks, or he had enough money to chug his way back up to Maine for a bit, spend the rest of the summer, take some odd jobs, buy himself enough gas to get back down to the Gulf of Mexico for the winter.

But, Jesus Christ, he was 42 years old. And after all this time, and other loves, and other lives, and houses, and babies and boats and cars, the girl that got away - his one and only What If - had finally admitted that she had loved him too.

That should mean something shouldn't it? That's shit for poetry right there. That's a country song and a French epic and a Shakespearean sonnet rolled into one.

So why didn't he feel better?

Because for right now, for today, it did him no good. He had fucked up any groundwork he had laid with Julia - goddamned beautiful Julia, who could, to this day, shock him, surprise him, make him laugh, make him feel horny, make him feel happy, piss him off and kick his ever-loving ass if she so desired.

And she may have loved him. Yes, she may have. But that was past tense.

She wouldn't take him seriously.

Not from just where she was standing.

But from where he was.

He saw the light go off in her hotel room. He checked his ropes, closed up the hatch, pulled off his shirt and put out his lamp. *All alone. A stupid guy, on a goddamned boat.*

Chapter 20
I Do

  She ran. She pulled the ring off of her finger and she just ran.

CHAPTER 21
Lawfully

She wasn't exactly sure what happened to get her on the road - she had just gotten into the car and drove. It wasn't until she was about to cross the Sagamore Bridge on Route Six on a Saturday night in March that she realized that she didn't have a plan. At all.

What the hell was she doing?

She just needed to see him. Talk to him.

She could figure it out from there.

But where would he be?

Julia's car had died earlier in the week. She had driven it since she received her license at sixteen and a half, having carefully saved her babysitting money and waitressing cash in a jar hidden in her mattress for several years, she had handed over the money to the slightly impatient used car dealer, counting out the last five dollars in change. It was hard saying goodbye to something she had worked so hard towards and maintained so lovingly, but the powder blue Ford Escort's chassis had rusted by the back right wheel well and the body of her baby was riding on the tire.

Will had been sweet to let her borrow his white BMW 325i for the weekend so that she could go and visit her mother - he would be away at a real estate conference in D.C. And suffice to say, it was the most beautiful car she had ever driven.

Julia had spent Friday night in her mom's apartment. They had laughed and talked and cooked dinner, Kevin and she watched late night episodes of Deep Space Nine and their mother had to get up and tell them both to go to bed. Saturday morning Mama had made pancakes and tottled off to work and Kevin had gone off with some of his guy friends. "Guy friends" was what he called them back then, before he had had the nerve to tell Mama they were his boyfriends.

Julia was determined to tell them that night, about the ring.

The huge ring she had smuggled into the mattress for her weekend home, in the same space where she had buried the treasure of her car money, and then college money when she would leave for school. Years of saving, of hiding, of keeping the secret of something to look forward to, a way out, an escape. Was this the next thing for her to look forward to? Was marriage to Will the next step in her life? Was this the next thing she would save and save and save for?

And then Saturday night came. Dinner had passed, and Mama had gone to bed, and Kevin had come and gone and she still hadn't told them. Will had given that ring to her on Valentine's Day, almost a month ago and she couldn't pull it out to show them. The incredible two carat stunner. Julia could barely look at it, it shone too brightly.

Julia had her pajamas on, slippers on her feet, she had washed her face and pulled back her hair. She took off her necklace and watched her face in the old mirror of her and her sister's old bedroom as she pulled out her earrings. She knew she had to get out of there.

She had to leave. Her breath came short and fast and her heart pounded in her ears. She was going to leave. There was no time for getting dressed, no time to think. It was all encompassing - get out, run! - the overwhelming atavistic need to migrate to where he was. He would comfort her, he would calm her brain, she needed to be able to figure this out.

She slipped out of the apartment, started the quiet engine, and just drove.

The bridge had been quiet and the miles of scrub brush trees marked her path to where he was.

She hadn't spoken, heard from, heard about him since she had left Osterville that Saturday morning.

How will he make this better?
It doesn't matter.
I will know what to do when I see David.

She pressed down the accelerator, and the lovely car smoothly sped along Route 6, almost like it was happy to be out of the city, on the open road.

Her fervor pushed her foot further down, closer every minute to the Regatta and her house and just close. *Close. I want to be close. Just for a couple of minutes. That's it. That's it. I'll figure it all out when I get there.*

She was about a mile or two from her exit when she stopped.

Or to put it more exactly, pulled over. For doing 112 mph in a 50 zone.

As was the typical response of a Massachusetts State Trooper, he pulled her to the side of the road and then let her sit there for about fifteen minutes.

It was in those fifteen minutes that she realized that she was an absolute idiot.

Where was she going? Oh God, what was she doing?

You mean other than 62 miles over the posted limit?

For all she knew, he might not even be there anymore.

License and registration.

It was her, boyfriend, *I mean, fiancé's* car and she wasn't used to driving it.

Quit his job? Moved on? Would that really be unlike him?

So you think that's an excuse for that unsafe speed?

No.

No sir, I'm just…

Where would she go? And when she did see him, what would she say?

Have you been drinking Miss?

No, no officer, not at all.

God, Julia. Three weeks. You were with him for three weeks. Get a fucking grip.

Excuse me, sir?

You've been with Will for six months, and you're running to see a man who may no longer be there. Physically, or emotionally, ever think of that? Ever think he'd not want to see you, Julia?

Or that maybe he has someone else?

Men do that you know. They move on. You did. Pretty damned fast, I might add. Like your driving. And it's not as though he didn't have other prospects.

Oh.

And even if you did find him and he did want to see you, what then? What would you do? You'd go back to Boston, you'd go back to your job, and then what? Try to find time for him? You would, you'd do it, out of that same need you feel right now, the need to be near him, to hear his voice. And then time would pass and you would come to resent the long drives, and the tearful phone calls, and all that time he would come to expect from you and what then, Juju?

What then?

I don't know, Officer. I don't know.

You're driving away from a man who has given you the space and time to do what you want to do, who is willing to commit to you as well as commit to the work you want to do, who understands the world you are about to enter, who can be your guide, who has given you a ring worth David's yearly salary, and who's car you are about to get a very large speeding ticket in.

Think about it. Really, logically. You are a practical girl.

You like William.

I do.

You like David.

I did.

That's right. All things being even, although deep down I know that they're not, I think you know what the right decision - the smart decision - really is.

Go home, Miss.

And drive safely, please.

Julia called Will's hotel room number that he had been sure to give her when he had left.

"Hello Julia, God, it's late isn't it? It's like three in the morning."

"I know, I'm sorry, Will, it's just that I have to tell you something."

"Yes, what is it?"

She took a deep breath, "I got a speeding ticket. In your car. A big one."

"How much?"

"$367."

"Wow." Will said, incredulously. "How fast were you driving?"

"About sixty something over the speed limit." She muttered.

"Ah, not used to that engine, are you?"

"I'm sorry, William."

"Don't be. It's not my worry anyway."

"No, it's not, I will pay it…"

"Yes, because it's your car now."

"What?"

"Well, I know you felt bad about your old one and I know that you need it and I was going to surprise you when I got back but I just bought myself an M3 here today and I thought I would just give you that one, it's safe and dependable and it's a couple of years old, but it's still a great looking car…"

"Are you kidding me?"

"No. Why would I kid about that?"

"Because it's your car."

"And?"

"People don't give people cars. Yeah, in commercials at Christmas on TV, but you don't actually give someone a car."

"But you need it."

"It's a car."

"Julia, yes. It's a car. Take it. I am happy to be able to do that for you. Why do you think I asked you to marry me? I want to do things like that for you. I want to help."

She sighed. He had come to her rescue. He was her White Knight. "I know you do. Thank you, William."

"You're welcome."

"I will be thinking of you in my dreams."

"So will I." She smiled into the receiver. "Goodnight."

"Goodnight."

William would help. He wanted to help. She had struggled and pushed her entire twenty-two years to make it somewhere, anywhere, to get herself into a good school, while girls around her neighborhood got pregnant and left, she pushed her teachers, herself, her family to give her more, to work herself harder, to make the grades that would send her to the best colleges, to study and work to secure her place in this world, the successful world, the better life, the Dream.

Two decades of continuously looking forward, strategizing and planning, and here was the future she had worked so hard towards, the future denied her sister, and their mother, and her mother and their neighbors and almost everyone around them, was on the other end of the phone, out in her mother's driveway, tucked into the mattress of Julia's childhood bed.

She slipped her hand up and inside the pilings, scratched the sharp corner of the box with her finger and caught hold, drawing it out and putting it down, clicking open the top lid and sliding the magnificent ring on her finger.

Julia would sleep through the night, her hand resting heavily upon her chest, and show her mother and brother at breakfast. And they all screamed and laughed their joy and promised to dance at her wedding.

William never asked where she was headed when she got the $367 speeding ticket.

And the night her heart had begged her to flee to David - the boy she had fallen for late one night as she lay still in his sleeping arms - was lost as an unread footnote in the epic mythical romance of Prince William and the Fair Julia.

CHAPTER 22
Tearing Asunder

He was just drifting off to sleep when he heard a sound - a slap, slap, slap.
What is that?
Footsteps?
Coming fast down the wooden gangplank of the dock.
He turned on his light, and opened the door of the cabin. She was standing there, on the dock, where she had skidded to a stop, still in her t-shirt and jeans from earlier tonight, but her feet were bare, her hair loose and her eyes hard and shining. "Juju, you okay?"

And she said to him, "David, I'm sorry. I'm sorry to bother you, but, I'm starting to figure out, that you, you know, you've meant more to me - in my life - than I realized. Or maybe, let myself realize. And I said something about pretending. Pretending that we were young again, right? But I don't think that's what I want. But I wouldn't mind trying to at least, go back, you know? Maybe just go back, for a little while, just go all the way back, you know, to the Cape?" She shrugged a shoulder, she wasn't sure how he would react.

And for once she couldn't read his face, she couldn't see what his eyes were trying to say.

Her bravado, her runaway emotion had gotten her this far, on sheer hope that he would respond, but she didn't know what else to say, or how to convince him, "If you think that would be okay."

All of the logical and rational thoughts of how and when and why and should he and could they went out of his head, and he ran, ran at her and she saw him and his eyes finally and he grabbed her in his arms as she leapt onto the deck of the boat, his hand in her hair, his mouth, after all these years, after all this time, finally once again, to hers.

CHAPTER 23
No Ending and No Beginning

His arms came around her and drew her body tightly to his bare, hard chest.

He put his large hand in her hair, and pulled back to look into her eyes. He smiled softly at her, trying at least to assure her that he would like nothing more than to kiss her for as long and as much as she would like. He couldn't say anything at first, and then his warm lips pressed insistently on hers, their tongues softly touching. He asked silently, with each kiss, permission to kiss her again, waiting only to hear her answer in her eager lips.

His hard line of stubble that surrounded his mouth scraped gently against the pulp of her lips, making them tender, hypersensitive, as if every nerve in them had been startled awake, made alive with electricity. She felt the deep current of blood through her body shift and fall like water from the sweet and tender pressure of their kisses, sliding down her spine and pooling gently in her center.

It had been so long since she had been kissed by someone to whom it wasn't routine, who wasn't just performing the sexual maintenance of a long term relationship. David wanted her.

Just her. Not her "presentation," or her earnings, or her potential Return On Investment, or her developing assets - *those assets stopped developing a while ago* - but all of those things that she had long believed were the hallmarks of a real, mature relationship. And yet, come to find out, maybe they weren't. David had not been looking for a long term business partnership, he had just been looking for her.

Julia could feel the waves of the ocean, fluid, natural, ebbing and flowing together, lapping the boat beneath them, but David stood firm on the deck, pressing him to her, holding her to his hard chest with each new swell.

She could feel the heat of his skin as her hands skimmed over his broad shoulders as he explored the sensitive skin of her throat with his lips, his tongue. Her eyes closed, as she soaked in his sweet attentions. But she forced herself to open her eyes, to see him, to look at him, to take him all in, to know exactly what she was doing. She pulled gently away from his arms. And his eyes opened, looking slightly befallen as her warmth moved away from him. She stood back on the deck, and reached her hand out to his ropy arms, running it over his unexpectedly smooth skin.

He stood there patiently, as she moved slowly around him, coming close, pulling away, and then fitting herself into the strong lines of his body, touching, nuzzling, tasting. It took every ounce of strength he had not to grab her, pull her to him again, hold her and kiss her gorgeous mouth. But he would wait, trying his best to be patient, to not make a sound, to not move, to just savor her attentions, even though every touch caused him to absolutely burn.

She could see that his skin was freckled even where his shirt would have covered, if he had been wearing a shirt. The sight of his chest, narrowing down to his barely covered hipbones, and that beautiful curve below the small of his back as he had stood in the door of his cabin, well, that had been inspiring enough, *I mean, well done, David,* but to feel his soft skin stretched tight over muscles made hard through days at sea, to feel them move, to tense and relax as her hands, her mouth made their way around him, she couldn't restrain the pounding of her heart. She also became more than well aware that under the thin fabric of her t-shirt, she had failed to strap back on her bra when she made her mad desperate run to see him.

Oh well, she sighed in gleeful resignation, if his now visible reaction to her was an indication, it wasn't as if she was going to need it any time soon.

She pressed herself against his back, sliding her hand around to him. His breath caught fast, and his eyes rolled back as the intense intake of pleasure momentarily stopped all thought in his head. She kept her hand steady, firm as she moved around to face him and she took his rough palm in hers and guided his hand under her t-shirt to her already taut breast.

"No," he growled, "inside."

She smiled, "You're shier than you want people to think, Mr. Diemand."

"You're ballsier than you want people to remember, Miss Santos." He lifted her off of her feet, and pulled open his cabin door, depositing her on his floor, unseeingly closing the door behind them. "This is just for you and me." He closed the curtains in the small cabin.

Satisfied with their privacy, he eagerly took up the task at hand with first his large fingers, then his warm mouth, in the cool cabin air, sending lightning shocks of pleasure through her body. Her lovely sounds encouraged him as the deep pulsing ache he had ignited in her made her slide herself closer and closer to him.

"Hold on a second." He pulled back.

His body, his fingers, his mouth were wrenched from that tender business. Now she was the one to almost whimper in distress.

She opened her eyes unseeing, breathing out heavily, almost painfully. "No." She moved into the lines of his body again, kissing, handling, grabbing, wanting him to feel as much incredible building pleasure as she was at this moment.

"I promised myself a long time ago," he managed out, "I wouldn't say anything stupid," he breathed between, speaking into her delicious kisses, her hands finding their ways in to familiar and unfamiliar territories around his body, making what he had to say and do now almost impossible to accomplish. But he had to do it. He pulled away again, his eyes suddenly solemn, serious, searching for hers. "Julia, I really think you should know..."

Oh no.

"David..." She had seen this look before, many years ago. And she knew what it meant.

"No, I think I have to say this, just one thing."

"Please, David, as great as this is, I don't think I can really handle..." She stepped back.

He stepped to her, "Listen to me, I have to tell you...."

"No, no you don't. This is going along just fine. This is what I want."

"Just hear me out..."

"I'm too old for this, Dave."

"I think..." He grabbed her elbows, trying to look into her eyes.

She put her hand to her head, shielding them. "You don't need to do this, I'm not some scared little girl who needs reassurance about what's happening here..."

"That I..."

"Please..."

"...know that you are..."

"Dave...."

He broke into a devilish grin, "incredibly hot."

She looked at him, waiting for him to finish some deep, emotional, long-awaited confession, only to hear the most adolescent, infantile, stupidly male Maxim Magazine words come out of his grinning mouth.

It was infuriating.

And stupid.

And in this situation, perfect.

And he knew it. He could barely contain himself.

She couldn't help it - she looked at him biting back his lips, his eyes playful, she just burst out laughing, "God, I've missed you."

Her confession made his grin broaden, stretch up into the corners of his eyes, and he took her into his arms, "Yes, you have," he answered back. "But right now, more than that," he then whispered, growling throatily in her ear, "I want you naked, over there, in my bed." And he kissed her again. The raw need in both his voice and in his kiss made her center of gravity shift to somewhere below her kneecaps.

She followed him a little unstable, further into the cabin of his boat, past the small table, past the chairs, and they undressed one another and found their way to his bed. He stood back to once again admire her, to take her all in, after so long, but this Julia - older, wiser, and aching - would not wait for him at the pillows, and she pulled him to her, against her, and finally, gratefully, to her. He laughed at her eagerness, but happily obliged, enjoying her readiness, and he made playful love to her in time with the rippling movements of the tide.

He lay with her after, still thick and heavy inside, until the beating of their hearts slowed and their breathing calmed. It was familiar but somehow new, their hands clasped together, he looked into her eyes. The playfulness had subsided and there came a realization, that they could never put words to what they were both feeling, couldn't confess how it had affected them, or maybe not just yet. But he could see it in her eyes - those magnetic eyes that caught him in their thick honeyed gaze - her sweet expression, that she knew what he was really trying to tell her before all the gentle bites and the rough kisses. And that maybe, just maybe, she had been saying the same thing all along.

CHAPTER 24
By The Power Vested In Me

He spread the blanket up and over them, "I'm sorry that it's cold in here," paying careful attention to get it down across her legs and feet.

"Mhm, you've always been very warm." She pulled him back down to her, and he slid easily into the loop of her arms.

He lay soft kisses on her neck, her skin still humming with sensitivity, "You will need," her shoulder, "to stay close," her collarbone, "You know," back up her neck, "so you don't catch," up to her ear, "pneumonia."

"And die?"

"And die."

"I could just put my clothes back on."

He stopped busying himself with her ear, and looked down at her, mockingly hurt, "Well, why would you want to go and do that?"

She giggled, "I don't know what I was thinking."

"Plus, I think I threw them overboard."

"Shut up, Diemand."

"Make me."

Over the course of years, this moment had come up in David's mind once or twice.

Okay, who was he kidding?

The particular scenarios of Julia's return, or David winning back her heart, or their chance meeting in some strange town where they had somehow traveled to by coincidence, had come to his usual very pornographic conclusions many, many a time over the course of the years. She was his What If, and *who hasn't fantasized about the one who got away?* But what he had failed to accurately portray even to himself were the complete array of sensory and emotional details that Julia was currently, and wonderfully, providing him with.

The sheer silken touch of her hair as it swept back from her shoulders, as he collected it in his hands, or she trailed it across his chest, the velvet quality of her tongue in his mouth, across his stomach, around him, her scent all over his own skin, in his sheets, the deep magnet lock of her eyes as they looked into his, her teasing smile, her taste like salted honey, her sweet little murmuring sounds as she softly spoke his name, the musical tones of her trembled out sighs, her small hands soft, then firm as they made their sensual way around the both of them.

He wanted to watch her, he wanted to touch her, he wanted to move her, he wanted her to move, he couldn't speak and then he couldn't stop the words from coming out of his mouth - how beautiful she was, how incredible and *Julia* - he wasn't sure at times where the floor was or if they could touch the ceiling above them. He could only feel that she had made his heart pound so deeply in his chest, he could feel it from his sternum to his spine, practically vibrating his bed that he could only assume was below them. This moment, this incredible collection of moments, was far greater, far more wonderful than any he had ever imagined. But why was he so surprised? So marvelously and happily surprised? She always had found a way to exceed his expectations.

He pulled her close to kiss her again and took her hand in his, lacing their fingers together, interlocking the two of them in as many ways as he could think of, as though it was his only chance to keep her here tied down to earth here with him, as her naked breasts heaved against his chest and she called his name into his mouth.

She said into the darkness of the cabin. "I have to go help your sister in a few hours."

"Mhm." He scraped his stubble against the back of her neck, down her shoulders, "Can you stay until then?"

"I'd like to," she hummed, and ran her hands up the arms that were surrounding her, settling them on his biceps, holding him, holding her, "but then there's that long walk upstairs…"

"The Walk…"

"We need a way to stop time."

"An apocalypse."

"Zombie?"

"Is there any other kind?"

"I wouldn't want an apocalypse, the kids."

"Okay, time-stopping it is."

"How does it not affect you and me and my children?"

"I don't know, it was your idea, Space Nerd."
"You chose it, help me out."
"I should have paid more attention in Senior Physics."
"You seemed good with Anatomy and Physiology."
"Stop flirting with me, I'm tired."
"Oh ho, sir, now you're getting arrogant."
"Cocky." He pushed himself against her.

She felt what he was referring to, "Hey! You just said you were tired."

"My library is still impressive and fully functional." He added, "Your fault, you are sexier than you were before. How is that even possible?"

"Theory confirmed, you're losing your eyesight."
"And you perhaps are losing your judgment."
"I could be."
"So, should we talk about it?"
"I don't want to." She pulled his hands free and placed them over her breasts, pushing her hips gently into him. "I'm not exactly sure what's going to happen, David."

He took the hint, "Fine with me."
"You are smarter than you used to be."
He laughed a little, "It's something."

She slept afterwards, gathered to him, his arms around her gratefully. He looked down at her peaceful face turned up, her arm over his waist, her hand on his side, her lovely smooth thigh resting on his, extending her long leg between his. He could feel her steady breathing, on his arm, his chest.

For the first time in perhaps a year, he didn't want to sleep. He wanted to lay here and breathe. To sip, to gulp, to just take her all in as she slept so peacefully beside him now. This night had become so incredibly full - a whole new world of What Ifs. He pressed his lips to her forehead and breathed in her satisfying skin, giving a silent thank you. Somehow, some way, he had gotten back here, to this place. He had been given a chance to be in this place with her at this moment.

He stifled a chuckle at his own amazement. *How the fuck did this happen?*

How did I deserve this?

David had saved no lives, helped no futures, ensured the safety and security of nothing. So how could this have happened to him? He had embarked on no Hero's Journey. He hadn't even really dug for the prize at the bottom of the box. So why? Why had it happened to him?

Maybe because he had basically loved her in the only ways he could for the past twenty years.

So, how would he not screw up this marvelous, amazing gift this time?

CHAPTER 25
Down the Aisle

He had dozed off. "Oh shit." The clock read 8:45 am.

"Fuck." Julia had heard his tone and leapt up out of bed, gathering her shirt, wiggling into her underpants, throwing him his, pulling her hair back into a quick ponytail, "You've gotta shower and shave."

"I'll grab my stuff."

"Hurry."

"On it."

They ran up the dock, carrying his dob kit to the lobby, up the stairs rather than wait for the elevator, and knocked breathlessly on the door of the groom's room. Julia shoved Chris aside with a quick "Good morning," she heard a grunt in reply. She pushed open the bathroom door, threw his supplies on the counter and turned on the water in the shower, "Go," she instructed to David who started stripping off before she finished closing the door. "You wanna..." he grinned and started...

"Are you kidding me?" she swung the door closed.

"Doesn't hurt to ask," he yelled through the door.

"It will if you don't get ready in time!"

To which she bolted out of the door and ran up the flight of stairs to the bridal suite, "Okay, whattya need me to do?" to a roomful of Diemand females. Every blonde head turned their blue eyes to her. It was like entering a hotel room of Stepford wives.

"Where were you?" turned Dee in the make up chair. The stylist waved.

"Oh, hi Marsetta," Julia waved slightly, realizing that this was the most unkempt that Marsetta had probably ever seen her. *Not presenting well at all.* She spoke to Dee, "Uh, David and I went out, for breakfast. You know, to talk."

"You and Davey?" Joan inquired.

"Yes. Davey."

"Oh yeah?" Dee asked.

"Yes. We worked it all out. We're good now. No problems. Best buds."

"Good," Dee turned back to the stylist that Julia had recommended. "We're set here, but if you could go and check to see if my second dress and shoes are okay down in the dressing area off the ballroom..."

Goddamn second dress..."Yes." Julia nodded. "I will."

And Joan added, conspiratorially, "And you might want to..." The Diemand's oldest sister did not finish the sentence, but merely made a frown-y face and pointed to her own breasts, first one and then the other, in a quick gesture that made Julia suddenly very aware that she was, in fact, still braless under her T-shirt.

She quickly grabbed her own biceps and backed out of the door. "Yes," she nodded. "I will go down and be sure everything's tucked away where it's supposed to be..." She closed the door and bolted.

Joan's only comment was, "Wow, little Davey had a really nice breakfast."

Dee shot her sister a look.

Julia smacked her own head, *Oh my God, how flipping unprofessional!*

But no time to dwell, she could jump in the shower, oh my God, she had to shave again, okay, no, she would run downstairs, check on the dress and shoes and then run up to shower... but she should stop at her room and grab a bra or something... but then she should just...*Oh crap.*

Pull yourself together woman.

This is what being emotional got you. This is what happens when you let feelings get the better of you, these are consequences of irresponsibility. You got to spend the night with him, you woke up late, and now you need to make it right. She took a deep breath in through her nose, straightened her shoulders, and let it out through her mouth. *Get that guy out of your head, Missy, he will not fuck up this day.*

She headed downstairs.

With purpose, but without a bra.

Julia stalked to the elevator, bouncing and uncomfortable with each step and of course, OF COURSE, the couple - yes, the one that she had verbally assaulted inside the elevator just a few days ago - stepped off onto the floor, smiling and laughing, arm in arm, until they saw her. She watched their faces simultaneously darken, and they shrunk even further into one another's arms. She felt her own face grow red, and her chest thumped with something besides unrestrained flesh, but she politely put her head down and they, grim-faced, hugged against the opposing wall.

She stepped onto the elevator and sighed with relief when the doors closed in front of her.

She made it down to the lobby and found the head of the day staff.

Her phone buzzed: 'Dressed. Need help?'

She texted back: 'You worry about Chris. I'm in lobby with manager.' *Who is currently enjoying the view.*

Gary was just stopping at the desk to grab his keys, but had stumbled and fumbled a couple of times, just staring at her boobs, despite her efforts to conceal her supportless condition. *Jesus, Gary.*

And that is when Julia glancing over the front desk saw Laura walk into the hotel.

Julia stepped out from behind the desk. She hadn't seen Laura in years but she knew exactly who she was - David's fiancée.

Her tiny little frame encased in a flowing peach gown, brought in at the waist, sitting softly on her little shoulders. Her itty bitty feet in golden high heeled slippers only she and possibly the real Cinderella could fit into. Her blond hair cut in pretty layers, she had obviously had it blown out just this morning, her makeup flawless, Laura's appearance was one of careful planning and execution and here she was, at the wedding, no Plus One in sight.

Julia's heart sunk. *She was here for him.*

Today was the day. The day she was due. Of course she was here for him.

And as if on cue, David, his hair combed up and back like Julia had suggested out on the boat, clean shaven, resplendent in his black dinner jacket and pants, the snow-white of his shirt showing off both his sailor's tan and his gray green eyes, stepped off the elevator. He spotted Julia first, his arms spread wide, beaming at her, "Tuxedo is to woman, what lingerie is to man," grinning devilishly.

He saw her look and his brows lowered, "What is it, Juju?"

"David?" Laura called.

David's face went white at the sound of her voice and he saw her, "Laura?"

Julia rocked back on her heels.

David was stuck in the spot where he stood. Laura came running to him, not noticing makeup-less, braless Julia standing next to her handsome ex-fiancé.

"Hello, David."

"What…" he stammered, "What are you doing here?"

"I wasn't going to come, David. But I thought, I thought today, of all days, I should. I should come and see you and I don't know. I think it's time we talked." She laughed breathlessly, nervously, gazing up hopefully at his narrowed eyes. "This is a celebration of your family and I've always loved your family and I thought it was my fault that we couldn't be celebrating this together…"

"Your fault? I don't… I don't know what…."

Julia started to back away. He noticed her movement and turned to her, "Julia, no, don't…"

Her eyes wide, "David, I can't…"

Laura finally saw her, "Julia?"

"Hello, Laura," she replied quietly. "You look wonderful."

"Thank you," Laura frowned slightly, "I'm sorry, I didn't think you'd be here." Then a look of realization came over her face, "Oh yes, Deidre told me that she was going to have to call you…"

"Laura…" he started, warning.

Julia stopped him, "No, it's okay. Yeah, it's weird. Just, it's my hotel. I'm just helping with the preparations for the morning. I'm not…" she decided, just then, in that second, her throat burning, "I'm not staying…"

"No," he blurted out forcefully, whirling back to her, "Don't go." His brows were pulled down low over his eyes, his mouth twisting painfully.

"I can't… I can't. You have more important things to work out." She backed up towards the stairwell, her eyes swimming in their sockets.

"Please, no."

"Ten years versus three weeks, David." She cracked out a smile at the two of them, standing there, looking so beautiful, so perfect together, like she and Will used to, "Far more important things." She shrugged a shoulder, pulling her lips tight, "And honestly, so do I."

"Juju," he pleaded softly.

But she had ducked through the door and was gone.

"What did you do?" Chris bored through the doorway of the bridal suite.

The Stepford Diemands exploded at the sight of the groom. "Bad luck!" and "You're not supposed to see the bride!"

"You invited her!" he thundered.

"Who?"

"Laura. She is here! In the lobby, downstairs. Julia saw her."

Dee's eyes widened.

"You invited Laura!"

"Well, yes," Dee was thinking back, her eyes shifting left and right until she pulled out the response from her memory, "but she declined! Her card said regrets!"

"The best man is freaking out! And your planner is gone!"

She put her hands to her newly made up face, "Oh, poor Julia…"

"Yes and this is your fault. You and your shit with your brother, can't you just give him a fucking break?"

"This is not my fault. I didn't know all the information! How was I supposed to know?"

"About Julia and David?" Joan interjected.

Dee spun on her sister, "How the hell do you know?"

"Dad told me."

"Dad told you?!"

"Dad thought he'd marry that girl actually. Goodness, that was a long time ago." Joan shook her head.

"What the hell?!"

Chris spat out, "He probably didn't tell you because he figured you'd try to conspire some crackpot system to get everyone together and end up fucking everything up, like you did when you wanted to be with me in college."

"Oh my God," the bride groaned. "What has happened? My wedding day, I just wanted people to be happy."

He roared. "Then let them be!"

"I know I'm sorry, Chris."

"I'm not the one you should be apologizing to."

"Oh, you're right." Dee gathered her wedding dress up and under her as her sisters watched in coordinated dismay, "No!" "What are you doing?" "Where are you going?"

Julia opened the door to the bridal suite the bride was about to barrel through. "Juju! I was just coming to find you."

Julia walked in stiffly, braless, makeup from last night, her ponytailed hair must have looked as though she had put her finger in a light socket, but she stood stock straight, gestured smoothly and easily, and commanded the room of blondes with her articulate words and practiced poise. *Spock, this called for Mr. Spock,* she reminded herself. "Deidre, I need to tell you that Amy will be here in about twenty minutes and she will be handling the remainder of the day. She knows the timeline, and she's the one who we talked to about the cake for you, remember? Marsetta knows her too."

"Julia, I can't tell you how sorry..."

"Just let me get through this, Dee, okay?" Her friend nodded, and Julia continued, "I've spoken with Mr. Cavanaugh and explained to him that my presence today will most likely be a hindrance, and he agreed that my responsibility is toward making this day a magical beginning for the bride and groom, and no one else. These two - Chris and Dee - are the priority. And I hope that you, as the bridal party, remember that. I am removing myself from the equation, so you, along with my replacement, will take up that responsibility."

Dee started, "Julia..."

But Julia couldn't stop her speech, "I wanted to let you know how much it has meant to me to be able to see you... all... again, to be included in this journey with you. When you first called me, I was so shocked. I hadn't heard from you Dee, in God, ten years? And when you told me that you and Chris were getting married, I was so happy." She paused, a breath. "And when you asked me to help, I couldn't believe it, I couldn't believe my luck that I got to be a part of the joy of this day, this week. Particularly when my present situation has been so... trying. It's meant so much to being around people who I used to be friends with, laughing again, spending time with those of you who remember who I used to be, before Will and the kids, you know?" She wiped a corner of her eye. "This week has made me remember so much about love, and friendship. And there is so much of that surrounding me as I leave here today, and I will remember that and you for it. But I don't think it's wise for me to stay." She didn't duck her chin, she didn't falter, "You're in good hands with Amy as your point person and the rest of the staff, and you know I wish you all the best."

"But, what about you, Julia?" Chris asked.

Her voice broke, "Don't," she croaked out, but then smiled tightly, "Don't worry about me, okay? You all right here have an opportunity in front of you to be happy right now. So, just take it." She laughed a little bit, running her hands down the front of her, smoothing down her shirt, "Take it and run with it and don't look back."

No one moved.

A thunderous noise came from the hallway, "My loving sis-ter!" A bitterly sarcastic voice came in through the door, "Where the hell are you?" David stomped in to the room, and stopped short at the circle of people, surrounding Julia.

"Julia," he said, quietly surprised, "I thought you'd left."

She looked around, "Just going now."

"You don't have to."

"Yes, I do."

"I want to talk to you, but you know, not in front of all these people."

"I don't think that's smart."

"No one here would accuse me of being smart, Juju."

"David, stop."

"No, I won't."

"David," his sister pleaded.

"No!" he yelled at her. "You don't get to say anything!"

"And you," yelled Julia, "don't get to yell at the bride!"

If the room had gone quiet earlier, it was like tomb right now.

He pulled his head back in surprise at her outburst.

And she went at him.

"You are going to suck it up, David. Do you understand me? It's not your day. It's Dee and Chris' and you will go out there and you will be best man and you will give one hell of a speech because that is what you are supposed to do. It's your only goddamned job."

"Hey.." he stammered out.

"No!" She pushed her face up to him, and went a little farther, "Today you are going to get off of your goddamned boat, and you will help people other than yourself. I have been and always will be your friend, but understand one thing - you are going to set the record straight with everyone here, get off your self-pitying ass and make it work. Because not everyone has had the advantages you have had, and it is up to you to help people, David. You know that. So, yeah, maybe you probably will hurt them, too, but we can't live only taking care of ourselves. It just doesn't work that way. Other people are important. Their plans, their ideas, their weddings - whether you think so or not. Get today straight, Diemand and so for once in your goddamned life, shut the fuck up and do what your family wants - No! - *needs* you to do!"

David's mouth was wide open. He couldn't speak, and she didn't want him to. And she withdrew and walked out of the room.

David looked at every one of his family members staring at him, at the door, shocked at what that woman had just said to their baby brother, and he saw what could only be naked agreement in their eyes. He waved them off and stalked off to follow her.

And Joan leaned over to Dee and confessed, "Oh my God, I almost applauded."

Dee agreed, "I love her. I love her so much."

Julia had handed off the file gratefully to Amy and gathered her bags and her dog to walk out to the lot to her car. Her sunglasses firmly in place, the tears slid down her cheeks as she unseeingly popped the trunk and strode up to its tail end. David stepped out, his hands jammed deep into his dress pants pockets.

He cleared his throat, "You quoted Star Trek."

"What?"

"Just now. You quoted Spock, in uh, Wrath of Khan I think." He started, "I have been and…

She finished, "always will be your friend…I…paraphrased." She nodded. "It's true."

"I know…"

And she breathed out, "I think we have to say, that this is it, David."

"That's that. Again."

"Yes. And you know it is, too," Julia sighed, she opened the back door and Star hopped in and lay down.

"Don't tell me that."

"You know what I am going home to face, David. There's no room for this." She pushed her hand back and forth between them, "And you know I'm right."

David stared at her face, and then broke off the look.

Julia's eyes filled, "Go to Laura, David. Talk to her. Straighten it out. She obviously still loves you. You have the chance I don't have and the only thing I can tell you is to take it."

"Julia," he shook his head, "I'm not sure that's the chance I want."

She looked at him fully, "It's the only one you've got."

His mouth tightened and he looked up at the sky.

She walked around him, put her things into the trunk. "You couldn't believe I could just jump husbands - go from one to the next, do you?"

"That's not what I was asking…"

"I know that, now. It's just that's what it would have come to. Eventually. We're too old to pretend, remember?"

He looked at her, eyes searching, and then finally, nodded.

"Good luck, David."

"Good luck, Julia." He bit his lips, and he tried, just once again, "Hey, I'll probably see you around."

Oh God, he looks so handsome. He could have been Prince Charming.

Words wouldn't form.

He said it.

Why can't I say it back?

Because this is it. This has got to be over, so he can go on with his life, and I can go on with mine, whatever the hell it's going to be. She shook her head, "I don't think so."

He was quiet as she pushed down the trunk lid, then, "You're doing it again." He kicked at the limestone beneath his black dress shoes.

"What?"

He looked right at her, "Making the decision for both of us."

She tilted her head, "I guess, yeah, I am. I just think this time I might be making the right one."

He nodded again, and then relented, his usual devilish smile tried its best to twitch up the corners of his eyes, but he ended up just smirking bravely, brokenly, his hands once again, deep in his pockets, "At least kiss me fucking goodbye this time," he tried, joking.

She went to him, put her arms around his neck, and looked into his eyes - they were greener than she had ever seen them. Her heart stuck deep down in her throat, but she had to say this, she had to at least give him this before she closed the window between them. For good.

"Goodbye, David," and before he could respond, she kissed him. She felt him lean slightly into her soft mouth. There were other words that had come to mind. Other words she could have said, but they lay too heavy in her throat, too dense to float on the air.

His arms came around her, pulling her as close to him as he could, his lips hot on hers, and he made an odd little noise. She pulled away slightly and he looked down at her face. He pushed back a hair that had curled out from her mess of ponytail and looked into her mascara-blackened eyes, "Funny," his lips twitched at the corners, "you look like a girl I knew once."

She pulled out of his arms. He stood there, shoving his empty hands into his pockets - he looked so wonderful just standing there in his immaculate white shirt, his crisp black jacket, his shining shoes in the startling white limestone parking lot, the beautiful gray hotel behind him against the backdrop of the sky and the ocean. She took in the whole picture, "And you," she breathed out, finally, "look like the man I never got to meet."

She tried to smile at him, but an ache pulled at her throat, and so she had to break away, duck her head, slide herself into the driver's seat, start up her car, back up and drive away.

And David watched her go. He turned and headed back to the hotel, hanging his head in what he had known was his inevitable defeat.

CHAPTER 26
I Now Pronounce You

She drove into the long driveway, lined with long boxwoods that had never seen a softball, a Frisbee, a basketball, a stuffed animal languishing in its bushes for more than an hour. She led the dog among the handpicked stones, her expensive shoes knocking a hollow pattern into the cool, damp air. She opened the front door with her key and let herself inside her house.

The house seemed odd, off balance, the familiar color continuity of carefully arranged shelves was interrupted by missing books, photos in frames had disappeared from their rightful places on the mantel, her keys were the only residents of the rings, and when she went upstairs, she noticed that her clothes in their closet hung empty and alone. He hadn't even bothered to push them all apart, spread them across the railing, her dresses remained unnecessarily crushed to the left, her shoes huddled underneath them.

William was gone and had taken his things with him.

Her life had been dismantled.

She sighed. The kids would be back tomorrow and she could focus on them. But tonight, she just wanted to sleep.

She crawled into her large king-sized bed, and laid her head on the pillow on the right side, where she had always slept. The dog leapt up and lay down against her. She wondered if William slept on the left at her house, or would he just do everything different now. And as she drifted off to sleep, her errant brain wondered also, if David would sleep on the left, or the right tonight.

She kissed the kids too much when she saw them, it made Annie giggle and made Billy push her away. She needed to make something clear, "You, young sir, are going to get kissed and hugged at least once a day. You decide when it happens, but just know it's going to."

He had snickered a little at that, but waved her off, "I'm good for today then?"

"Yes, you've made your quota."

So, the three of them went back to a different kind of life, sorting their laundry and making their lunches and going to the beach on sunny days, Julia actually sat with them on the dunes and built sandcastles, ruining her pedicures and missing workouts to go boogie boarding. The house had to deal with a lapse in daily attention; the dust bunnies collected under the sofas while they played cards; popcorn made its way into grooves on their reinstated movie nights. Julia found that she just didn't have as much time to obsess over the details of her showroom house, her showroom clothes, or her now nonexistent showroom life, not if she wanted to spend time with the kids when she wasn't working.

Cavanaugh had been very happy with how Amy had stepped in and handled the wedding in Julia's absence. Julia was pleased because she had trained the young woman and the girl was blossoming into a punctual, meticulous Manager of Romantic Fantasy. She took some of the pressure off of Julia, handling even some of the offsite events and wedding shows that used to eat up Julia's weekdays.

She saw William on Thursdays and Sundays, sadly, he'd never looked better. The usual stress that dropped his brow looked lightened; he seemed to smile with his eyes now. He would take the kids for the weekends while she would be working at the hotel, arranging the perfect nuptials for the brides and grooms of this year's Boston up and coming, even if she was in last season's Mahnolo Blahniks.

She even tried dating. When it was made known that she was suddenly available, guys she had talked to in the schoolyard, at the grocery store, at the library were asking her if they could call her. It was disconcerting at first. And she accepted the invitation of a certain Richard Brighton. He had picked her up in his Lexus, taken her to a restaurant in Boston and then tried to feel her up in front of her house. She had removed his hand, thanked him for the lovely dinner and told him to, instead, go home and fuck himself.

She had never been opposed to First Base, actually liked it quite a bit, but in the past twenty years, it had only been done by someone she knew for more than twelve hours. Truth be told, that accent shouldn't have even gotten him that far.

She thought about David, but she had put him out of her mind before, she could most certainly do that now. She wasn't completely Vulcan. She did have feelings. But sometimes having feelings wasn't necessarily constructive, or helpful. She used her powers of mind control as wisely as she could. Just like Spock.

Dee had tried to tell her things about his job or how things were going with Laura in their now weekly conversations and once a month lunches. But Julia was on to her and stopped her before she got too far, with just a curt but sincere, "Good for him."

But it wasn't until her son happened to inadvertently disclose the contents of his and David's amidships conversation at the helm of his boat, that it dislodged the last of her memories of David and how he had always made her feel. And it was hard to deny who he really was to her, and even who he had become over the years.

Billy's little confessional took her back again, back to the truth - not just what she had wanted to happen, not just the story she had wanted to tell her friends, her acquaintances, her children, her mother, herself, but the truth - and she really let herself feel that deep and long-rooted pang of missing him.

Billy and Annie were doing homework in the kitchen while she was pulling the dough out of the fridge in their kitchen, when her son ventured, "We should invite someone over for pizza night."

"Oh?"

"Um, I was thinking maybe, Jack, or Evan, or Pete, or maybe sometime, I could ask maybe my friend Tricia."

Tricia?

"Oooh," Annie started.

Julia gave her a look that silenced her, "Do you think sh... they'd want to come and make pizza with us?"

"Um, yeah, I guess."

"Do you want to give, uh, them a call now?"

"Yeah!"

Just a little while ago, Julia would have been on the phone, calling the moms and arranging a "playdate" so that her kids would have appropriate, supervised fun, but she knew that her boy had gone beyond this, and that she needed to just let him "Go ahead."

Bill was on his phone in about two seconds. Annie gave her a silent "Oooh!" and Julia just gave her a surprised look.

They communicated silently, conspiratorially, until Bill could be heard in the other room. Julia put her finger to her lips.

Bill came back in, "I tried the guys and stuff but you know, no answer, but uh, Tricia said she could come."

Julia suppressed a grin, "Sounds good. Can't wait to meet her."

"Mooom."

"We'll be cool, won't we Annie?" she said.

He gave them a look.

"I promise for both of us."

A lovely little blonde *(these blondes!)* came to their side door with a look of hope and fear mixed on her face. Bill had been standing in the kitchen trying to look casual but had been jumping up to look out the window every couple of minutes. Now that she was here, he opened the door for her and his handsome face broke out into a smile, Julia saw him welcome her in and the girl turned back toward the driveway and wave away her mom before hopping in the door.

"Hi, come in, I'm Bill's mom."

"Hi Mrs. Rosa, oh, wait, I'm sorry, are you still Mrs.?, I'm so sorry!"

"It's probably easier if you just call me Julia."

"Okay, Julia. "

"So, how did you two meet? In class?"

"Um, after school, I was outside waiting for my mom to pick me up and I was just sitting there, listening to music and he asked me if he could go through my iPod…"

"I told her that she's got some horrible stuff on there," he teased good-naturedly.

"I do not!" She retorted.

Oh, that smooth devil, Julia smiled to herself.

She didn't want to, but she did.

He had stumbled into Julia's room, carrying what looked like a box in his large hands. "Where's she?"

"Who?" She asked of the large random boy.

"What do you mean who? Your roommate. The girl you live with?"

"I don't know."

"You're not helpful."

She shot back, "And you haven't talked to a girl before."

"I have. Once." He smiled and dropped the box on her bed and looked over at her stereo, "What do you have?"

"What are you talking about?"

"Music, CDs," he flipped through her small collection. "Crap. Crap. Not bad. Okay, Good. Wow, No. Crap. Crap. Hey, I don't have this one, it's numbered." He held up a CD, her White Album by the Beatles, "this is an early release... hmm. You, pretty girl, suddenly became interesting." He then picked through the rest of her collection, changing his mind, "Ah, maybe not so much."

"Who are you?"

He walked out of her room, he yelled back, "Someone with taste apparently, who doesn't belong in the same room with someone like you."

She yelled back, "Um, excuse me, but what the hell is your problem?"

She poked her head out of the door, his lanky body was trailing down the hall. "My problem is, for the most part, your pitiful music collection."

He turned the corner into a stairwell. "Who are you to say... music is a totally subjective media..." She ran off to follow him, tripping down the stairs, seeing him duck into another hallway.

"Nothing is that subjective..." she heard him yell back. She ran into the hallway but he had disappeared. She peered into room after room after room, finally spotting him in a room with this great looking, burly, football player guy and her new roommate, Deidre sitting down cross-legged on the floor.

"Hey," Dave grinned. Then he said to the other two, "Told you I'd get her down here."

"Um, yeah, hey, you couldn't have asked me?"

"Then I would have had to introduce myself, explain what I was doing, that I was not psychotic..."

"So being an asshole was the less psychotic option..."

"In the interest of time, yes."

"Why did you need me down here so fast?"

"Dunno. She said she wanted us to meet you."

"So you came up, didn't introduce yourself, insulted me, and then ran away."

"I didn't run away."

"Yes you did."

"No," he smiled. "I got you to follow me."

She sighed, "So what is your name?"

"Oh, it's Dave. And you already know my sister, Dee, and this is Chris Billings."

Laura had left when he quit his job for the second time.

It wasn't the cause of the end, but it was the nail in the coffin. He had tried. He really had. He knew that Julia had been right - David and Laura deserved a second chance.

But deserving it and wanting it were two separate things.

At first, Laura had convinced him to go and ask for his job at her dad's accounting firm back. His name was still good in the city despite their "break," and now that it was over, he could easily go back to the work and retain his old salary.

He bit the bullet, went back, and bent his head to his computer screen from eight-thirty AM to six PM in a corporate office every single weekday. His tan faded and his salt-weathered hands grew smooth again.

Although he found out one day that he could see the Plaza from his coworkers' window.

She'd be proud of him.

Or would she?

He would walk at his lunch, but never in the direction of the hotel. He made his way around the Public Gardens, and out of the Back Bay, and down Beacon and up Charles and he would find himself in front of a school and he would sit and read, almost everyday. He didn't want to seem like he was some weird pedo, so he ended up chatting with an administrator during recess and, just purely out of curiosity, asked about any openings. They had responded enthusiastically, asked him to please come back, with a copy of his license, they needed a sub for their ninth grade ELA teacher, she was going out on maternity leave for the last month of the school year.

He got the job and walked back from their meeting to gleefully tell Laura's dad that he quit. Again. And Laura's stuff was out of the apartment they shared before the end of the workday. "Goodbye, David."

He had disappointed her again.

But at the school, he disappointed no one. He was helpful, insightful, funny, and managed a classroom of twenty-seven urban population students well enough in those wild last few weeks of school that the Admin were inspired enough to promise the remainder of her leave in the fall.

He decided not to pay out the Boston rent for either the apartment, or the expensive slip. Despite having plenty of money left from the work at the firm, he broke the lease and looked for a good spot to harbor the summer. He found a slip available online - in, of all places - Osterville, Cape Cod, Massachusetts.

A little further searching online found him a summer school opening at the high school. He called and they asked him to come down for an interview tomorrow - they were desperate and so happy to hear from a former employee - they needed a warm body for six weeks, starting Monday.

He packed up the SS Midlife Crisis that night.

David spent the summer teaching, sailing, reading and thinking. And what was nice was, he slept every night.

He had about ten days until school started and he would need to get back in Boston to look for a place and go to the meetings at the beginning of the school year. With the leftover cash from his summer gig, he was able to lease a little Toyota and he was driving out among the cottages to pick up a new bilge pump when he swung down a familiar road.

He slowed down almost automatically. He had wandered this street so many nights when he was younger and every time he passed it, he still stole a glance or two at the front yard, unknowingly searching for something familiar, even though everything that had happened in it - the fun, the laughs, the fights, the pain had happened twenty years previous.

He rarely saw anyone or anything of interest. The tenants coming and going on weekends mostly.

And yet today, there they were.

A tall, dark haired boy, gangly but gaining, hucked a huge purple ball at his sister, also lanky, stubbornly always a few years behind her brother, but her skin is the color of her mother's. A skin that tans so well in the summer sun of the Cape.

His car came to a halt almost automatically. David opened the door and stood up to see if this was all just a mirage - some sort of location-induced flashback.

Bill warily looked at the vehicle, but recognized the guy who took him out on the boat and who had introduced him to the Bad Juju-side of their mother. "Hey!" He called out, "Hi, Mr. Diemand, Dave! Where's your boat?"

"Um, hi Bill. It's at the dock, down the street. What are you guys doing here?"

"Mom found this place online and we came down last week. Kind of a last vacation before school."

"Oh yeah?"

Annie sung out, "She couldn't believe it, she just kept saying she couldn't believe it. She told us that her summer here was the happiest time of her life."

"Oh God, I know," Bill concurred, rolling his eyes.

And Annie went on, "Her first place of her own, her first hotel job, her first real love. Ooooooooooooohhhh!" Her daughter fake-swooned, imitating, "And you never really get over your first love!!!"

"It's true, Annie," a voice rang out, "and I'll remember that when you start talking to me about your buddy, Liam, again."

"Mom!"

And there she was.

In the doorway of the cottage they had shared for a summer. The orange light of the setting sun was in her hair, on her dress, down her browned legs and bare feet. And like it was one of the nights after she had gotten home from work, she greeted him as though he was expected. "Hi, David."

"Hi, Julia."

She turned her attention back to her kids. "Inside you two. It's almost dinner and I need you to set the table."

"Aw, Mom, Annie can do it."

"Mom! I did it for lunch!"

"Both of you can do it for me tonight. Team effort."

"Huh," David said.

"What huh?" She looked into his face.

"I don't know. Just never picked you for the sentimental type, Jules."

"Yeah well, you don't know everything about me, Mr. Diemand," she put her hands on her hips.

"Yes, like what was this first love's name?" His eyes darted back and forth, and he stroked his jaw, thinking, "Did it start with a B? Or a P maybe? Possibly a D-something? I think I remember Dirk, Derek, Da—rryl?"

"No, I think his name was Tim," she smiled slyly.

He grinned back. "Shut up, Santos."

She turned to go inside, "Come on, guys, the table. Dinner."

He stood outside her door, watching her gather her children into the cottage's side door into the kitchen, she put her foot on the step, and turned her head to see him standing awkwardly on her grass walk, "You coming?"

"Oh, um," he stopped, not knowing what to do, instincts and priorities pulling in opposing, and then similar directions, "I, uh, can't."

"Oh," she shrugged a shoulder, surprised. But then, she shouldn't be, "Okay…"

"No, you don't understand," he said quickly, almost too quickly, but he needed to make her understand, "I have an appointment. To go pick up a bilge pump, the guy's expecting me."

"Oh, well, you've got," she offered quickly to cover her embarrassment, "you know, to do that."

"Well, I uh, I do, actually," he nodded.

"Okay," she nodded with him.

He kept going, "And I've got to bring it back to the boat, I have to go back for school in a week and I have to fix it and I'm not with Laura anymore and I have a teaching job and…" he took a deep breath, he was nervous, *why the hell was he nervous?* "…the boat, I've got a slip in Osterville just down the street, literally down the street, so I'm not far and maybe you and I could, I don't know, go for a walk when I'm done, or something?"

"Oh wow," she was taken aback at his lengthy, breathless explanation. "Okay. Yeah, that sounds nice."

"Good." He clapped his hands together, and nodded, "Good. I will see you in a bit then."

"Come by when you can."

"I will." He couldn't pull his eyes from hers, but he knew he had to go.

She smiled at his hesitation and he smiled back. "Oh, okay," and he turned and took a couple of steps, and turned back. *Nope.*

She had already turned to go back in the door.

He started back for his car, but thought, and turned around again, "Juju!" he called to her.

She turned back at his nickname for her - "Yes?" - the one he had made for her in college, so long ago.

And he was there on her lawn, his finger to his lips, and she could see - *yes, there it was* - a devilish grin on his face, "So, Juju, I've been thinking..."

"Scary."

"Yes, so, when you said that the girls planned the... well, you know."

She carried his glance back to the door, warning: Children Present, "Yes."

"I was going to say you remember when we first - you know - kissed down the Cape..."

"Okay," she rolled her eyes, "yes?"

"Are you telling me – that all along - you planned... that?"

"Oooohhh," came from the window.

Julia stopped them with a quick glance, and then turned her attention to a waiting David, who was biting back an evil grin. She shook her head, "You know what, David?" And then she said it - finally admitting, "I'll probably see you around."

And then she simply smiled at him. Her smile was open, friendly, and even maybe a little, *hopeful.*

"Yeah," he couldn't help it. He smiled back, just as openly, just as hopeful, "probably."

Acknowledgements

I would like to thank the following people who helped, supported, listened, read, talked through, barely tolerated, and couldn't wait to see this book. I truly get why writers are notorious drinkers and I commend you all for not acting on your wishes to murder me during this process. I appreciate it.

First, thank you to Desiree Spinner of Desiree Spinner Events, (http://www.desireespinnerevents.com/). She was the first to really talk to me about the true nature of the wedding industry and she proved to be a fantastic resource in those first few weeks when I was figuring out what this story had to be about. Thank you Laura Welch, for being a friend, and providing the inspiration for Julia and David's little love nest down the Cape. So much fun, Katie Lamanna!

Thank you to the usual suspects - Leah Miles, Mary Donlan Phelan, Kathy Nestor Parker, Kathleen McDonald for your eagle eyes, your comments, thoughts, questions, and just making me a better storyteller in general. Ms. Miles, thank you for providing me with writing time while the kids spent time at your camp. You made me go back to my Sondheim!

Thank you to the additional Island Dwellers – Sean and Kelly Bishop, Paul Mailloux, Kat and Frank Parker, Penny & Dave Smith, Larry Lowe. Why aren't you in my kitchen right now?

Thank you to all of the Phelans and Blatchfords, as well as the former Phelans and Blatchfords.

Thank you to Anna and Pete and Mimi and Murphy and Tula. I love you every day, all the time, no matter what.

And finally, thank you to Peter Phelan. I love you. You inspire every word I write.

About the Author

I find these things difficult to write – a biography? Really? Because honestly, none of you really wonder about my personal life, do you? I don't know why you would. I have not had any hot and heavy affairs with any rock stars, and I don't have any old flames that I plan on revisiting any time soon. So, what to write? My life is truly not that interesting and I am no expert on anything. I just like to write stories that amuse me.

I am a mom to Anna, 10, and Pete, 12. I have a dog, Murphy, and a cat, Tula. My mom lives with us – we finally finished her room this year, thank goodness. My husband, Pete and I are constantly doing work on our house. We go out to Rolly's Tavern in Lynn when we want to be social and The Old Spot in Salem when we don't. We like to drink wine, swim, take the dog to the Dog Park, and we wish we were more frugal. My kids are funny and nice, and they bicker a lot.

I teach 7th grade ELA because no one wants to teach 7th grade. I mean, think about it. What a tough age. Do you remember what it was like when you were in 7th grade? I do, and it was awful, feeling so awkward, and uncomfortable. Yuck. I would never want to go through that again. And so, I think that's why I can work with them. I remember what it is like to be them. Plus, I like the kids I teach, so I guess that counts for a lot. My job is about reading, writing, and thinking so I feel I'm lucky in a lot of ways.

I love my family even when they make me crazy. I try to be self-reflective and think about how my actions have affected others but I end up just being gossipy. I try not to bite my nails. I like clothes but I end up ruining whatever I wear.

I am, for the most part, a nerd. I like the freedom to unabashedly love things that being a nerd gives me. I am introverted but you would never know it if you talked to me.

I drive a minivan and I don't mind. I had to get bifocals this year. I have lived in another state and I got to travel the US when I was young. I would like to take vacations in other countries someday soon. I cook – sometimes it's delicious, sometimes not so much. It is a crapshoot, really. I can say, very candidly, that I make GREAT pizza from scratch every Friday night. Ask my kids and anyone who has stopped over for a Pizza Night. It. Is. Awesome.

So, wait! I could say I am an expert on pizza-making. Thank you for the apprenticeship from 15-17, Papa Gino's.

But still, all in all, not that interesting. I do hope that you liked the book. And I look forward to writing another one.

If you liked "Plus One," read Sarah Phelan's debut novel...

It could have been a "Fairytale Romance" if that pesky "Reality" thing wasn't in the way...

Stay At Home mom and put-upon daycare provider Janie Hadley rarely gets a moment to herself never mind an entire night out, so when she's invited to a concert featuring the famous singer/actor Billy Smitts, Janie isn't looking for much more than a modicum of Tanqueray and a whole lot of letting-loose fun. But the morning after, Janie finds herself to be *plus* a killer hangover and *minus* a wallet. As our headachy heroine frantically calls to cancel her credit cards, the perpetrator stalks her to her house and shows up at her door with his famous, multi-million dollar smile and a dubious business proposition. Billy Smitts is on location for a few months and has run dry of twenty year old blonde, big-boobed nannies for his daughter. Much to Janie's dismay, Billy Smitts uses his trademark boyish charm as well as his enormous, ahem, *buying power* to manipulate his way past her protests and into her daycare.

Forced to "play nice" in front of the kids on a daily basis, a contentious friendship develops between the notorious celebrity and the Mrs. Perfect mom. Billy and Janie, the two most unlikely of allies, soon begin to realize that despite what the Outside World may believe, neither of them really does have it all, and the harrowing experiences they share cause them both to call into question whether they are better off facing life together, or apart.

Turning a tried and true romance novel premise on its ear, Sarah Phelan tells "Stay At Home" as a sweetly personal, intensely sexy, provocatively smart and brutally honest story where love refuses to play by the rules and how "happily ever after" doesn't always mean the same thing to everyone.